Escape to Lilacwell

Sasha Morgan lives in a village by the coast in Lancashire with her husband and has one grown up son. She writes mainly contemporary fiction, her previous series having a touch of 'spice', probably due to all the Jilly Cooper novels she read as a teenager! Besides writing, Sasha loves drinking wine, country walks and curling up with a good book.

D0474779

Sasha Morgan

Escape to Lilacwell

CANELO

First published in the United Kingdom in 2022 by

Canelo
Unit 9, 5th Floor
Cargo Works, 1-2 Hatfields
London, SE1 9PG
United Kingdom

A CIP catalogue record for this book is available from the British Library.

Print ISBN 978 1 80032 959 1
Ebook ISBN 978 1 80032 958 4

Look for more great books at www.canelo.co

Printed and bound in Great Britain by Clays Ltd, Elcograf S.p.A.

1

For Geoff, my late father-in-law, whose voice I can hear in Fletcher Hendricks, kind, old sage that he was

Chapter 1

Pulling into the crowded car park, Adira Summers squeezed into the tight space. With a heavy heart, she turned her mobile phone on. Immediately it bleeped into life with dozens of messages, as she'd fully expected. The first one being from her irate boss.

'Where RU?!' he'd blasted. The tone of his text matched him completely – oozing derision and impatience. Adira stared at the message for a moment. *Where am I? Good question*, she thought bleakly, looking out of the car window, still reluctant to open the door and get out.

It was raining. The sky was filled with metal-grey clouds, refusing any glimmer of light. Talk about symbolic. There didn't seem to be any glimmer of light in her life at the moment.

Being a successful barrister and earning a decent wage had originally been her main goal in life. As a student studying law at Oxford, her ultimate ambition had been to achieve what she had strived so hard for. And now she had it… well, it still left her wanting. The problem was, Adira didn't know what she *did* want.

Still staring glumly out of the window, she realised what she *didn't* want. To be here, stuck in this car park, stuck in this city and stuck in this job, she concluded closing her eyes.

Her phone rang. Willing herself to focus, she answered as brightly as she could muster.

'Hi Richard, I'll be there in five, horrendous traffic,' she lied.

'The meeting's about to start, Adira,' he stated flatly. 'It would be good if you could make it,' he added with sarcasm.

She chose to ignore him and just tapped to end the call. Taking a deep breath, she collected her bag and ran through the rain into the red-bricked building displaying the impressive sign 'Goldgate Chambers' in mirrored lettering. The chambers had been standing in Goldgate Square for decades, with its pretty, cobbled pathways and artisan shops. It had a deli to die for, a sweet, little bakery and a wine bar named 'Mario's', which the barristers from Goldgate Chambers often frequented. In short, Goldgate Square was a hip, vibrant place to be, tucked away in the leafy quarters of North London. Adira's friends envied her place of work; they envied her lifestyle even more. Living and working in London, mixing with the high-flyers, rubbing shoulders with the elite, left them feeling deflated in comparison to their own rather dull lives of nappy changing and play-dates. Adira couldn't see it. To her, the shine had well and truly worn off. Yes, at first it had been a whirl of rich clients, cocktail parties and Law Society dinners. She'd meet celebrities (either suing or divorcing), millionaires, and even royalty once, but nowadays even that didn't impress her. She'd seen it, done it and grown out of the T-shirt.

Walking towards the lift, Adira composed herself. The last thing she wanted was to appear flustered. In this job, image was everything. Cool and sophisticated, intelligent and competent, that's what her clients paid for. Entering the room with her shoulders back, she smiled with an air of confidence.

'Good morning, ladies and gentlemen,' she spoke clearly and swiftly took her seat. Luckily, they were still chatting over coffee. Richard had obviously delayed all present for as long as possible.

With a warning look, he coughed quietly. 'Well, shall we begin?' He gave his most beguiling smile, making Adira cringe. Buffoon.

After a long and laborious meeting, Adira escaped for lunch. In desperate need of a drink, she walked past the deli and straight into Mario's.

'A large Sauvignon Blanc please, Mario.' She stood at the bar. It was fairly quiet, with only half of the tables taken. Mario was the Italian owner and had often chatted to Adira, another one finding her work interesting.

'So, how's your morning been?' He passed over her much-needed glass of wine.

'Bloody awful actually.' Adira took a long sip. Hell, that was good. Her stomach rumbled. Just the one drink, then food, she told herself. On reflection, she was telling herself that quite a lot these days, '*just the one drink*'. A warning bell faintly rang inside.

'You look tired, Adira.' Mario looked genuinely concerned. She loved the way he said her name, making her sound exotic. Adira was of Hebrew origin and meant 'strong', as her gran was always telling her. Deliberately named so, after being prematurely born at seven months and fighting for survival. Her parents had willed her strength, peering into the glass incubator, gulping back the emotion as their tiny, fragile daughter lay wired up.

All the hopes and prayers had paid off. Adira had come through, battling against the odds; she'd lived up to her name.

'I feel tired,' she replied wearily.

'Bella, Bella, that's no way to be,' Mario shook his head sadly.

'I know,' Adira swigged back another mouthful of wine, 'it isn't.'

The weekend couldn't come quick enough for Adira. Stretching languidly in her bed on a sunny Saturday morning, she contemplated what to do with a whole free day in front of her. Normally she would catch up on work, read through briefs and make copious notes, but not today. The bright sunshine was too inviting to be cooped up indoors.

Adira had a sudden impulse to see her gran. Maybe subconsciously it was the radiant spring weather that had prompted her. Edie Wilde had always been the 'cool' grandma of the family. Whereas other grandmothers fitted nicely into the archetypical peg of grey hair, support tights and knitting, Edie was way outside the box. *Bohemian* was how she liked to be described, *embarrassing* is what her daughter, Cleo, often called her. It amazed Adira how her gran could have given birth to such a complete opposite to herself. Whereas Edie was flamboyant, quirky and had a passion for adventure, Cleo was pragmatic, logical and very matter-of-fact. Interestingly though, they had both studied medicine – well, in a fashion. While Cleo was a qualified GP, Edie had ventured into natural healing, believing nature always provided. Since being a tiny girl, Adira could remember how friends and neighbours and anyone recommended would call on gran for advice to aid an illness, much to Cleo's personal and professional chagrin. Edie would always be there to help, on hand with her vast experience and herbal encyclopaedia, mixing up some potion or another. Invariably, they worked. Headaches were eased by lavender balm, rashes vanished with Aloe vera gel, insomnia cured by chamomile tea, the list was endless.

Adira had loved staying at her gran's. Edie had converted her potting shed into a studio where she saw her patients. It was packed to the rafters with shelves holding multicoloured bottles containing herb extracts and oils. It seemed almost magical to Adira as a child; her eyes would scan the small, wooden room, taking everything in. Edie was also a massage therapist – something else Adira had admired, so much so that she herself had undertaken the necessary qualifications to train and become one as a teenager. This had allowed Adira an escape almost from the relentless studying her mother had pressurised her into. Cleo hadn't approved of her daughter wasting valuable time learning how to rub oils and goodness knows what into people's bodies. It all seemed ridiculous to her, especially when there were top A level grades to be gained and a place at Oxford university on the horizon. Yet Adira had fully benefited from the instant relief her gran's healing hands had given her during stressful times, like taking exams. Edie would knead out all the tense knots in her back and calm her aching muscles. It was pure heaven. Just the smell of basil and ginger oil being rubbed into her body was enough to still her.

What she wouldn't give for that now, she thought as she packed an overnight bag. Having rung her gran to arrange a visit, Edie had been delighted and suggested she stay the night too. Why not? Adira had replied, suddenly desperate to escape to the tranquillity of her gran's quaint village. Situated just outside Oxford, she had often taken refuge there whilst studying at university.

By early afternoon, her Mini Cooper pulled into her gran's driveway. There was Edie, stood at the front door waving, making Adira's heart swell with love. Where would she be without this wonderful woman who always managed to inject life into her?

'Hi love, had a good journey?'

'Fine thanks. Could do with a cuppa,' Adira laughed, grabbing her overnight bag and walking into her gran's open arms.

'How's my girl?' Edie pulled back to take a good look at her granddaughter. 'You look exhausted, Adira.'

'I know, so everyone keeps telling me,' she replied drily.

Edie gave her a thoughtful look. Then, deciding not to voice her thoughts, guided her in.

After a therapeutic walk in Bluebell Woods, a heavenly body massage and delicious chicken casserole, they both relaxed by the open fire with a glass of red wine. Adira couldn't remember the last time she had felt so peaceful.

'Are you happy, Adira?' Edie suddenly asked, as she watched her gaze into the flames.

After giving it some thought, Adira looked into her gran's eyes. 'No. I don't think I am.' She took another sip of wine and turned back to watch the fire.

'When have you been at your happiest?' pressed Edie.

Again, after giving the question consideration, she replied after sighing. 'Probably as a child, when you gave me that beautiful gypsy caravan for my tenth birthday. I felt so free, at one with nature, even though I was only in the back garden,' she smiled.

There was a pause before Edie spoke.

'Maybe that's something to think about.'

Adira frowned slightly, but was far too tired to talk anymore, her eyelids were practically closing.

'Time for bed, my girl.'

As Adira's head hit the pillow, she fell into the deepest, most blissful night's sleep she'd had in a long time, oblivious of the impact her gran's words would have.

'Adira, you're late again,' Richard stated in a flat tone.

Glancing at her watch, she replied, 'No, Richard, I think you'll find I'm actually bang on time.'

'Your client's coming this morning now, in about ten minutes,' he informed her officiously.

'Since when?'

'Since eight p.m. last night when I emailed you.' He smiled self-righteously and returned back to his laptop.

Smug bastard, Adira thought gritting her teeth. Did the guy ever switch off? At eight p.m. last night she had been travelling back from Oxford, not scouring her work emails. He'd obviously sent the message late, deliberately hoping she wouldn't read it – she hadn't.

It was an effort getting out of bed that morning to come back into work at all after such a relaxing weekend. That knot in her stomach started to tighten.

Grabbing the client's file out of the tray, she sat down at her desk and opened it. Quickly scanning the neatly printed notes told her everything she needed to know. A rich, successful man, divorcing his wife and wanting it to cost him as little as possible. *Same old*, Adira thought, rolling her eyes. So, it was down to her to squabble with the wife's representative and thrash out some sort of settlement, which, if either had any sense, could be reached between themselves, without the legal costs. Love and money, it made people do the strangest things, well according to her gran anyway. Thinking of Edie made her warm inside.

'Adira, your client's arrived!' called Richard, looking out of the chamber's window.

The warmth turned to cold. Adira joined Richard to see a chauffeur-driven Mercedes pull into the car park. Out stepped an immaculately dressed man with his nose in the air. Adira clocked the private registration plate 'DEM 5Y'. Sir Reginald Demsy strolled with an arrogant air of confidence into the building and Adira knew immediately he was going to be the worst kind of client.

The meeting was a farce. Reading between the lines, Reginald, as she was permitted to call him, had committed the classic, cardinal sin of cheating on his long-suffering wife with his much younger secretary. His opening line of 'my wife doesn't understand me' nearly made Adira laugh out loud, as did the admittance of attending a 'business trip' to the Seychelles with Chardonnay, who was there to take notes. *I bet that's not all she was taking*, Adira thought tartly, whilst keeping a straight face. A part of Adira wanted to let this man get screwed for every penny he was worth. It was times such as these that she questioned the morality of her career. Should she be helping people like Sir Reginald? Was it ethical?

Her mood didn't lift throughout the day. Constant telephone calls, countless emails to wade through and more of Richard's snide comments only added to that sinking feeling. Reaching for her mobile, Adira noticed a message from her gran. Opening it up she saw a photograph of a camper van. Frowning, she squinted to read the writing underneath:

> For sale £25,000 – Sheila is in great shape. Renovated in 2014, this Aussie import is in excellent condition and boasts a solid underbody that has been undersealed.
>
> The 2ltr twin-carb engine has done approx 9,000 miles and runs like a dream. Such a good-looking bus, but also fully kitted out for camping holidays, of which we have enjoyed trips to Devon, Wales and Derbyshire. 240v hook-up, Propex heating, inflatable drive-away awning/tent, gas fridge and cooker. A recently fitted new clutch.

Adira smiled, remembering the conversation from the weekend about her gypsy caravan. Typical gran. Edie had been searching for a way to make her happy again.

She stared at the camper van. Sheila did indeed look in good shape, with her pale blue and white shiny body. How cute, a VW Classic camper van. At £25,000, she wasn't going cheap, but didn't these VW camper vans hold their value? It certainly seemed that way, and she'd still have a substantial amount of savings left.

A growing sensation rose up in Adira, a heady mixture of excitement, anticipation and curiosity. Should she? It would only be for a year, she told herself, that gap year she'd never actually taken. Didn't she deserve it?

Adira licked her lips and read through the description again. She quite fancied travelling about in a sweet camper van called Sheila. She glanced round the office: there was Richard schmoozing some client on the phone, the rest of the staff had their faces glued to screens, tapping away on keyboards. She looked again at Sheila, calling to join her in the great outdoors. The impulse was too much. A force inside shot through her and she suddenly stood up.

'I've an announcement to make,' she blurted out almost hysterically.

The whole office stopped and stared at her. Richard smoothly ended his call and raised an eyebrow.

'I'm leaving.' There, she'd said it!

Richard blinked; the others gave a sharp gasp.

'With this notice? I doubt it,' he scoffed.

'I'll work what's left of my notice, after you've given me my annual leave,' Adira replied sternly, looking him in the eye. They both knew she'd hardly taken any of the leave due since working at Goldgate Chambers. Richard looked away with a scowl.

'Where are you going?' asked another barrister.

'As far away from here as possible,' she replied, collected her bag and marched out of the office with her head held high.

Chapter 2

Fletcher Hendricks sat on the bottom stair and cursed harshly. He did that a lot – curse, not sit about. He was a doer, always on the move – or rather he tried to be. Nowadays, it was taking him longer to get about, but then at eighty-five, who could blame him? He did. Fletcher hated the fact he was old. He loathed being constantly tired, his impatience grew as he witnessed first-hand the way his body refused to do as he told it, the frustration! And now he had something in his eye, which was practically blinding him. Fletcher had been reaching for his gardening diary on the top shelf in the library, when down it came with a thud, belting his forehead, whilst some debris from the shelf had flown right into his eye.

'Ah!' he'd roared, but to no one, except probably the odd mouse to be found in his rambling, old house. Stumbling into the hall, he steadied himself by grabbing the banister post and easing his body down. He took out a handkerchief and blew his nose. Wasn't that supposed to help? No, he remembered, you were supposed to put your top lid over your bottom eyelid, then blow. He tried again, his shaky hand only just managing to manoeuvre his eyelid. Yes, that seemed better.

Cursing again, he collected his diary from the bottom step and made his way into the kitchen garden. It was May, time to start planting the cabbages, cauliflowers, courgettes and broccoli. He had to dig over the herb garden and sow basil, coriander, parsley and dill; nurture them, watch them grow, given the hearty Lancashire weather.

Fletcher lived deep in the countryside in Lilacwell, an area of outstanding natural beauty near the Forest of Bowland. He was proud of his roots, having lived there all his life in the majestic, Georgian country house, The Laurels. It was his family home, passed on from generation to generation. Except Fletcher hadn't a son or daughter to pass it down to, only a nephew. Still, Jasper had been like a son to him.

Memories of Jasper's childhood often made Fletcher smile, a rarity in itself. He'd reminisce while gazing out at the now unkempt orchard of holidays spent there with a young, enthusiastic nephew, eager to help pick the apples and prepare them for cider making. Jasper had loved staying at The Laurels with his Uncle Fletcher. He'd doted on his every word, idolising the wise, old sage his uncle had been to him. Fletcher in turn had enjoyed playing up to the role, ready to offer guidance and counselling when asked, which he often was. Jasper had a connection with Fletcher which he struggled to find with his own father, Rufus. Fletcher's brother lacked the imagination and passion which a young boy growing up craved.

For Jasper, The Laurels held all the fun and excitement he could soak up in the long, hot summer days. The Georgian pile held secrets from the past, hidden amongst its stone walls. Fletcher would make up ridiculous, fictitious tales of various members of the family in an attempt to entertain his young nephew. Watching Jasper stare up at him by a crackling fire, eyes like saucers, hanging on his every word, made Fletcher a happy man. He came to life when Jasper stayed. Endless hours of fruit picking, horse riding, fishing and foraging in the woods filled Fletcher's days. He'd welcomed the distraction from having to run The Laurels and the land which surrounded it. It was hard work, sapping all his energy, and Fletcher often longed for a sense of freedom, without the worries of the estate.

Basically, it was all down to him. He had staff to keep, tenants' rent to collect and farmers to liaise with. It all took time, which he begrudged. Being the eldest son, he'd always known where his responsibilities lay. He was expected to take over The Laurels once his parents had gone. Meanwhile, Rufus, his younger brother, was free to do as he wished. Ironically, Rufus was the more sensible of the two, which probably meant he would have been a better custodian, or indeed a happier one, than Fletcher had proved to be.

Fletcher had never married, never having found that someone special to share his life with. Or, if he had, she'd slipped through his fingers. Never having children was the biggest regret of his life. However, as parenting went, it was obvious to see how his brother neglected *his* son, even to Fletcher. Perhaps subconsciously he had tried to compensate for Rufus's shortcomings, by taking on the character of boisterous Uncle Fletcher. Certainly, he relished his time with Jasper, it gave him the perfect excuse to act the goat, brought the child out of him. It made a refreshing change to being grown-up and responsible.

His head ached with responsibilities. It took some co-ordinating running The Laurels, or at least it had. These days, he employed a manager to collect the rents and oversee any issues regarding the land he owned. Whereas at one time the impressive country house bustled with scullery maids, gardeners, a butler and housekeeper, now it had only an elderly cleaner popping in once a week (almost as old as Fletcher himself) and a man from the village who cut the grass. A rather sorry state from what had been. Gone were the days when The Laurels had hosted midsummer evening parties, with dancing on the lawns and laughter echoing round the orangery; warm, cosy Christmases where the hall was decked with holly, berries and mistletoe and the family all congregated once a year. Now it stood forlornly empty, apart from its only occupier.

Like Fletcher, The Laurels was gradually winding down, being sapped of its vigour. Sadly, the sparkle had faded.

—

'That's a nasty bump, Fletcher.'

'It's nothing, Lilly,' he dismissed and turned away from his cleaner's close scrutiny. He knew she meant well, but he resented the concern. As the years had tumbled on, so had the fear of his independence fading. His ultimate dread was to be taken away from the precious home that he'd known all his life and put into care. The very thought gripped him and often kept him awake at night. It was in those dark moments when he was at his worst, though he'd never admit it to anyone, especially those who cared about him. And plenty did, including Lilly Grimshaw and her twin sister Ruby, the three of them having practically all grown up together.

Lilly and Ruby, like Fletcher, had never married and lived in a pretty, little cottage nearby. Lilly had kindly offered to clean his home years ago when the last house-keeper at The Laurels had had enough of Fletcher's cantankerous nature and bolted, unfortunately taking the butler with her, leaving a rather lonely Fletcher to fend for himself. Being in her late seventies, Lilly was barely able to whiz round with the hoover, but she did her best, knowing it was the company Fletcher craved more than a tidy home. She and his nephew seemed to be the only visitors these days and he couldn't remember the last time Jasper had been at The Laurels.

'You ought to go to the doctors, you know,' insisted Lilly. 'You could be suffering from concussion.'

'Don't be daft, woman,' Fletcher snorted. The last thing he wanted was to see some quack who'd alert the social services and whisk him off in no time.

He opened the kitchen door and slammed it shut with force.

–

Lilly shook her head in despair as she watched him through the window, marching off to the kitchen garden in wellington boots. Typical Fletcher, stubborn as a mule.

The phone rang. Quickly making her way to the hall, Lilly picked it up a little breathless.

'Hello, The Laurels.'

'Hello, Lilly.'

'Jasper!' she beamed. 'How are you, dear?'

'I'm good thanks, and you?'

'Well,' she sighed, 'just about managing that stubborn, old uncle of yours.'

Jasper chuckled down the phone. 'How is he?' He stopped laughing when hearing Lilly pause.

'Jasper, I think he needs help.'

'Is he ill?' came the immediate reply.

'No, but he isn't looking after himself properly. He's banged his head, a lump's come up and he refuses to see a doctor.'

'Is he there?' The concern in his voice was evident.

'No, he's in the garden, tending to his beloved vegetable patches. Shall I get him?'

'No. No, don't tell him I've rung, Lilly.' He stopped in thought for a moment, then made a decision. 'I'm coming to see him.'

'When?' she replied with surprise.

'As soon as I can arrange it.'

'Good, Fletcher would love to see you, especially as he missed you at Christmas.'

Although the remark was meant innocently, it dug deep into Jasper's conscience. He should have gone back home to England to see his family, but work had been hectic and completely took over.

Swallowing, Jasper said his goodbyes and sat back in his swivel chair. Turning to the huge office window, the magnificent views of the tall buildings against a cloudless, blue sky shone before him. There was Dubai in all its glory, with its bustling streets, bright lights and lazy beaches stretching out, waiting to be enjoyed. And he had enjoyed it, so much so he had extended his contract for another couple of years. Now, after that phone call, he had begun to have doubts. Had he done the right thing?

Chapter 3

'Your usual, Fletcher?'

'Aye, lass.'

The young girl parked a pint of real ale in front of him.

'Ouch, that looks sore,' she winced at closer inspection of the bump on Fletcher's head.

'Don't you start,' he grumbled into his beer.

Cassie smiled to herself. Being a local and working in the pub meant she knew only too well how awkward Fletcher could be. Her dad was a farmer and a tenant of his, so she'd known him all her life. Cassie also knew that deep down Fletcher was in fact a softie and had a kind heart. More than once, he'd bailed her parents out when money was tight, allowing the rent to run over whilst getting back on their feet. As a teenager, she had happy memories of working in Fletcher's orchards and always recalled how well he'd treated the small set of fruit pickers earning cash as students. She also recalled the dishy nephew he had that had spent a lot of time at his home, as did most of the girls that had caught a glimpse of him about the estate.

Cassie had had an idyllic childhood growing up in the village, so much so she couldn't wait to return from university. Having completed a degree in Hotel Management, she had taken on the role of assistant manager at the Inn at Lilacwell, an award-winning country hotel, boasting Michelin stars and luxury accommodation. The place oozed rustic character, with its stone floors, inglenook fires, antique furniture and four-poster beds. Yet for all the Inn's splendour, it still held an intrinsic down-to-earth charm, welcoming visitors donning either dressy heels or muddy walking boots, and, of course, dogs were always made a fuss of, even having their own baskets and treats in the rooms.

The rear of the Inn gave magnificent views of the River Hodder, filled with salmon and fresh trout. The Inn lay nestled deep in the valley, surrounded by forest, so whilst being an area of outstanding natural beauty, it also meant a mobile signal wasn't guaranteed. This fact in itself brought visitors flocking, desperate to get away from the demands of everyday life. The Inn at Lilacwell was a haven, a retreat, a place to unwind and deeply breathe in that clean, country air. It was both a romantic getaway that lovers gravitated towards and a country lodge for shooters and fishermen. The official owner was the Duchy of Lancaster, as it was situated on an estate owned by the Queen. However, the Inn had been leased to the Davenport family for the last century. The current proprietor, Charles Davenport, looked upon the hotel as all his ancestors had, as a much-loved family business.

Fletcher knocked back half his pint. It was thirsty work digging and planting vegetable patches, but enjoyable. It gave him a sense of satisfaction, being in the outdoors, working his land. Although he hated to admit, his back ached and that thumping headache refusing to fade made him feel worse for wear now.

Slowly making his way to sit down, Fletcher glanced up as Charlie passed him.

'Hello there, Fletcher,' he smiled at one of his oldest customers.

'Charlie,' he nodded back, then recoiled in pain as his back niggled him.

'You OK?' Charlie halted, looking concerned.

'Yes, it's just newness wearing off,' came the flippant reply, however unconvincing.

'Shall I get you a menu?' Charlie didn't want Fletcher having to move again, looking uncomfortable as he did.

'No need, I'll have the fish pie please.'

'No problem, I'll get it ordered for you. How about another pint?'

Fletcher looked down at his nearly empty glass. Another beer to dull the pain sounded like heaven.

'Aye, another please.'

It was only when he'd finished his favourite meal, sunk two pints and had a whisky in his hand that Fletcher managed to relax. Warm and now reasonably comfy sat by the open fire as it sizzled and snapped, his eyes grew heavy and closed.

Cassie saw him asleep and went over to gently take the tumbler of whisky resting on his lap and placed it on the table in front of him.

'The old boy looked tired,' remarked Charlie as he passed again.

'I know,' she agreed. 'He needs someone to look after him,' she spoke quietly.

'Hmm, don't let him hear you say that,' Charlie replied with a wry grin.

Half an hour later and now closing time, Cassie gently nudged Fletcher awake.

'Fletcher, let me give you a lift home,' she whispered.

Slightly startled, he rubbed his eyes and yawned.

'Much appreciated, lass,' he replied gruffly, glad his aching bones didn't have to haul him home tonight. The thought of his warm bed was tempting enough to get back as soon as possible, rather than wandering down the dirt track and shortcut through the woods to The Laurels.

After bidding Cassie goodnight, Fletcher paused for a moment under the lantern hanging from the cast-iron arch at the top of his footpath. He surveyed his family home in the moonlight. How magnificent it was, with its sandstone walls and large sash frames. The slate roof had two tiny attic windows peeping out from it. To the left side was the elegant glass orangery, shimmering as it reflected the stars in the night's sky. How beautiful, he thought.

Had it been daylight, his critical eye would have noticed the broken slates on the roof, the peeled paint on the window frames and the odd smashed glass pane. But it was dark and the full moon and starry night added a touch of romance to Fletcher's gaze. For the millionth time, he only wished he was opening the door to a full house, bursting with family.

–

Jasper had finished for the day and closed his laptop. An analyst in oil research, he had completed his report for a network of local and international energy market players. Satisfyingly, Jasper had finished it earlier than expected. The reason being, he was eager to go home. Back to England, back to Fletcher, who was now constantly on his mind. Ever since that phone call and hearing Lilly's concerns, he'd grown more and more resolute in flying home and seeing his uncle. Despite looking forward to staying at The Laurels, a part of him was apprehensive, however. Exactly what state was his beloved old uncle going to be in?

His mind cast back to childhood days, filled with joy and exhilaration that Fletcher had provided in abundance. He really had given him the most captivating time in his country house, which exuded history and times of yesteryear. Jasper pictured himself as a little boy, running through the vast corridors being chased by Fletcher; creeping through the dark, secret passageways by torch-light, gripping his uncle's hand tightly; and galloping on horseback through the rolling hills with the wind gushing past him. It all seemed like a lifetime ago now.

Jasper's eyes misted over. How could he bear to see the most precious gentle giant decline into a frail, elderly man?

Once again, that needling voice whispered inside, digging well into his guilty conscience: *He needs you now. It's your turn to look after him.*

Jasper swallowed, then rang through to his secretary.

'Zara, have you a moment?'

'Of course,' came the immediate reply.

Zara was used to Jasper's instructions. Although always courteous, she knew he wanted an instant response due to the tone in his voice. She'd grown to read and understand him very well, professionally anyway. Zara craved more. She didn't just want a working relationship with Jasper. So, dropping everything in a second to attend to him would be a pleasure – literally.

Zara had totally fallen for his dark good looks and charisma. He had real English charm. She had instantly seen what a gentleman he was, with his impeccable manners and approachable way. Experience told her that not all people were as good to work for. Zara had appreciated the way Jasper had treated her as his equal, even though he held such a prestigious position in the company. And she'd been at pains to show it – well, as much as she could under the circumstances. All he had to do was say the word.

They'd been out together, but mainly business lunches accompanied by clients; not what you'd call dates, except for one evening dinner in a high-class restaurant as a thank you for all her efforts in the office. Only then had he opened up and spoke about his home in the UK and his family. Zara yearned to learn more about him, but it seemed there were limits to Jasper. Apart from that one evening, when he had driven her straight home after eating (much to her disappointment), it had been strictly business.

Not to be perturbed, Zara had upped her game, taking extra care of her appearance. Her long, black hair hung heavy and glossy past her shoulders and those big, brown eyes, darkened with liner and smoky eyeshadow, always took everything in. Her clothes, whilst covering every inch, as was expected, still fit closely enough to hint at what lay beneath. Once or twice, she had caught Jasper discreetly glancing – well, he was a man after all – and she had smirked to herself with satisfaction. Just give her more time and she'd crack him.

Entering Jasper's office, she had her notebook and pen at the ready.

'Zara, can you book me a flight to the UK?'

Looking slightly surprised, she blinked.

'Immediately please,' he said with force.

'Y-yes…' she stumbled, then quickly recovering, asked, 'Your report to the—'

'Done,' he cut in, 'and ready for you to submit.'

'Certainly. I'll get you on the next flight tomorrow.'

'No. Tonight.'

Again, Zara was a touch taken aback and was itching to know why Jasper had to go home so urgently.

'When should I book the return flight?' Those brown eyes searched his face.

'I'll do that. Just get me to Manchester ASAP.'

Feeling somewhat deflated, Zara nodded politely and did as Jasper instructed.

Three hours later, Jasper was checking in at the airport. He felt better already, seeing it as a step in the right direction. In just eight hours, he would be home. He would see and breathe in the fresh, green grass and hear birdsong. He'd be able to drive through quaint, leafy lanes and drink real ale in country pubs. Ah, bliss.

'Enjoy your flight, sir,' the desk attendant said with a plastic smile.

'Thank you,' he replied and took his boarding pass.

Chapter 4

'I blame my mother for this,' hissed Cleo as she took in the sight before her. There, pulling up the driveway was a sky-blue camper van, complete with her excited daughter at the wheel.

'You've got to admit though, Cleo, we've not seen her so happy in a long time,' conceded her husband, Pat.

'But to chuck it all in!' trilled Cleo.

'Shush, don't ruin this for her,' he warned, already predicting an almighty row between wife and daughter. That's what they were notorious for, their blazing arguments. Little wonder Adira had often sought solace with Edie. And now his mother-in-law had excelled herself, encouraging their daughter to take off in a camper van, he thought wearily. 'Come on, united front,' he told his wife, as positively as he could muster.

Together they plastered on smiles and went to greet their precious daughter, who was about to 'find herself' at the cost of her glittering career she had busted a gut for.

'Well, what do you think?'

It was hard to be negative and tell her what they really thought, especially at seeing her face lit up with such glee and anticipation.

'It's...' Cleo faltered, looking the van up and down.

'Smashing, love,' finished Pat.

'I know! Come and look inside her,' Adira beamed.

'Her?' Pat replied with a frown.

'Sheila. She's an Aussie import,' laughed Adira as she ushered her parents into the cosy interior.

'How sweet.' Cleo was genuinely beginning to melt. But then it would be hard not to at seeing the cute kitchenette with a small sink, gas hob and distressed wooden cupboards. The fabric furnishings matched the outside sky blue of the camper van.

Adira had put up a flora material padded noticeboard with criss-cross elastic. It held photographs of family and friends, in case she got homesick, not that she anticipated for one moment she would, such was her eagerness to get on the road and escape the rat race. The camper van was kitted out beautifully and also had a small shower unit and toilet towards the back.

'Adira, it's fantastic!' Pat was hugely impressed. Despite his wife's reservations, he could see the attraction this little van had. A part of him envied his daughter. If only he had had the same backbone at her age. He glanced sideways at his wife. Was that a wistful look he noticed in her eye? Maybe she was thinking the same deep down. There could be no disputing Adira's utter joy, it was practically radiating from her. 'So,' he swallowed the lump in his throat, 'where do you intend to go first?'

'Up north. Scotland, I think,' she replied, beaming.

'Scotland?' snapped Cleo, earning herself a scowl from Pat. She softened her voice. 'Why Scotland, Adira?'

'Just fancy it,' she shrugged. 'You never know, Mother, I could stumble across some ancient castle in the Highlands and end up marrying a dark, swarthy laird.'

Pat smiled wryly.

'More like catch your death of cold,' Cleo said, rolling her eyes.

Adira looked thoughtfully on, and not for the first time was amazed at how different her mum and gran were. Polar opposites. She knew full well how Edie was going to react when she travelled to Oxford next week to show her the camper van. Edie would be in raptures, touching all the knick-knacks, marvelling at the quaintness of it all. She would fully appreciate the reasoning behind Adira's decision to trade in the glitz and glamour of London city life, plus the stress and strain, in place of roaming the countryside and making new discoveries. Freedom, it counted for a lot – well, to Adira it did anyway.

In her quieter moments, she did reflect on and agonise over if she was doing the right thing, of course she did. After all, she *was* giving up a lot. But, only for a year, she'd told herself. Enough time to spread her wanderlust wings and take stock. It wasn't all about throwing caution to the wind. Adira had sufficient savings to live off for twelve months, plus she envisaged doing some form of work, circumstances permitting.

To onlookers, especially her colleagues, it might appear she was being frivolous; having a romantic, rose-tinted outlook of a life on the road. Being a free spirit seemed almost too clichéd for the successful pen-pushers she had sat alongside at the chambers, but Richard, surprisingly, had remained silent following her announcement of leaving. Often, she would catch him looking at her with a quizzical expression, before quickly averting his gaze when making eye contact. The only fellow worker who had wished her well had been Rory, the maverick of the office, who hardly conformed to the clean-cut image of a top-class barrister, with his unruly curls, slightly unkempt clothes and love of beer over any top vintage wine. His northern accent stood out like a sore thumb too, but he never let that hinder him.

'Good on yer,' he'd bellowed, thumping her back. 'Wish I had the balls to do it me self.'

Adira had smiled with affection at him. Out of all the office, he'd be the one she would miss. No one else. As soon as they'd learned of her departure, they'd all scavenged for her work like vultures, each eager to get the most prestigious files. It pleased her that Rory had landed the Sir Reginald Demsy case.

So, all in all, when Adira had been handed her flowers and listened, whilst cringing inside, to the false farewell speech made by Richard, laced with resentment, she had bid her goodbyes and never looked back. As she'd walked towards her car, Rory had chased after her.

'Adira!' She'd turned to find him running across the car park, shirt untucked, tie skew-whiff, panting, out of breath. She'd suppressed the giggle threatening to escape. 'Adira, this is for you,' he'd smiled and handed her a small present. 'Open it up.'

Passing him her flowers, she'd ripped the gold wrapping paper off. It was a key ring, with a miniature campervan pendant.

'Oh Rory, that's so sweet of you.' Her eyes had filled.

'See ya, mate.' He'd hugged her, squashing the roses in between them. 'Have a ball,' he'd whispered.

And that's exactly what she intended to do, despite sensing her parents' trepidation. Adira wasn't a fool, she knew them only too well. Behind the brave gusto they had summonsed up, she realised it was a front. For her. They were putting on a cheery display and she loved them for it.

Chapter 5

Lilly was attempting the ironing, while Fletcher stood looking broodily out of the kitchen window. He was bored and needed something to do.

'I'm going for a walk,' he told her decisively.

'It looks like rain, Fletcher,' she warned.

'I won't melt.' He reached for his wellington boots and dragged them on.

Lilly shook her head, did he ever stop? Then she realised that it was probably best he didn't. It was his land that kept him going. Whether he was tending to his vegetable plots or surveying the estate, it gave him focus. In a way, Lilly admired his grit and determination, but occasionally she wished he'd slow down, just a little. After all, he was in his eighties. *Like you*, a voice inside reprimanded her and made her chuckle.

Fletcher slammed the door behind him and strode with purpose to the far fields and woodland. His eyes narrowed as he assessed the land. There was a fallen tree that needed chopping for firewood, its branches had blocked a portion of the stream trickling through the leafy woods. He noticed the five-bar gate which led to the dirt track was lopsided. Marching towards it, he saw that it had broken from its hinges. Fletcher managed to drag it back and prop it against a nearby hedge. He'd have to get Colin, his estate manager, to repair it. Another job.

His gaze then followed the clear, babbling brook that wound through the trees and he couldn't resist a walk beneath the lush, green canopy of branches, enticing him like a guard of honour to explore. Fletcher was at his happiest amongst nature. If only it wasn't for the pain in his joints that constantly persisted. He knew deep down that he ought to seek medical help, but always that menacing thought of pesky, young doctors sticking their noses into his business threatened him.

Gone were the days when he could nip into the surgery at a moment's notice and be seen by Bill Baines, the old village doctor who understood him. In and out in no time, with a trusty prescription, without any interference, that had been Bill. Nowadays, they wanted your inside leg measurement before they'd agree to see you in two weeks' time! Bloody ridiculous. Then would come the inevitable questions, 'Do you get any help at all, Mr Hendricks?', 'How are you coping, Mr Hendricks?', 'Do you require any assistance, Mr Hendricks?'

No he damn well didn't! What he wanted was to be left in peace. If the social services got inside The Laurels, they'd have a field day. The very thought sent him cold. He'd be packed off in some home full of old codgers. For Fletcher, despite all his aches and pains, never really considered himself 'old' as such. In his mind, he actually wasn't; but his body couldn't keep up with his alert brain, it simply refused to do as it was told. It was his stubbornness and possibly his prejudices that kept him from doing the sensible thing. Seeing a doctor would open up a can of worms, of that he was convinced.

He continued his journey until he felt the faint drops of early rain. The sky above had turned grey and still, threatening a storm. Quickly as he could, Fletcher made his way through the fields and back to The Laurels.

Lilly had finished the ironing and had just put the kettle on.

'Just in time for brew.' She helped him take off his coat. The doorbell chimed. 'I'll get it,' she said, scurrying to the hall.

The bell rang again.

'Hang on, I'm coming,' she muttered. Then, when opening the door, she gasped. 'Jasper!'

Fletcher, on hearing her, practically ran through to the hallway.

'Hello,' smiled Jasper, 'and how are you, Lilly?' He hugged the tiny, frail woman carefully. Then, turning to his uncle, he beamed. 'And how are you, Fletcher?'

'Never better, never better,' he lied, while thumping Jasper on the back.

–

Never better? Like hell, thought Jasper as he lay back on his pillows that night. He was in his old room, up in the eaves. Sighing, he put his hands behind his head and closed his eyes. What was he to do? Although he had only just arrived, already the thought of flying back to Dubai leaving Fletcher to rattle about in this great house, alone, gave him an uncomfortable feeling – one which was growing rapidly. He'd been quite shocked at his uncle's decline; watching him struggle with his cutlery, seeing his hands tremor gripping his whisky glass and slowly sink into his armchair with shaky legs, made him want to weep.

A desperate urge gripped him to turn back the clock to the days when Fletcher was full of life and vitality.

He'd been his world as a little boy, a figure to look up to. Uncle Fletcher always had the answers, knew how to put things right. He'd been his idol, his tower of strength. Now he was weak. A weak, old man who needed his help. With a dull realisation, Jasper knew the roles had reversed. It was his turn to look after him. Like it or not, Fletcher needed him. By the look of things, his uncle wasn't going to give in and receive any form of help easily. And just how was Jasper going to help, living thousands of miles away in Dubai? He had to think of a plan, and fast.

He cursed himself for not having come sooner. How had it happened so fast? The last time Jasper had seen Fletcher, he had seemed more agile. *But how long ago was that?* his conscience pricked him. Obviously quite some time ago, judging by his deterioration.

A branch scraped across his window in the night's breeze. He opened his eyes. The moon was beaming through the thin curtains, faintly illuminating the bedroom. This had always been his room, tucked up snug under the beams. He'd loved it as a child. The small leaded window gave panoramic views of the rolling green hills, woods and streams. The bare wooden floorboards creaked and the tiny cast-iron fireplace still smoked when lit. A far cry from the spacious bedroom in his Dubai apartment, where the huge king-sized bed stood by the balcony doors overlooking the bright lights of the city and the air conditioning hummed quietly in the background. But he realised with sudden clarity that he didn't miss it. He was beginning to appreciate more and more just where his loyalties lay.

Jasper enjoyed Dubai, he really did. It was hard not to when everything was on offer: golden beaches, clear blue oceans, high-class restaurants, designer shops, a glittering career and women, well… Although disciplined, he knew he pretty much had his pick. Not that he took advantage, but he was a man – and one that women found attractive. Zara for one. Once or twice he'd been tempted, she was very easy on the eye after all, but she was also a colleague and Jasper knew more than most never to mix business with pleasure.

For a moment, he contemplated Fletcher and wondered why he had never married. Always, his uncle would brush off any questions about his relationships, declaring he'd simply never met the love of his life. Jasper had struggled to believe this though, especially when considering how vivacious Fletcher was, how magnetic his personality. He was fun to be around, his sense of humour and outlook on life was refreshing. He had charisma and people sought his company. Jasper recalled the parties he'd hosted, when The Laurels had been packed with guests laughing and chatting, delighting in Fletcher's hospitality. In his day, he'd been a looker and had cut a very handsome chap, always impeccably dressed, hair sleeked back with Brylcreem.

Jasper had a photograph of his parents and Fletcher, all huddled together smiling into the camera, with The Laurels in the background. It was his favourite one of his parents and his uncle. So why? Why had Fletcher never married? He'd been handsome, brilliant company and owned a country estate. It beggared belief. And to top it all, he'd have made a fantastic father. Jasper would have had a cousin to share the magical childhood he had had at The Laurels. But no, it had never happened for Fletcher.

Jasper's head ached. His eyelids grew heavy and gently closed. He was jet-lagged and his troubled mind was weighing him down. Soon, his breathing became steady and controlled and he fell into a deep, deep sleep.

Chapter 6

As predicted, Edie was in raptures over the camper van.

'Oh Adira, she's lovely!' she exclaimed. It tickled Adira that her gran had referred to the camper van as 'she', like her.

'I know. I can't wait to get going.'

'No regrets then?' Edie grinned.

'Absolutely none. Leaving that job is the best thing I've ever done. I can't tell you how much better I feel already.'

'Good.' Edie squeezed her, then guided her into the kitchen. On the table was a wooden box, filled with all sorts of bottles and containers.

'What's this?' Adira asked.

'It's a stock of basic medicine,' Edie told her. 'Didn't want you to go on the road empty-handed.'

'I see.' Her brow furrowed, trying to decipher what was in there.

'There's the everyday ingredients to warn off infection, or—'

'Just what do you think's going to happen, Gran?' Adira laughed.

'There's nothing like being prepared,' Edie replied rather indignantly.

Adira shook her head with affection. Her gran meant well and Edie's formulas had often proved fruitful in the past. It would be handy to have some in whilst she was travelling.

'Thanks, Gran.' She hugged her hard. 'I'm going to miss you.'

'Oh give over, you'll be far too busy enjoying yourself.' Edie hugged back and willed herself not to get emotional. 'Oh, and I've also got this for you.' She pulled out a large UK map from the side of the box.

Adira chuckled. 'I do have satnav, you know.'

'Yes, but those things don't always work,' Edie dismissed, making Adira smile again.

She looked at the kitchen clock, it was ten a.m., almost time to go. Adira was due to set off late morning to allow herself a good day's drive. She planned to make several stops on the way to Scotland, taking her time to appreciate the journey and stay in new places. That was about all her plans consisted of, deciding to take each day as it came. That, after all, had been her intention in the first place. At the risk of sounding like a hippy, she had well and truly got into the travelling mode and wanted to 'let go', it being such a stark contrast to the rigid work pattern she had been forced into over the years. On reflection, Adira grasped that perhaps she was also escaping from the monotonous, stringent regime developed from revision and exam taking too. This was truly the first time in her life that she could completely relax. It was only a year, then she could easily get another job. Perhaps she would move out of London? Who knew? And who cared, thought Adira. For the time being she was a free agent and she intended to make the most of it.

'Where will you stop tonight?' asked Edie.

'Dunno,' Adira shrugged. 'Wherever the mood takes me.'

Edie took in her granddaughter's free spirit and marvelled at the change in her, compared to the tired, serious-looking girl that had visited only a few weekends ago. Why her own mother hadn't seen how exhausted she'd looked was beyond Edie. Typical Cleo – high expectations and no pleasure, she thought with a tinge of regret. Why couldn't her daughter lighten up? Surely now, even she must see how happy Adira was.

'Well, you've certainly got the weather.'

'I know, it should last too.' Adira had looked at the long-range weather forecast. It was early June and, luckily, the warm spell would see her nicely on the way to Scotland. Today's conditions were ideal for driving, as her dad had told her after looking the camper van over. He'd tested the air pressure in the tyres and checked the oil and water. He also had insisted that Adira join the AA and download their app, just in case of emergencies. All good advice, which she'd taken. And now, it was time to go.

After putting gran's medical kit in the camper van and the map on the passenger's seat, she gave Edie one last hug. Her heart was pounding, this was it, freedom at last.

'Text me when you arrive tonight.' For the first time, her gran looked concerned.

'I will.' Adira climbed in and slammed the door shut. 'Wherever that will be,' she mouthed through the window, then blew a kiss.

Edie stood at the bottom of the drive and watched her go, until the sky-blue van disappeared round the corner.

'There she goes,' she whispered, 'God speed my love.'

Closing her eyes, Edie prayed she'd done the right thing, knowing full well where the blame would lie should anything go wrong. She could see her daughter's finger now, pointing straight in her direction, that look of derision scouring her face. 'It's all your fault,' she'd say, making Edie feel the inadequate mother she perpetually did. It had always been the case between them. Chalk and cheese, complete opposites – only in this case never attracting. Especially when it came to Adira.

In the very beginning, Edie had fully understood her daughter's overprotectiveness with Adira. She had been born prematurely, only just surviving as a newborn. Flashbacks of that tiny scrap of pink flesh, wired up in the incubator fighting to exist, were enough to make any mother overprotective, of course they were. But it hadn't ended there, Cleo's safeguarding gradually morphed into something a little more sinister than just a watchful eye. She became obsessive about her daughter's safety, paranoid about where she was, who she was with and what she was doing. Cleo vetted Adira's friends, making sure they were from the right background, living in a good area. Then inevitably came the boyfriends, raising Cleo's paranoia. Once she'd secretly followed Adira on a date, to make sure she was OK. Cleo hated the idea of her precious daughter going into town, what if he tried to get her into a pub and drink underage?

Edie had learnt all this from Pat, her son-in-law. He had confided in her after his attempts to try to calm Cleo down and just let Adira live her life had proved futile. Cleo simply wouldn't listen; she knew what was best for her daughter, she'd tell him, like he didn't! Edie had intervened and tried to reason with her, make her see sense. This had had some effect. But, in time, as Adira's A levels had loomed, Cleo began to pile on the pressure once more. She devised revision timetables, banned the TV and took away her stereo. All for her own sake, she'd tell Adira, who had protested fiercely. In the end, Adira had buckled down to get the results needed for Oxford University, but not because her mother wanted her to, it was an escape route. Adira was urgently seeking a way out, Edie knew. She couldn't wait to leave home and her mother's regime. She hated it. Growing up under Cleo's scrutiny was suffocating.

Her only respite had been Edie. Often she would stay with her and together they'd talk. Edie tried to be impartial, not wanting to be disloyal to her daughter, but it was hard when seeing the effect Cleo was having on her granddaughter. It was clear that Adira had been pressurised, especially regarding university and her chosen subject. Cleo had pushed heavily towards her studying law, seeing it as the perfect option for such an intelligent girl. Adira had once mentioned maybe working in a solicitor's office, like one of her friends had, but Cleo had dismissed the suggestion and told her to aim high, train to be a barrister and earn lots of money. From then on, Adira's path had been set, and her mother was right behind her all the way, whether she liked it or not.

Luckily, Edie knew, Adira had enjoyed university life. More than anything, she had flourished with the independence it gave her. Not surprisingly, she hadn't gone home much, but chose to visit her gran, who lived nearby. Cleo was just plain relieved that her daughter had made it into Oxford, telling her friends and anyone who'd listen how clever Adira was. Ironically, having Adira away at university made Cleo calm down and actually focus on her own life. To her husband's relief, she slowly but surely grew back into the Cleo he had first fallen in love with. Whilst still serious in nature, she had lightened up a little and often made suggestions of weekends away, dining out, concerts and nights at the theatre. All the things they'd once enjoyed together. Edie had been delighted by the change. In short, Adira moving out had given them *all* space. And whilst also delighted by Adira's success as a barrister, she still sensed a restlessness in her granddaughter. But had Edie gone a bridge too far by encouraging Adira to go off travelling? She hoped not.

–

After a while, Adira grew tired and was in need of a break. She decided to follow the signs leading her to the Cotswolds. She'd once visited there as a child and remembered enjoying the old-world country villages. At the time, she had been reading *Cider with Rosie* at school and the idyllic childhood of Laurie Lee had resonated with her.

Coming off at the junction on the motorway, she drove to a quiet road and pulled in to study the map her gran had given her. She couldn't recall the place she'd previously been, but plumped for a village called Bourton-on-the-Water. The name sounded rather quaint and it piqued Adira's interest. She quickly searched for it on her phone and soon learnt it was known as the Venice of the Cotswolds and was famous for its honey-coloured stone architecture and charming village scenes.

Sounds lovely, she thought.

However, on entering the place, Adira had instant reservations. Yes, it truly was a picturesque, beautiful village, with its arched bridges spanning the river Windrush, but unfortunately the world and its wife thought so too. It was packed. A victim of its own beauty, she concluded, wading through the traffic, stopping for people crossing the road, armed with cameras. It was way too much of a tourist attraction for her.

Disappointed, Adira drove straight through and stopped at a garage on the main road outside the village to refuel. Once there, she bought a sandwich and a coffee, then parked in a space at the side.

Feeling a tad disheartened with her first choice, she consulted the map again whilst eating. She thought of travelling further up north, given the favourable driving conditions. If she rested for half an hour, then nipped to the garage loo, she'd be able to drive for another three hours, Adira estimated. This could take her as far as… Cheshire, she decided. Yes, Cheshire sounded like a plan.

Looking at where exactly in Cheshire to stop, she once more searched the area on her phone. Liking the sound of Alderley Edge, famed for being the champagne capital of Britain, with its quality restaurants, trendy bars and even trendier boutiques, Adira chose to stay there. She was also intrigued by the Wizard's Well – a place where, legend had it, King Arthur was buried beneath the hill in a stretching honeycomb of caves! Adira laughed to herself. Yes, she'd go and explore Alderley Edge.

It was early evening by the time Adira reached Cheshire. Tired and hungry, she followed the signs to Alderley Edge. Immediately she was struck by the opulence of the area, expensive houses in pleasant countryside that was obviously popular with the wealthy. Where could she park? This didn't look like a place to have a local campsite nearby. Instead, a rather swanky hotel was set back off a busy road.

Adira's stomach rumbled. She'd only eaten toast and a sandwich all day and all the driving was taking its toll. She considered the options – or lack of them: the hotel looked like the only choice.

In the end, she took the bull by the horns and drove her camper van up the wide, gravel driveway to the front of the hotel. Parking Sheila up and feeling a touch self-conscious, she entered reception. Wearing a loose, cotton tie-dyed dress and flip-flops earned her one or two curious stares. However, the young man on reception was most polite.

'Can I help you, madam?'

'Err… yes please.' Adira lowered her voice and leaned forward, 'Could I possibly park my camper van in your car park overnight? I've been driving all day and I'm—'

'Exhausted?' he smiled.

'Absolutely,' she nodded.

'There's a staff car park round the back,' he quietly told her. 'Providing you dine with us, I can't see it being a problem.'

'Oh, thank you!' she gushed.

'What time shall I book dinner for you?'

'About an hour? Give me chance to change,' she whispered awkwardly, looking round at the cliental.

'Very good, madam,' he smiled and gave her a surreptitious wink, before taking her details.

After washing, sprucing up her hair and changing into the trusty little black dress she was thankful she'd packed, Adira walked back into the hotel with confidence. Giving her name to a waiter, he showed her into the restaurant. As a single diner, Adira had discreetly been given a table in the corner, behind a pillar. She was glad to be out of the way of other diners. It didn't stop her from hearing them though.

'OMG, I can't believe what she was wearing!' said one high-pitched voice, instantly catching her attention.

'I know, unbelievable. What was she thinking?' drawled another, promptly followed by a low chuckle. 'God knows what she's going to bring to Mauritius, probably halter-necks, capri pants and a whole range of maxi dresses.'

This was met with splutters of laughter.

'*Soooo* last season,' cooed another.

'Oh yah,' someone agreed, 'very yesterday,' then quickly added in hushed tones, 'Shush, she's coming.'

What was wrong with halter-necks? Adira wondered. *She* had a halter-neck top. What a bunch, Adira thought, but couldn't help eavesdropping further.

'Hi, Melissa darling! You look divine. How's Jamie?'

The sound of air kissing, 'M'wow, m'wow,' came next.

'He's busy training for tomorrow's match,' was the smug reply. 'He's been made captain.'

'Lovely. Well done him.' The flat response sounded anything like a congratulations.

Alderley Edge was clearly full of WAGs, as well as the wealthy. Not Adira's kind at all, but still, after visiting the Wizard's Well tomorrow, she'd be out of here.

The next day, after having gone on a pleasant walk to discover the cave with an old man's face carved into its rock, Adira was left feeling somewhat deflated. Somehow, she had expected more, but no, that's essentially what the Wizard's Well was: a rock, which had the image of a face carved into it. She was beginning to have second thoughts about the whole travelling thing. Had she made a hasty decision to repent at leisure? She had a whole year stretched out in front of her. Then, mentally shaking herself, she got back into her camper van. Ignoring the map this time, she decided to just drive off and land where the mood took her. Less planning (look where that had got her) and more spontaneity. Onwards and upwards!

It was early evening and the sun had been shining through the windscreen all day, making the van hot. Adira was getting tired and decided now was the time to stop. She desperately needed to cool down. Having only stopped once on the motorway, she was more than ready for a cold drink and something to eat. She had turned off the motorway at a junction in Lancashire a while ago and was now driving through stunning countryside. Winding the window down fully, she heard wood pigeons cooing through the trees as they rustled slightly in the refreshing breeze. A faint smell of wild garlic floated in the air.

Adira slowed down to really appreciate her surroundings, it was so therapeutic – something she desperately needed after the fairly disastrous start to her adventure. The sound of running water caught her attention and she pulled into the roadside and turned off the engine. What she wouldn't do to sink her hot, swollen feet into a cool stream, or splash her dry, tired face. The urge became too great. There and then, she decided to find somewhere nearby to park up for the night and sleep under the stars in this beautiful place she had stumbled upon. The only sign she had noticed, whilst driving through the country lanes, told her she was in the Forest of Bowland. Adira consulted the map Edie had given her. Squinting, she found her destination and learned it was a designated area of outstanding natural beauty. *It certainly is*, she agreed. *There must be a campsite nearby*, she thought.

She turned the key to start up the engine, but nothing happened. Oh hell, please don't say Sheila was packing up on her! Another twist and the camper van spluttered and shot forward into life, making Adira jump. With a huge sigh of relief, she carefully drove along the road, looking for a place to stop. She saw a dirt track that veered off to the left and followed it. It led to a stone post, with a wide-open entrance, almost inviting her into the lush, green field beyond. There was no sign marked private land. Then she heard that wonderful sound of running water again, enticing her. Without another thought, Adira drove onto the field and parked along the edge, by the stream canopied by a cluster of trees. It seemed a nice, quiet spot. The clear, fresh water bubbled, intoxicating her. Glancing around, she saw no one, not a soul. All was still and peaceful; ideal for taking a dip and revitalising her sticky body.

Chapter 7

Jasper's spirits had been raised slightly, having spent the day with Fletcher. The initial shock of seeing him had sunk in, but spending time with his uncle told him that although his body was aging, his mind certainly wasn't. His conversation was as entertaining as always, peppered with humour and fascinating tales from the past. It made Jasper smile the way Fletcher exaggerated and spun a yarn, maximising his storytelling. He'd never lost the talent of keeping people interested. Little wonder Jasper had loved staying with him as a child.

Fletcher had taken the opportunity to be completely open with Jasper. Whilst not mentioning his own physical ailments, he did spell out his wishes on the event of his death. It was no secret that Jasper was the sole inheritor. However, Fletcher had been at pains to stress that The Laurels was to remain in the family.

'It's part of who we are, Jasper. It's in the blood. Do you understand?'

It had been the first time Jasper had seen his uncle so earnest, so adamant to emphasise the point. Jasper was slightly offended. Did he think he would sell The Laurels the moment he inherited it? Then again, it did make him consider what exactly would happen. Could he see himself living at The Laurels, deep in the countryside? It was a far cry from Dubai and the career he had built up. A very successful career, which had made him good money. Whilst he stood to gain a lot from inheriting the family estate, it also meant giving up a lot to sustain it. The enormity of the future had begun to weigh heavy on him, giving him mixed, confused feelings. Deep down, Jasper couldn't even contemplate losing Fletcher.

'This place needs attention, Jasper. You can see for yourself. But there's only so much I can do.' They were sat outside on the patio in the sunshine and Fletcher was in good spirits. The warmth of the sun soothed his aching bones and the pre-dinner drinks he had poured them were having a desired mellowing effect. Plus, having Jasper there had given him a huge lift. His nephew was just the tonic he needed.

'I'd like to take a good look at the place, see what needs doing.'

'You do that.' Fletcher threw back his drink, then looked him solemnly in the eye. 'It's time to pass on the baton.'

Jasper swallowed, then tried to make light of the conversation. 'There's life in the old boy yet,' he raised his glass to salute him.

Fletcher barked out a laugh.

'Let's have another drink,' he replied with a wink.

After dinner, Jasper decided to make a start. He was going to survey the house and land and make notes on any immediate repairs that needed doing. Fletcher had mentioned his inspection of the fields and woodland at the back of The Laurels. Apparently there was a fallen tree and a broken gate. There could be more damage that he'd missed, given the amount of land on the estate.

Jasper set off with a notebook and pen and headed for the fields. He noticed something in the distance, a blue vehicle parked by the stream. Stopping in his tracks, he watched carefully. He couldn't see anybody about. Who had trespassed on their land? Maybe there was a group of people. Squatters even? He needed to suss out who was there before approaching them, so he walked into the woods for cover. Making his way through the trees, he strained to see it was a camper van. A trendy Volkswagen, one that probably a group of students were holidaying in.

Jasper walked with forced purpose on the mossy ground, snapping twigs and branches, eager to get a closer look. Then, when only yards away from it, he saw a bikini-clad woman gently ease herself into the stream. Jasper gulped and froze. She had long, blonde hair that hung in tendrils down her back. His gaze homed in on her svelte, toned body, glistening with droplets of water. She looked like Aphrodite, beautifully elegant in the shimmering pool as she splashed water onto her face. And what a pretty face it was, dotted with freckles from the sun. Jasper drank in the sight before him, he was transfixed.

Then, realising how this must look and not wanting to be accused of being a Peeping Tom, he very quietly retreated back through the woods. There only appeared to be one person, a young woman travelling on her own. Hardly a threat, but even so, she was on private land and needed to be told. Perhaps it would be better coming from Fletcher? No, that seemed so lame, sending an old man over to approach her. It should be him. He'd go back in an hour or two, once she'd finished her swim and was dressed.

'There's someone parked on the back field,' he told Fletcher as he entered the drawing room. It was getting dusk now and Fletcher was settling down with a whisky.

'Who?'

'A woman in a camper van. She's set up camp by the stream.'

'Why didn't you tell her to push off?'

'Err… I thought I'd speak to you first.' He avoided Fletcher's scrutiny.

'Oh well, I'll tell her in the morning.' He was tired and didn't want bothering. 'Leave the lass be until tomorrow, she's not doing any harm.'

Jasper wasn't sure he agreed. Part of him wanted to go back to the field and see what she was up to. Then he resisted. What if she'd noticed him through the woods and knew he'd seen her bathing?

Fletcher was right, what harm could such a young woman do? Apart from assault his senses that was.

Chapter 8

Fletcher woke early morning as the sun through his curtains. Feeling rather revitalised after a good night's sleep, he decided to rise and make the most of the day. The house was in silence. Jasper obviously wasn't yet up and Lilly wouldn't be arriving until later.

After finishing his breakfast, he remembered what Jasper had told him the night before. He put on his boots and made his way to the field where the trespasser was. He was surprised at Jasper not confronting the woman when he'd seen her yesterday evening.

Striding through the dewy grass towards the blue camper van he saw a figure with long, blonde hair sitting in a deckchair. As he approached her, she looked up startled.

'Good morning, miss,' he nodded his head.

'Hello…' Still she looked apprehensive.

'You do realise that you're on my land?' He looked directly at her. This made her fluster even more.

'No! Sorry, I didn't.' She seemed genuinely shocked and moved to get up.

Fletcher felt a tinge sorry for his abruptness. He waved her to sit back down. 'It's all right, lass, sit down.'

'I'm really sorry, I'd no idea… The gate was wide open and… I just—'

'The gate's broken. I've propped it against the post.'

'Oh, I see.' Her face fell.

Not wanting to make her feel any more embarrassed, Fletcher rubbed his hands together and smiled. 'Lovely morning, isn't it?'

Sensing the old man wanted to talk, rather than send her away immediately, Adira asked if he wanted a chair to sit on.

'Aye, lass.' He nodded again. 'And how about a cup of tea?'

Adira smiled. 'I'll put the kettle on.'

Soon they were sat opposite each other in the glorious morning sunshine exchanging pleasantries. Adira had told Fletcher of her plans to travel to Scotland in the newly bought camper van and he had explained how he owned the surrounding land and lived in The Laurels. The two chatted amicably for a few minutes when suddenly Adira leant forward towards him.

'That's some bump you have on your forehead.'

'Now don't you start,' he gently warned, taking a sip of his tea.

'Seriously, it needs attention.'

'I'm not going to no quack,' he replied gruffly.

Adira knew she'd hit a nerve by his response.

'I could give you something for it.'

Fletcher's head shot up in surprise. 'Like what?'

'Witch hazel, it'll cleanse and bring the inflammation down. Just a minute.' Adira got up and went inside the van. She soon reappeared with the box that Edie had prepared.

'What you got there?' frowned Fletcher.

'It's a stock of herbal medicines.'

His frown deepened, making her laugh.

'No need to look so worried, it's only nature bottled up and ingredients that have been used for centuries. In many ways, it's better than drugs that are dished out all too readily.'

Fletcher nodded thoughtfully, maybe she had a point?

Adira pulled out a small brown bottle and unscrewed the lid. Tipping a few droplets onto her fingers, she moved over to him. 'I'll just rub a little into your bruise. Relax.'

Fletcher did as he was told and closed his eyes. The liquid felt cool and calming. The smell was pleasant too, he thought, as her soft touch skimmed over his forehead.

'How did you get this?' Adira asked, still gliding her fingers gently over his skin. He found it very therapeutic.

'Book fell on me head,' he murmured back, 'and something went in my eye.'

'Open it up, let me see.'

Fletcher stared up as Adira assessed.

'Hmm, it looks red and slightly inflamed. I'll give you a compress to ease it and take the sting away.'

'Thank you,' he quietly replied, feeling completely tranquil.

When she'd finished rubbing in the witch hazel, Adira opened various other bottles and, using a glass dropper, mixed up a potion into an empty jar. Then she took a small piece of towelling from a bag. Passing them to him, she gave instructions on what to do.

'How come you know all this. You're not some kind of witch, are you?' He gave a mischievous chuckle.

'It's all down to my gran, she's a naturopath. Knows a lot about the healing qualities of plants.'

Fletcher was intrigued, what a curious lady she was. Suddenly he realised he didn't want her to disappear off his land just yet. Interesting people like her didn't crop up in his life very often. In fact, not many people cropped up in his life at all these days! 'You don't have to rush off, you know. Take your time. In fact… I'm sorry I don't know your name?'

'Adira,' she smiled.

Adira, even her name was different. 'Well, Adira, why don't you come up to the house for dinner this evening? As a thank you for this.' He lifted up the jar.

'Oh, how kind. Thank you very much…'

'Fletcher,' he supplied.

'That would be lovely, thank you, Fletcher.'

'Right, see you then.' He nodded once more and set off.

–

Jasper eventually rose from a deep sleep to find Fletcher rinsing his eye in the bathroom.

'What's that, Fletcher?' he asked, pointing to the jar of liquid stood on the windowsill.

'It's an eye compress. That young woman gave it to me,' he said while wiping his eye with a towel. 'You know, the one in the camper van.'

Jasper stood still for a moment.

'You've spoken to her then?'

'I have that, and a very pleasant girl she is too. Her gran's some sort of white witch,' he laughed to himself.

Jasper blinked. 'Pardon?'

'She's sorted me bruise out too, look it's gone down.' Fletcher looked in the bathroom mirror, then faced Jasper. It had slightly. His uncle's forehead no longer protruded with such a huge bump. 'Rubbed it with witch hazel.'

'With what?' asked Jasper sharply.

'Witch hazel.' Fletcher laughed again. 'Jasper, put your face straight. No need to look so suspicious, you'll see for yourself what a grand lass she is.'

Jasper stared at him. 'Will I?'

'Aye, she's coming for dinner.'

—

Adira hummed to herself as she strolled up the driveway to The Laurels. Wearing a red, strappy sundress which show-cased her golden tanned skin, she admired the beautiful building before her. It really was an impressive country house, with its sandstone walls covered in ivy, large sash windows and elegant orangery. Her critical eye quickly noted its faults though, spotting the odd cracked roof tile and window pane.

Adira's thoughts turned to how Fletcher had seemed almost defensive about seeing a doctor. She suspected he was a man who was too proud to ask for help, or even admit he needed it, including when it came to the welfare of his property, not just himself. Surely it wasn't just him rattling around this huge house? How on earth could he maintain the upkeep of such a large place, especially at his age? Intuition told her that Fletcher was lonely. He had been eager to talk to her that morning, and her a stranger at that, who it transpired had been trespassing. The shame! Then she giggled, wait till she told her gran.

She rang the bell and waited. The door soon opened and a pair of brown eyes the colour of melted chocolate stared into her. Caught slightly unawares, Adira stalled. The eyes belonged to a handsome face, with a strong jawline, slightly shadowed with dark stubble.

'I'm...' she stammered.

'The lady who's camping on our land?' The face broke into a grin. 'Hi, I'm Jasper, come in.'

'Adira,' she smiled backed. So who was Jasper? Fletcher never mentioned a son, although he did resemble him.

Jasper had the same thick, wavy hair, albeit dark and cut short. As he led the way through the hall into the drawing room, she observed his broad shoulders in the Oxford shirt he wore and his muscular legs in close-fitted jeans. Well, this was a turn-up for the books, she thought rather pleasantly. Then she smirked wryly to herself; just wait for his wife to appear.

'Ah! There you are, Adira!' called Fletcher, like a long-lost friend. He was by a drinks cabinet. 'What can I get you? Thought we'd enjoy pre-dinner drinks first.'

'Oh, whatever you're having, thanks, Fletcher,' she replied, just as familiarly, causing Jasper to raise his eyebrows slightly. The easy casualness wasn't lost on him, making Adira suddenly feel slightly self-conscious. Her sharp eyes also clocked that Fletcher was only pouring into three glasses, so no one else was due to join them. This settled her for some reason.

'There you go,' Fletcher passed her a tall, cut glass, jangling with ice cubes. 'Can't beat a stiff gin and tonic,' he winked, making her giggle.

Again, she noted those chocolate brown eyes bore into her. Did Jasper resent her being here? It was hard to tell, he had that kind of poker face, however handsome, which didn't give anything away – all dark and brooding. Her gaze met his defiantly.

'You've met Jasper, my nephew then,' Fletcher continued, seeming totally oblivious to any undercurrent between the two.

'Yes,' she replied.

'He was the one who first spotted your camper van,' Fletcher chuckled.

There was an awkward pause as Adira's eyes slid back to Jasper's. Was he blushing slightly? When exactly had he seen her camper van? More to the point, when had he seen *her*? Please not when she had taken a dip in the river. His face didn't flicker, he really was hard to read.

Then Jasper spoke, changing the subject. 'Dinner's nearly ready.' He turned to her and smiled charmingly, 'Beef casserole OK?'

'Lovely, thanks.' She wondered if he'd cooked it. In fact, she was beginning to wonder quite a bit about this man full stop. He invoked an interest inside her. She watched him leave the room and admired his physique once more.

Fletcher nudged her playfully. 'Don't mind him,' he teased, 'I think I startled him when I mentioned you being a witch.' He winked again.

Adira couldn't help but laugh, he was the most mischievous, old rogue.

'Hardly a witch,' she replied drily.

'Hmm, I'll wager you could bewitch Jasper though,' he said thoughtfully, gauging her reaction.

'I doubt that.' She took a long, hard drink to steady her nerves. She felt a tinge shaky all of a sudden.

Fletcher might be old, but he was no fool. He'd detected a frisson of attraction between his nephew and this pretty, young woman. And why not? They looked good together, he concluded.

—

Fletcher had hit the nail well and truly on the head. Adira had indeed got under Jasper's skin. Later that evening, in his attic bedroom he had found himself once again contemplating, but not over his uncle, this time it was their dinner guest who had dominated his thoughts.

Images of her laughing easily with Fletcher who had harmlessly teased her filled his head. She had a natural, pretty look, her skin had a healthy, golden glow and the sun had highlighted streaks in her long, blonde hair. Even her fragrance haunted Jasper, a light, floral scent which he couldn't inhale enough of.

Stop it, man, he roughly reprimanded himself. She was a virtual stranger, who he happened to have witnessed bathing. This then brought him back to his dilemma of whether she had sussed him. Fletcher hadn't helped matters, blurting out that he was the one who had first spotted her. He knew the possibility had crossed her mind judging by the way she had looked at him. He was sure he hadn't given anything away, he was renowned for his straight face in the boardroom when others had threatened to lose their nerve. Jasper was a master at 'keeping his powder dry', to quote one of Fletcher's sayings.

It half unnerved him, though, the way his uncle had so easily warmed to her, and she to him. It appeared to be a mutual connection, one which had been created all too speedily for Jasper's liking; perhaps because this behaviour was the polar opposite to his. Always he would act under caution, it was just his nature, his make-up. That's why he had proved to be so good at his job. Never completely trusting anyone, unless he really knew them, had served him well over the years in the cut-throat world of business. Jasper made sound judgements. People trusted him. If Jasper Hendricks was on board, the powers that be could rest assured. He stood head and shoulders above the highest of flyers with his astute, cool exterior. Whilst negotiating deals, he appeared calm and composed, never getting hot under the collar, unlike many of his counterparts. Often, his colleagues would joke about him being the perfect poker player, to which Jasper would simply reply he didn't gamble. Taking risks wasn't his forte; he made sure he won. If they'd seen how Jasper was with his family and friends, they would probably be quite shocked. For it was them who saw the deeply caring Jasper, who would protect them at all costs.

Whilst he had grown up being closer to Fletcher than his own father, he still held his parents in high esteem and he had taken after Rufus with his rather cautious nature, but his mother, Alice, had passed on the compassionate, loving genes which ran through his blood. As a child, he'd often wished for a sibling, maybe Fletcher had in some way filled that gap.

Jasper couldn't help but smile at the way his uncle had performed over dinner, regaling his stories from the past, half of which he was convinced he'd invented, or certainly embellished beyond recognition of the truth. Adira had loved hearing them, giggling along, encouraging Fletcher even more.

Then the vigilant side of Jasper kicked in. What if there was more to Adira than met the eye? Already, she had influenced his uncle with her herbal 'medicines', supposing she had an agenda? The more he considered it, the more plausible it became. Fletcher was an old man, with an estate. If he so chose, he could very easily leave a substantial amount of money to anyone he should befriend. Jasper had watched Adira walk up the path through the hall window. He had seen her admiring The Laurels. What had she been thinking? Had the pound signs flashed? Was she really a barrister, or had that been a ruse to look respectable? He remembered how her eyes had darted about the place, taking everything in – the paintings, antiques and silver. He also noted how quick she'd been to offer help, show concern over Fletcher's ailments. That jar on the bathroom windowsill shot into his thoughts. What exactly was in it? What else was she going to 'prescribe' him?

Jasper shifted uncomfortably in his bed. His mind was going into overdrive. Probably too much wine at dinner, he told himself.

He heard Fletcher whistling softly as he shut the bathroom door. Well, Adira had certainly cheered him up, no doubt about that.

–

Adira strolled back to the camper van in the soft, silver moonlight. She'd stayed much longer than anticipated, time having flown. Fletcher was such entertaining company, but that she had expected. In a way, he reminded her of Edie, being quite a character, in an unconventional kind of way. Quirky, would be a word to describe them. Perhaps that's why she had gelled so well with Fletcher, he was a comforting grandfather figure.

And Jasper, well he was food for thought. He'd certainly piqued Adira's interest, but in which way, she wasn't quite sure. There was no denying how attractive he was, but he wasn't overconfident with it, unlike some men she had known. Often, when working alongside handsome barristers, they had flaunted their good looks by being openly flirty, expecting her to be flattered by the attention. Personally, she found it a turn-off and didn't find it particularly professional when seeing the same behaviour with the pretty women in the chambers either.

Adira wasn't a prude, far from it, but firmly believed that the workplace was just that, a place to *work*. One or two of her male colleagues had asked her out, to which she had very politely declined. Instead, she had chosen to date men outside of her chambers. Rory had been different, she had enjoyed a few drinks with him after work, but that had been purely platonic, as friends meeting up.

Jasper was different too, but in a completely separate way. He was self-assured, in an understated manner. Comfortable in his own skin, surmised Adira. There was a definite edge to him, of that she had no doubt. Clearly he was protective of his uncle, and rightly so, and she detected an air of distrust oozing from him. For once, Adira couldn't quite put her finger on what gave her that uneasy impression. Jasper had been amiable, he'd joined in the conversation, often sharing banter with Fletcher, and had briefly talked about his life in Dubai. In return, he had politely enquired about her and had appeared rather impressed to learn she was in fact a barrister and had even heard of Goldgate Chambers. He also seemed to admire her decision to buy the camper van and get away from it all – well, for at least a year anyway. So, he knew she was no 'hippy' about to squat forever on his family's land. On the face of it, she was just a harmless passer-by that Fletcher had invited for dinner. So why had he looked at her in that brooding way?

Adira had been accustomed to meeting new clients and quickly judging their characters, getting a sense as to what made them tick. Always her instincts, her gut feeling, had been proved right. Look at Sir Reginald Demsy, she'd got his measure immediately. Yet for some reason Jasper was an enigma. One minute he was all smiles and pleasantries, the next he was sizing her up with narrowed eyes. Once or twice, she had met his scrutinising gaze head-on, as if challenging him. He didn't respond, just coolly sipped his wine.

Truth be told, Jasper unsettled her, and she hated to admit it. Unacquainted with this position, it made her feel vulnerable. Adira was used to being in control, both in her public and private life. She could be assertive when needed in court and knew what she wanted from a relationship. All she knew about Jasper was that she found him attractive, yet wasn't sure if she actually liked him.

Soon, she had made her way across the field back to Sheila, gently lit up by the stream and waiting for her. Fletcher had roared with laughter when she had told him of the camper van's name. He'd also shown concern when Adira had mentioned that Sheila had momentarily conked out on her shortly after arriving in Lilacwell. He'd insisted the camper van be checked over, earning her another 'look' from Jasper.

Entering the cosy van, Adira put the stove on for a cup of Horlicks. She looked up at the small roof window, out onto the clear, starry night sky. How beautiful it was and how fortunate she was to have found such a place.

Chapter 9

The next day brought more glorious weather. The bright morning sunrise warmed the valley, which didn't encourage Adira to get behind the driving wheel too soon. In fact, with Fletcher's permission, she fancied staying in Lilacwell a few more days before setting off again. Deciding to explore the village, she headed to the local inn which he had mentioned last night. She took the track she had originally driven down, drinking in the idyllic scenery. In the distance lay the Bowland Fells with shades of every green. Fir trees surrounded the area, interrupted by stone walls and clear running waterfalls. Adira heard a wood pigeon call far from a verdant forest and breathed in the fresh country air. It was heaven.

For a moment, she compared her surroundings to that of North London, where the traffic stood pumping out fumes, whilst commuters frantically went about their business in silence with fixed expressions. It was a world away, and a world she was well shot of. In such a short space of time, Adira was coming to the conclusion that she was no longer a part of the London life. In many ways, she wondered if she truly ever had been. All it had taken was a couple of days in a camper van to realise how much that life had been crushing her. How right her gran was to send her that picture of Sheila to entice her out of it. Where would she be now if Edie hadn't taken the initiative? In that office with the rest of them, tapping away at their keyboards, staring at screens. She shuddered at the thought.

As Adira walked to the end of the track and onto the main road into the village, the first view of the Inn at Lilacwell stood before her, every bit as impressive as The Laurels, with the same sandstone and Georgian pillars. Set in stunning grounds and a winding gravel driveway, Adira saw the open studded oak door and was too tempted not to visit.

She entered the inn to find it fairly busy. Obviously a popular place to dine, given that most of the tables were taken. It had a faint smell of beeswax and polish. Rays of sun blasted in through the small leaded windows, highlighting a touch of dust from last evening's open fires. It was exactly what she expected of a typical country inn. And so different from the corporate bars and pretentious restaurants in the capital. The atmosphere was friendly and comfortable, the clientele varied yet relaxed, ranging from local farmers propping up the bar, to the archetypal country set in tweeds with Labradors sat obediently by.

A young woman serving behind the bar smiled up at Adira. 'Hello there, what can I get you?'

'A Coke please.'

After handing her the drink, the girl spoke again. 'Visiting Lilacwell?'

'Yes, just for a few days. I'm camping nearby.'

At this the girl laughed, making Adira frown.

'Oh, so you're Fletcher's squatter then?'

Adira looked surprised, making the girl laugh even more.

Leaning over the bar, she informed her in a hushed tone, 'Everybody knows everything here in Lilacwell.'

'Ah, I see,' grinned Adira, 'and have you been told all about my magic potions?' she replied with humour.

'You mean the witch hazel and eyewash?' she played along.

Adira got friendly vibes. She had an easy way about her, with a natural look. Her chestnut hair was cut short into a wedge. She guessed they were a similar age.

'I'm Adira by the way.' She held out her hand, which the girl shook.

'Cassie. I'm the assistant manager.'

'It's a beautiful place.' Adira looked all around her at the stone floors, inglenook fires and wooden panelling holding paintings of country scenes.

'It sure is,' Cassie agreed. 'So, what's the crack with the herbal remedies?' Curiosity had been aroused already amongst the village and she was never one to miss an opportunity, not when she had the 'witch' herself stood in front of her.

Adira smiled at the openness of her, that was the vast distinction between living in London where nameless peoples scurried about their business, oblivious to those around them. Here, it seemed everyone, especially a newcomer, was of paramount interest.

'Well,' she replied, then took a long drink, 'my gran's a naturopath and she's taught me all she knows. I'm actually a trained massage therapist.'

'Really?' Cassie asked, curious.

'Yes, so if ever you need to relax those muscles full of tension, I'm your man,' Adira winked, making Cassie laugh again. She liked this new visitor, with her strange ways and unusual name. She understood Fletcher's interest. Adira was fresh blood to Lilacwell, and the villagers, she knew, would want to know every single thing about her.

'Hmm.' Cassie paused in thought. 'You could well have fallen upon a good idea there.'

'Sorry?'

'We've talked about having a spa treatment room here at the Inn, offering guests beauty therapies and massages, that kind of thing.'

'Good idea,' agreed Adira, 'you've certainly got the custom.' She glanced round at the many tables occupied with ladies of various ages. They obviously had money to spend staying at the Inn, so why wouldn't they buy beauty treatments as part of their stay?

Cassie was looking at her pensively.

'Would you consider offering advice, on how to set it up, what we'd need, that kind of thing?'

'Well...'

'Even if you're not planning to stay here long, perhaps you can help to get the room ready and give directions on packages we could offer?' Cassie gave her most beguiling smile, then threw in the clincher, 'I'll make sure you're paid well.' Aha, that made a difference, judging by the look on Adira's face.

'It's very tempting, but to be honest, it depends on whether Fletcher agrees to me staying in his field.' She had intended to work where she could, but envisaged bar work, or fruit picking – not doing what she really took pleasure in and was good at. Adira knew the money to be made in this line of business and was reluctant to look a gift horse in the mouth.

'Oh don't worry about Fletcher,' waved away Cassie, 'he'll love having you about.'

Adira was inclined to agree deep down, but didn't like to assume. At least this way she could offer him some rent for staying on his land. Then a thought suddenly occurred to her. 'When did Fletcher tell you about me?'

'He didn't. Lilly, his cleaner, told Lisa, who lives in the cottage next door to her and works here, she told us all.'

Adira stared at her. 'Oh, I see.'

'Like I said,' laughed Cassie, 'everybody knows everything in Lilacwell.' Then, with a slight smirk added, 'Met the nephew yet?'

'Jasper? Yes, I've met him.' Why was Cassie's mouth twitching?

'What d'ya reckon?'

'Pardon?'

'Easy on the eye, eh?'

Adira couldn't keep her face straight, suddenly loving the frankness of Cassie. It made such a refreshing change to be with people who were honest and direct, instead of the closed, calculating environment she was used to. Giggling into her drink, she chose her words carefully, knowing every word she spoke would be repeated.

Looking straight at Cassie, she replied, 'He seems a very nice man.'

'And?' she pressed, raising an eyebrow.

'Let's just leave it at that, shall we?' Adira smiled neutrally, making them both chuckle. Something told her it would be fun to spend a little time here, working with Cassie. What was the harm? She wasn't in any rush. Adira had her certificate in massage therapy in a folder, along with her insurance policies, driving licence and emergency contacts. What a lovely environment to work in, she thought as her gaze shifted round the Inn again. Then suddenly she caught sight of dark, wavy hair above a newspaper. She froze. Surely, it wasn't?

Down came the paper to reveal those brown eyes piercing into her. Jasper. Had he heard her conversation with Cassie? They stared each other out for a moment before he finished his coffee, stood up and walked towards her.

Adira's heart started to beat frantically. She swallowed, forcing herself to stay calm.

'Hi, Adira.' Again, he was giving nothing away.

'Hello, Jasper,' she replied, desperate to sound equally casual. She turned her head sharply to see Cassie at the far end of the bar now, busy serving.

'So, it looks like you'll be staying a little longer then?' He tilted his head slightly, still looking into her eyes.

'Err… yes, that's if Fletcher doesn't mind.' Shit. He'd heard every word.

'I'm sure he'll be delighted.'

What was that supposed to mean?

A spark of anger ignited her. 'He'll hopefully appreciate the presence, once you return to Dubai.' She saw his jaw tighten; there, that struck a nerve.

'Hi, Jasper!' called Cassie from the end of the bar. Obviously, she hadn't been aware of him sitting close by either.

'Cassie,' he nodded with a smile. Then, turning to Adira, he evenly said goodbye and strode out of the pub. A few heads turned, watching this tall, handsome man in black jeans and fitted black T-shirt which emphasised his broad shoulders and muscular arms. Adira refused to let herself be one of them.

Chapter 10

Fletcher was staring into the mirror in the hall when Jasper returned to The Laurels.

'My eye looks fine now, see.'

Jasper closed the front door and peered into his face. Sure enough, the redness had completely gone.

'How does it feel?' he asked.

'Much better, not sore anymore. I've a lot to thank that lass for.'

Jasper's concerns were beginning to grow again. 'Yes, she's getting quite a following already in the village,' he replied drily, making Fletcher chuckle.

'Lilly wants something for the arthritis, maybe Adira can help.'

Jasper closed his eyes. He imagined some sort of pop-up mobile hospital in their field, with villagers lining up outside the camper van, waiting to be seen by Adira. 'Fletcher, you must remember, we don't really know Adira—'

'I know she's mended me eye and forehead,' he butted in, 'and… I like her.' Then, turning to look Jasper full in the face, he asked, 'What's not to like about her?'

Jasper stalled. Good question. What had she done wrong?

'She parked illegally on your land,' he offered, sounding rather lame.

'By mistake! And besides, I told her not to dash off. What harm is she doing?'

Again, Jasper hesitated. Perhaps he did need to calm down. He recalled how aloof he'd acted in the Inn and regretted it. Cassie seemed to have got on well with her and she was a good judge of character, meeting lots of people in her profession.

Fletcher assessed his nephew, sensing his unease. How like Rufus he was. It saddened him to see the worry etched on his young face. 'You know, Jasper, I think you need to chill out a little.'

Jasper grinned, it sounded strange coming from an eighty-five-year-old, almost role reversal.

'Look at you all tense,' Fletcher said.

Instantly, he heard Adira's voice, '*If ever you need to relax those muscles full of tension, I'm your man.*' He could feel his pulse pick up at the thought of Adira rubbing soothing oil into his body.

Fletcher's brow puckered. 'Are you all right, Jasper?'

'Yes,' he shot back, not meaning to sound so abrupt. 'You're right, Fletcher, maybe I should—'

'Pay her a visit,' Fletcher interrupted again. This chap needed cheering up a bit and who better than a pretty, young lady like Adira to do it?

Jasper mulled it over for a few seconds. He had wanted to find out more about Adira, especially if she was still going to be here, near his uncle when he returned to Dubai. It was in his and Fletcher's interest to get to know her. Research he liked to think it.

'I will.'

'That's my boy!' Fletcher slapped him on the back.

When Adira returned to the camper van later that afternoon, an envelope was stuck to the door. She opened it and read.

> Dear Adira,
>   Hope you don't mind me asking, but I believe you're good at sorting out people's ailments. The thing is, I don't know if there's anything wrong with me, or if it's my husband. Can we have a chat? Cassie tells me you'll be working at the Inn, so I'll introduce myself.
>   Very best,
>   Lisa.

What?!

Adira re-read the note in disbelief. Then couldn't help but giggle. This village, it really was something else.

Shaking her head, she entered the van, but hadn't been in there long when she heard a tap at the window. Looking out, she saw an old lady wave at her. Adira opened the door.

'Can I help?'

'I hope so. Can you give me something for my aching joints, dear? The stuff I've been taking is useless. Lilly, Fletcher's housekeeper by the way.' She held out a gnarled hand.

Adira shook it and saw her wince slightly. Poor woman, her joints did look swollen and twisted.

'Come in, Lilly. I was just about to put the kettle on.'

'Well, isn't this lovely!' Lilly's eyes darted around the interior of the van. 'Very cosy, I must say.'

'Thanks. I've heard a lot about you,' Adira smiled, putting a cup of tea in front of her.

'All good, I hope.' Her eyes twinkled.

'Yes, Fletcher and Jasper speak very highly of you.'

'Fletcher speaks highly of *you*,' the old lady grinned, reminding Adira of her gran. A pang of homesickness struck her. She so wished Edie was here to meet all these eccentric people.

'And what does Jasper make of me?' she asked half joking.

Lilly laughed. 'Oh, don't mind Jasper. He's a grand fellow, just a touch defensive of his family.'

'Yes, I got that impression.' Did she ever. 'So, about your arthritis.'

Lilly looked up expectantly, all ears.

'Turmeric can help relieve the pain, you can buy capsules, just take one a day.' Adira knew Edie took turmeric and swore by it.

'Oh, thank you, dear, I'll try it.'

'If you don't feel any better though, I would advise you see a doctor,' she added, keen to stop the word getting out about her being the go-to for any illness.

Lilly sighed. 'I know, and I will, if there's no change. But according to Fletcher, you're a miracle worker.' Her eyes twinkled once more.

What an endearing old lady.

Then a thought occurred to Adira. 'I've had a note from your next-door neighbour.'

'Oh Lisa, yes, she said she'll be seeing you too.'

'Right…'

'The lass wants to start a family, but apparently it's just not happening.'

Adira blinked, still not quite believing how upfront the residents of Lilacwell were. 'I'm not a doctor, you know…'

'We know.' Lilly looked earnestly at her. 'She just wants a chat, dear.'

Adira took a deep breath. Where on earth had she tumbled upon?

Alone and needing to clear her head after Lilly's impromptu visit, Adira decided to go for a walk, somewhere peaceful and tranquil to collect her thoughts. The most obvious place to her was the church and its grounds. Following the quaint signposts in the village led her to Saint Jude's, a beautiful sixteenth-century stone church, complete with an impressive bell tower. She pulled on the solid wooden door, but it was bolted. So, Adira thought she'd stroll through the graveyard towards the back of the church.

To her, graveyards were a place of calm and serenity. She'd always found it therapeutic, wandering amongst the aged tombstones, each telling their own story, windows into lost lives; it fascinated her. Adira slowed down to read them, choosing to find the oldest in the graveyard. One or two dated as far back as the mid-sixteenth century; she could only just make out the names and dates. Many went back to the First World War; poor, young soldiers laid to rest in their prime. Then, a name suddenly caught her attention:

GRACE CONWAY 1891–1941
DEVOTED WIFE AND MOTHER

Grace Conway? That name resonated with her. Conway was her grandmother's maiden name. She was sure Edie had mentioned a Grace in her family at some point.

Adira reread the gravestone. It didn't give too much away, just her name, year of birth and death and the fact she had had a husband and child. Could there be a connection? Curiosity mounted inside her. It was such a pity the church was closed. Adira longed to look inside and talk to the priest, maybe look at the church records. Would they give any more information about Grace Conway?

Was it her imagination, or did a sense of completion sweep over her? An essence of fulfilment grew inside, as though she was meant to be here, in Lilacwell. Adira stood, rooted to the spot. She felt a calling, as though a spirit or suchlike was trying to connect with her. She shivered and rubbed away the goosebumps appearing on her arms. *Don't be silly*, she told herself. She was just tired. It had been quite a day.

-

It was dusk as Jasper walked through the field armed with a bottle of wine. It was intended to be an olive branch. In the distance, he could see Adira, sat by a small campfire. How romantic it looked, he thought, seeing the amber flames light up her face as she sat peacefully.

She turned on hearing him approach. Was that trepidation flashing across her face? He hoped not.

'Hi, thought you might like to share this?' He held up the bottle – immediately realising how clumsy that sounded. Why would she want to share a bottle of wine with him? 'Let me rephrase,' he quickly added. 'I'd like to apologise for being abrupt with you earlier in the pub. May I join you?'

Adira was staggered, then, after a few seconds, answered, 'Yes, of course. I'll get a couple of glasses.'

Hell, this was unexpected. He was looking devilishly handsome in a white, open-necked shirt exposing a hint of dark chest. Adira caught his faint aroma of lime and bergamot. Willing herself to stay composed, she quickly checked her reflection in the window, wishing she'd washed her hair. Never mind, she'd have to do. Then inwardly chided herself for caring.

She passed him the glasses and brought out another deckchair. He appeared relaxed pouring the wine.

'Cheers.' He handed her a glass.

'Cheers.'

There was a short silence. Adira waited for him to speak first, after all he'd come to her.

'You've probably figured that Fletcher means the world to me.'

Adira was touched by the announcement, and if being honest, quite surprised at the warmth of it.

Jasper didn't wait for her to reply. 'I worry about him, Adira.'

She looked up into his troubled, beautiful brown eyes.

'Oh Jasper...' was all she could say.

'I'm dreading going back to Dubai... I don't want to leave him.'

'Then don't.'

He gave a sharp laugh. 'It's not that easy. I've signed a two-year contract.'

'Is there no flexibility?' she asked.

He half-smiled. 'We can't all be like you, just take off in Sheila.' He was attempting humour, to lighten the mood, which she understood.

'Fletcher seems a tough, old soul,' she replied encouragingly. 'He's managed so far.'

Jasper shook his head. 'No, Adira, he needs someone here. He's eighty-five, riddled with pain and stubborn as a mule. This place is too much for him now, he's as good as told me.' Another short silence followed.

'I take it you'll be inheriting The Laurels, as Fletcher's next of kin?'

His eyes narrowed. 'Yes. Why do you ask?'

'Well, putting it bluntly, if Fletcher died tomorrow, what would you do about your career in Dubai?' Asking difficult questions was part and parcel of her job as a barrister, it didn't faze her.

Jasper considered it.

'I suppose I'd have to try to negotiate some form of resignation, due to personal circumstances.'

'Well then, couldn't the current situation be regarded in the same light?'

Jasper looked at her. She spoke complete sense. In just a few short sentences, she had totally summed up the predicament. He grasped what a good barrister she must make. Beauty and brains – a lethal combination in his book. The sudden urge to lean forward and kiss her empowered him. He took a gulp of wine.

The fire crackled and an owl hooted in the nearby trees, breaking the spell. All was still.

'I'm sure you'll work it out,' she quietly spoke, then sipped at her glass.

Jasper looked into the flickering flames for a short while.

'Here, let's have a refill.' He poured them both another glass. Eager to change the topic, he told her she had Fletcher's absolute consent to stay as long as she liked in his field, which was an understatement. When Jasper had mentioned it to him, his uncle was delighted to learn of

Adira working at the Inn. This made her smile with real affection.

'He's quite a character, isn't he?' she laughed.

'He certainly is. Made a wonderful uncle growing up here.'

'I'll bet.'

They looked at each other again. Jasper swallowed. They both took long drinks.

'I've had a visit from Lilly,' Adira continued.

'Hmm, I heard as much, and a note from Lisa.'

'Are there no secrets in this place?' she asked in good humour.

'Nope.' He shook his head. They both reached for the wine bottle and their hands touched, sending electric waves through Adira. Her eyes flew to his face. He gulped. 'I better get back. Fletcher will wonder what's happened to me.'

She didn't respond, still quite shaken by the effect of his touch.

'Goodnight!' he called over his shoulder.

'Goodnight,' she replied hoarsely.

Chapter 11

'So, this is the room I was thinking of. What d'ya think?' Cassie pushed open the door to reveal a spacious room with two skylights. It was situated right at the top of the Inn, high up in the eaves.

'It's certainly big enough,' replied Adira, 'and plenty of light. Yes, it's good.'

'Excellent. I always thought this room was destined for great things; it seemed a shame to waste such a space.'

Adira nodded her head in agreement, then looked to the floor. 'I'd get rid of this carpet. What's underneath it?'

'Let's see.' Cassie rolled up her sleeves and knelt down in a corner of the room. Gradually pulling the carpet up, she exclaimed, 'Look!'

Adira quickly hurried over. 'Wow, let's get it all up.'

Together they managed to heave the carpet into a roll, to reveal the original tile flooring. It had a Victorian pattern in burgundy, cream and black tiles.

'It's amazing, why would anyone cover up such beautiful tiles with carpet?'

'I know!' gasped Cassie, thrilled with the find. 'I'll have them cleaned and polished.' She clapped her hands in glee, 'It's going to look fab-u-lous!'

Adira smiled, Cassie's enthusiasm was infectious.

'What will you call the treatment room?' Adira asked.

'Oh, I hadn't thought…'

'Naming it gives it kudos, like it's a special place, rather than just "the treatment room".'

'You're right.' Cassie chewed her lip, pondering a name.

'Give it some thought. Now, we'll need a massage bed, obviously, and very subtle lighting, plenty of shelves for storage and the walls need to be painted a gentle, relaxing colour.'

'OK, I'll get some colour charts.' Cassie was busy making notes on a clipboard. 'What about stock, all the essential oils and mixing lotions?'

'I'll make a list and give you details on where to buy them.'

'Thanks,' she beamed, thoroughly enjoying herself. Cassie had been excited to get this project off the ground. 'Would you need an assistant, help of any kind?'

'It would make sense to have a second therapist on hand, for when I move on.'

Cassie's face fell. Hearing Adira say that brought into focus she wouldn't be a permanent fixture.

'What about advertising with leaflets?' Adira suggested.

'I'm onto it. We're using the same printers who produce our menus.'

'Good. Thought about any kind of promotion?'

'I have actually. What do you think about the Inn having a hog roast party? We could hand out flyers and offer special discounts for the first week of opening. Plus, a good old shindig would be great for the village.'

'That's a brilliant idea! Especially with all this hot weather.'

Cassie looked elated with Adira's reaction.

Just then, there was a knock at the door.

'Ah, Lisa, meet Adira.' Cassie ushered the young woman in.

'Hello, Lisa, pleased to meet you.' Adira held out her hand.

'Hi, Adira, did you get my letter?' Lisa looked rather shy, hiding behind her long, brown fringe.

'I did, yes.'

'Do you mind if we talk?' Lisa asked Cassie.

'No, of course not, I'm just going anyway.' Cassie made her way out. 'Bye for now.'

Adira was keen to make one thing straight before Lisa launched into anything. 'Lisa, I must stress, I'm not a doctor.'

'I know, but I just thought you might be able to suggest something.'

'On?'

'How to get pregnant. I mean...' she laughed nervously, 'we're doing everything we should, but...'

'Have you sought medical advice?'

'Not yet.'

Adira could see the young woman was reluctant to go down that route right now and her heart went out to her. She did actually recall a conversation she'd overheard Edie have years ago. In a similar scenario, her grandmother had advised the woman to try to reduce her stress levels, explaining how tension built up in the body could have a physical impact. She had suggested passion flower relief tablets or a flower remedy oil. Never had Adira envisaged repeating this, but maybe it could be worth a try?

Having outlined what Edie had suggested years ago, Lisa looked stunned.

'Is that all?'

'It's all about learning to relax,' Adira explained. 'You could always try it, to start with, that is.'

'Yeah, definitely, thanks.' And with that, she smiled and went. Consultation apparently over.

As Adira made her way back down the stairs and into the reception area, she saw Cassie talking to Charles, the owner of the Inn. Cassie waved her over, with animation.

'Charles is just telling me the room upstairs was once the bathroom in the servants' quarters years ago.'

'Really? That explains the beautiful tiled floor,' Adira replied, smiling at Charles.

'I believe you both have big plans for it,' he returned with a grin.

Then Cassie suddenly exclaimed. 'Adira, I've just thought of a name. Let's call it "The Bath House".' Her hands drew quotation marks in the air.

Adira's eyes widened. 'Good idea. We could give it a Victorian look, keeping the original feel.'

'Now that I do like,' approved Charles.

'Think wrought-iron light fittings, gothic-style candle holders, copper planters and wooden towel stands,' went on Cassie.

'And Victorian prints of bathhouses framed on the walls,' gushed Adira.

Charles laughed at the two of them.

'I'll leave you ladies to it,' he said, walking back to his office.

'Have we been given a budget?' whispered Adira, hoping they hadn't appeared too keen.

'Don't worry about that,' assured Cassie. 'They'll be queuing up to visit The Bath House.' The pride in her voice was evident. Adira couldn't help but echo this.

Together they made a good team. Never once had she felt this way in London.

Chapter 12

Jasper had asked for a meeting with Colin, the estate manager. He was eager to discuss matters with him, not believing for one moment Fletcher's version of the estate being 'just grand'. Colin had confirmed his reservations. Far from being 'grand', it was actually on its last legs, not that he had been that brusque, but Jasper could read between the lines; 'needing attention,' 'limited funds' and 'lack of work force' could only mean one thing – the estate was on a downward slope. Action needed to be taken.

Not for the first time, Jasper was anxious about how bad things would have got had he not been here to put things in place, because that's what he fully intended to do. No way could he allow himself to return to Dubai without leaving some form of action plan. Talking to Adira had put everything into perspective. Regardless of the contract he'd signed, family came first. To be fair, he doubted whether it would prove such an arduous task manoeuvring himself out of it, the Emirati businessmen he worked for were honourable people, who, like him, considered family with paramount importance. If push came to shove, he felt sure they would support him. So, with that in mind, Jasper was focused. He had a plan, and that always brought out the best in him.

'Colin, I want a thorough report on every single job that needs attention on all the land and buildings, plus the contact details of all the tenants.' He'd been direct, making the manager stall a little.

'That… could take some time.' Colin looked at Jasper. He knew who he was dealing with. Often, he would skirt around the edges with Fletcher, only telling him what he wanted to hear. Not so with Jasper. Time was of the essence; he would be leaving for Dubai soon.

Jasper returned the stare. 'If you need help, get it. I want that report by the end of the week, Colin.'

'I understand,' he nodded. Colin was relieved, not only for the offer of assistance, but that finally someone was taking the reins. This place needed strong direction, a firm lead from the boss.

They were in the estate's office, in the adjacent field to The Laurels. A footpath from the back garden led through a small cluster of trees situated at the far end, which hid the building. Good job it was out of view, as it was crumbling, had a leaking roof and gaps in the stonework where the breeze whistled in.

Jasper took a look around him. 'Are the rest of the outbuildings in this state?'

'No. They're worse.'

Jasper rolled his eyes. This was going to be a mammoth task, but, as he kept telling himself, it was his future. As Fletcher had said, he was passing the baton on to him.

'I want to see the accounts.' Asset-wise, it was looking pretty grim, but he needed to know the income, outgoings and cash flow. The orchards were still producing good fruit and the fields a good harvest, that was something. But Jasper could see much of the land was wasted. He was eager to put it to good use and, funnily enough, Adira's camper van had given him the seedling of an idea.

'Certainly.' Colin rose from his desk and opened a filing cabinet. Taking out two folders, he placed them in front of Jasper.

'When was the last time Fletcher looked at these?' Jasper asked.

'He hasn't. Not in years anyway,' Colin replied, slightly red-faced. Looking decidedly uncomfortable, he coughed and turned away from Jasper's glare.

The suspicious side of Jasper began to simmer inside him. Was Colin hiding something? Could he be trusted?

'How long have you worked here, Colin?' His eyes bore into him.

'Ten years,' came the stilted reply.

'And in all that time, Fletcher has never examined or queried any of the bookkeeping? Just signed cheques without question?'

Colin's face turned puce. 'Err… actually, I'm an approved signatory.'

'You're signing the cheques?' asked Jasper flatly in disbelief, making Colin cringe.

'Yes,' he squeaked.

'Not any more you're not.' Jasper collected the files and stood to his feet. 'That report, by Friday,' he ordered and slammed the door behind him.

Raging, he marched all the way back to The Laurels. My God, this was far worse than he had thought. His uncle had well and truly taken his eye off the ball, practically giving his estate manager the purse strings! What on earth was Fletcher thinking?

Then he stopped. *He's an old man*, the voice inside him reasoned. *He's a tired, old man who just wants to end his days in peace and quiet, no hassle, no interference and preferably no pain either.* Jasper's eyes began to fill. He hated the thought of his uncle being taken advantage of.

Just then, he saw Adira walk across the field to her camper van. He remembered having similar thoughts about her too. Was he being paranoid?

Fletcher was snoozing in the library and Lilly was tackling the ironing in the kitchen when Jasper returned.

'Been busy, dear?' asked Lilly as the steam hissed over her.

Jasper shook his head. That was another thing that needed changing. Lilly, bless her, was far too old and frail to be tending to Fletcher. He needed a younger housekeeper who could manage The Laurels properly. He looked around him again, this time taking in the dusty worktops, dirty floor and piles of dishes on the draining board. In fact, the whole kitchen needed ripping out full stop.

'Very busy, Lilly.' Then, seizing the moment, whilst Fletcher was out of earshot, decided to take the bull by the horns. 'Lilly, can I have a word with you?' He nodded towards the armchair by the wood burner.

Looking up surprised, she turned off the iron and sat down.

Jasper pulled a chair up to sit opposite her. 'While you're doing a terrific job looking after Fletcher, I think it's time you put your feet up. All this work can't be doing you any good,' he tried to justify.

'But I enjoy doing it,' Lilly replied, somewhat confused.

Jasper tried again, as sensitively as possible. 'I know you do, Lilly, but perhaps we could ask someone... a little more able to do the cleaning, you know, the strenuous jobs, and you can still come and do…' He looked wildly around him.

'The ironing?' Lilly suggested.

'Yes! You can still do the ironing and we'll get someone else to do the rest. How does that sound?' He gave her his most endearing smile.

'Like hell you will,' came Fletcher's voice from the doorway.

There was no way some stranger was snooping about his home. *No bloody chance.*

Jasper closed his eyes and sighed. 'Fletcher, it's not fair expecting Lilly to cope on her own.' He lifted his hands, 'The Laurels is huge, it needs more than one cleaner—'

'Housekeeper, dear,' butted in Lilly.

'Sorry, housekeeper,' replied Jasper with forced patience.

Fletcher looked warily at him. Whilst he conceded Jasper had a point, he was still adamant about his privacy. Then an idea sprang to mind, causing a wry smile to spread across his face. 'I'll get another cleaner Jasper. Just you leave it with me.'

Jasper narrowed his eyes. What was the old boy up to now?

Chapter 13

Adira was in Charles' office, ordering all the stock for the new spa room. It felt rather liberating, having carte blanche to choose whatever she wanted without any restraints. Now and then she would run certain items past Charles as he passed in and out of the office. He would look at the screen, then at her and say, 'If you need it, get it.' A refreshing change to the controlling management of Goldgate Chambers. She bought quality oils from reputable stockists. When it came to the decorative side of things, she did endeavour to keep a lid on it. Less is more, was her mantra whenever tempted and she decided to make a list of the pictures, mirrors, candles, towel stands and light fittings to run past Cassie before completing the order.

Charles bobbed his head round the door.

'A visitor for you at the bar, Adira,' he called, then left before she had chance to ask who.

Approaching the bar, she saw Fletcher chatting to Cassie.

'Do you want to see me, Fletcher?'

'Aye, lass. Let me buy you a drink. Come and sit down.'

Soon they were sat opposite each other at a small table by the window, overlooking the river. Once again, she was reminded of just how stunning Lilacwell was.

'The thing is,' Fletcher began, 'Jasper tells me I need another cleaner. Lilly can't do it all.'

'She can't,' chipped in Adira, picturing the poor old lady's gnarled hands. 'Only the other day she was telling me how her arthritis troubles her.'

Fletcher looked out of the window in contemplation. Or was it guilt?

'I know how it looks, Adira, but it suits us both. I don't want no stranger in my house and Lilly wants a purpose. We both want the company.' He spoke in a quiet voice, sounding almost defeated, so unlike Fletcher, and she wasn't sure what to say. 'Jasper is right, the place does need bottoming, a damn good clean.' He looked at her. Adira began to wonder where this was leading. 'So, I'm here asking you to do it. I'll pay you of course.'

Her eyebrows shot up. 'Me?'

'Yes, don't you see, you're young and fit enough to do it and I wouldn't mind you in the house.'

In a way, Adira was flattered, but she had reservations.

'I couldn't take your money, Fletcher, not when you've allowed me to stay on your land. I actually was going to start paying rent, once I'm working here.'

'Nonsense,' he replied. Then his face lit up, 'Let's do a deal if money isn't to change hands. You stay on my land as long as you want. Use water, electricity when needed and you... well, you can clean my house.'

'But who'll clean it when I move on?' she smiled, not really wanting to put a dampener on his suggestion.

'Oh, let's cross that bridge when we get to it.'

Typical blasé Fletcher, she thought.

He leant forward and whispered, 'Hopefully Jasper will be off my back by then,' and winked, making her smile again. It was hard to say no to such a loveable, old rogue.

'And how do you think Jasper would react to me sorting out The Laurels?' Her head tilted to one side.

'Jasper will be delighted, I'm sure.' Was that a smirk he was trying to disguise behind his pint glass? Then he suddenly added, as though just remembering, 'Anyway, Sheila needs looking at. You mentioned she'd stalled on you.'

'Do you think something could be wrong?' Adira remembered the van stalling a few times when she'd charged the battery too.

'Well, you certainly shouldn't be driving far without checking, Adira.' She could hear her dad's voice in his warning. 'I'll get someone to take a look to be on the safe side.'

'Oh thanks, Fletcher, that's kind of you.'

'You scratch my back and I'll scratch yours,' he replied with another wink, making her laugh.

That night as Adira lay in her little campervan, tucked up snugly in bed, she reflected on her journey so far. It wasn't panning out the way she had envisaged at all, having stayed for days at her first stop, and continuing to do so for the foreseeable future, or at least till the spa was established and now Fletcher's house was deep cleaned. But was she happy?

Yes, she was. Very much so in fact. She had met some lovely, genuine, down-to-earth people, it was costing her nothing to live in an area of outstanding natural beauty and she had been offered two jobs, both stress-free. She was sleeping better, waking up with zest and was looking the healthiest she had in years. So why move on just yet? Plus, she was wary about driving Sheila without having the engine looked at. The thought of breaking down alone in foreign territory was a daunting one. On a more intrinsic note, Adira also wanted to explore more about Grace Conway. A deep-rooted, innate gut feeling refused to disappear.

Chapter 14

'Zara, I'm extending my stay here in the UK. Have there been any repercussions from the report you circulated?'

'Not so far, Jasper.'

'Good. I'll keep in touch. In the meantime, I want any feedback immediately.'

'Yes, of course.' After a short pause, Zara asked, 'When do you expect to return, should anyone enquire?'

'The directors know my circumstances and it's nobody else's business when I come back.'

'I see,' she stiffly replied.

'Contact me when necessary,' he added.

'Will do.'

'Bye.'

Jasper put the phone down. He was in the library, which he now used as his study, having cleared the huge, old desk standing in the corner collecting dust. He'd positioned it nearer the large sash window to gain light and a better view of the gardens. The library was the quietest room, away from Lilly in the kitchen and Fletcher in the drawing room. There was also a better Wi-Fi signal. He had considered setting up his workstation in the estate office, thereby keeping an eye on Colin, but decided against it. He wanted to strike the right balance by maintaining an appropriate distance, but still having the estate manager accountable to him.

He was going through the report which Colin had submitted. Jasper had immediately noticed that a couple of tenants were behind with their rent. Colin had assured him he was on the case. Other than that, it was pretty much what Jasper had anticipated. The repairs to some of the outbuildings couldn't be justified, especially when considering their use. He was contemplating having them demolished. He planned to replace them with more functional buildings, fit for purpose. A lot of the stone could be reused, but new roofing, fittings and insulation would prove more cost-effective.

-

Fletcher had sat and listened to Jasper's proposals, giving his full consent. He'd been impressed with his nephew and damn right grateful of his input. It felt like an enormous weight had been lifted from his shoulders. Fletcher was also thankful for Adira agreeing to clean The Laurels, although he hadn't quite got round to telling Jasper that yet. Thankfully, Jasper had been too preoccupied with the estate. It had been over a week now since his arrival and the impact he had made was phenomenal. It was so reassuring having Jasper about the place. A part of Fletcher wanted to cling onto him and he felt guilty for feeling this need.

-

In Dubai, Zara was having similar thoughts, although she was left with a feeling of desire rather than need. When Jasper had asked her to arrange his flight to the UK, she hadn't imagined him staying too long. He did have a job to do here in Dubai, after all. She'd been rather offended at his clipped tone on the phone earlier, especially as it had been nine whole days since last seeing her. And not to be informed of his estimated return was a further snub. Of course, Zara had asked the question, eager to know when *she'd* see him again, not really expecting anyone else to ask. Zara knew full well that Jasper would only have taken leave after settling it with his counterparts. Something was afoot, she was convinced. But what? She was starting to worry that Jasper may not come back at all, or if he did, then for how long? Was he preparing to hand in his resignation?

The thought gripped her. How would she cope without seeing him sat behind his desk? Those brown eyes scanning her work she had meticulously prepared for him; seeing his dark head bent in concentration; his broad, muscular shoulders stretching across his swivel chair, as he gazed out of the office window. It was purgatory him not being here – he was her daily fix. She had been longing to hear his voice and was overjoyed at seeing his name flash across her telephone, but hadn't cared for his no-nonsense, formal attitude. Although he had always been professional and business-like, Zara sensed a warming to her, the longer they had worked together. And why not? She was an extremely conscientious personal assistant. She was diligent, loyal and obliging – very obliging, if he only said the word. Just a tiny indication, that's all she needed. Zara had been at pains to show Jasper how discreet she could be. If it was purely a matter of keeping things private, avoiding any awkwardness in the workplace, she was a master of discretion. It was a case of giving him the green light, the go-ahead, subtly.

Trouble was, it just wasn't happening. For all her efforts, her painstaking attempts to snare Jasper were met with… nothing. Zero. Zilch. To be quite frank, she found it insulting. Never had she struggled previously. Usually the men came to her, to be flippantly batted away. Occasionally she had made a play for one or two, who had been extremely flattered and showed it. But with Jasper it was the opposite.

As soon as she'd clapped eyes on this distinguished Englishman joining their company, she knew he had to be hers. As luck would have it, the original PA assigned to Jasper had taken maternity leave, thereby leaving the position free for Zara to fill. It was fate, she told herself. They were meant to be together. Her belief was strengthened when learning Jasper had had his contract extended. More time together. Only once or twice had her efforts been rewarded with the odd glance. Her lips curved, remembering the evening when she had worn a low-cut dress that had accentuated her cleavage. The man was flesh and blood, like the rest of them, she reminded herself. It was just a question of time before he resisted. But was time on her side if he was in the UK?

As promised, Adira was reporting for duty that morning. Fletcher met her at the kitchen door, as arranged. She couldn't help feeling there was a sense of secrecy about the whole thing, the way he was talking in hushed tones.

Lilly was surprised yet delighted to see her, which further puzzled Adira. Why hadn't Fletcher told Lilly she was coming to help clean the house?

Once Fletcher had explained the situation, she too seemed somewhat relieved that it wasn't a stranger that had been employed.

Adira suggested they start in the kitchen by clearing out the cupboards, scrubbing the shelves and bleaching all the worktops.

'A lot of clutter could go, don't you think, Fletcher?' she asked, staring round the room.

'Absolutely. You just do as you think fit,' he told her.

'I'll make a pile of everything that's going, for you to agree first.'

'Righto.'

Lilly looked from one to the other, slightly over-whelmed by the sudden change. 'What should I do?'

'Could you wash all the crockery we're keeping? So it's nice and fresh to put back in the newly cleaned cupboards?' Adira suggested, hoping to please.

'Good idea,' her eyes twinkled, glad to be of assistance.

Fletcher beamed, that's what he liked, teamwork.

'And you, Fletcher, I want that kitchen window washed and polished. In fact, all the ground-floor windows could do with the once-over.'

Oh, he was part of the team then. He had intended to browse over the *Racing Post* that morning. 'Ah, right...'

'Well, come on then, let's get moving,' Adira chivvied them along.

Within an hour, she had emptied all the cupboards, made a pile for the charity shop and one for washing.

Adira was knelt inside a floor cupboard, scrubbing at the mouldy shelves when Jasper entered the kitchen, halting when he saw that pert, round bottom staring up at him. He'd know that perfect behind, tucked into skinny jeans, anywhere. Her T-shirt had ridden up her back, giving him a glimpse of soft, brown flesh. He forced himself to look away and saw the back of Lilly busy washing up and Fletcher outside cleaning the window. What was going on?

After a few seconds, he coughed, causing Lilly to turn around.

'Oh Jasper, there you are, dear.'

Adira stopped scrubbing. She eased herself out of the cupboard, conscious of how dirty and sweaty she must look. Wiping her forehead with the back of her marigolds, she smiled up at him. The look on his face told her everything. He'd no idea of her working here.

Jasper turned to see Fletcher through the window, who was looking somewhat sheepish. Adira clocked it all and fought the urge to giggle.

Finally, his gaze rested on her. She looked flushed, her hair was tied into a ponytail with tendrils falling down. He swallowed.

'Meet our new housekeeper,' chuckled Lilly.

Chapter 15

As the summer days happily rolled on, so did life in Lilacwell. True to his word, Fletcher had sent a mechanic to look at the camper van. Good job, as it transpired the fuel pump had broken. A new one had been ordered, so Sheila was officially off the road until that arrived.

Adira had completed tidying the kitchen, the bathrooms and had planned to make a start on the drawing room at The Laurels when she got a call from a very excited Cassie.

'It's finished!' she gushed. 'The Bath House is ready.'

'How does it look?' asked Adira, smiling at Cassie's fervour.

'Divine!'

'I'll come and take a look later this afternoon.'

'I'm just designing flyers for the hog roast promotion.'

'Good. That should generate a lot of interest.'

'OK, see you later. You're going to love it.' And with that, off Cassie went, leaving Adira shaking her head in amusement.

Entering the drawing room, she was again taken with the grandeur of The Laurels. How it must have looked in its heyday, she thought. Now, the mahogany wooden floor needed a polish, the Persian rug a good vacuum, the pictures and tables dusting and all the cut glass and decanters on the drinks cabinet washing. Her head turned towards the huge chandelier which sparkled in the sunlight. That would need dusting too, but she didn't fancy climbing a ladder to do it. Certain jobs would have to be done professionally. The second- and top-floor windows required a cherry picker to clean them, plus all the cracked panes had to be replaced. There were also the broken roof tiles to sort out. She'd have to speak to Jasper and get it all organised.

Adira could hear him speaking on the phone next door in the library. Judging from the sound of him, he was certainly putting the estate manager through his paces. Moments later, he passed by the doorway.

'Jasper!' she called.

He turned back and leant on the door frame. He was looking more relaxed than she had ever seen him, in grey jogging pants and a white T-shirt. His hands were in his pockets. He waited for her to speak.

'Can I have a word please?'

'Sure.'

'We need to hire a cherry picker to clean all the windows, plus get the cracked panes replaced, as well as the broken roof tiles.'

He nodded. 'I'll speak to Colin, get him to sort it. Fancy a coffee? I was just about to make one.'

'Lovely, thanks.'

'I'll bring them through.' Then he added, 'In fact, I'm going to order a decent coffee machine. This house is sadly lacking one.'

Adira laughed. It also made her wonder just how long Jasper intended to stay.

Minutes later, he entered the drawing room carrying two hot cups and tipped his head towards the chesterfield sofa. 'Come on, break time.'

Adira was glad of a sit-down. It was tiring work, constantly on your feet cleaning. She'd not exerted herself in this way for some time, having worked behind a desk for so long.

'Ah, thanks.' She blew on the steaming coffee and took a sip.

'So when do you start work at the Inn?' Jasper's brown eyes closely weighed her up.

'Soon. The new spa room's ready. I'm going to take a look at it this afternoon.' She then turned her head to face him. 'I still intend to finish cleaning The Laurels.'

'Good,' he nodded.

'When are you going back to Dubai?' she asked.

'To be honest, I'm not sure.' He sighed. 'There's a lot to sort out here first.'

'Fletcher will be pleased,' she smiled.

Their eyes met and a short silence followed. It was interrupted by his phone ringing in the library.

He rolled his eyes. 'Better get that.'

Adira watched him leave. She heard him next door and to her shame remained still to eavesdrop the conversation. Who was Zara? Just a colleague, or a woman waiting for him in Dubai? She couldn't explain it, but something inside made her ill at ease.

'It's amazing, Cassie!' Adira's eyes darted round the treatment room. It had been painted a subtle hessian colour, matching the cream in the floor tiles. Framed prints of Victorian bathhouses and spas filled the walls, highlighted by spotlights in the ceiling, whilst candles in wrought-iron holders dotted the shelves. Copper planters holding lush, green foliage added a lovely natural touch. A sea breeze aroma filled the air and the sound of the tide lapping against sand could be gently heard in the background. The massage bed stood in the centre of the room, covered in white towels.

'Thanks.' Cassie gave a wide smile, obviously pleased with the end result. 'So how many hours would you like to work?'

'Pencil me in for two days a week.'

'OK. I'll advertise for a part-time therapist today. Hopefully the vacancy will be filled soon after the hog roast.'

'Everything set for that?' asked Adira, interested to know.

'Yep. The marquee's booked, as is the folk band.'

'Sounds good.'

'Me and Lisa will be posting flyers tomorrow. Fancy helping?' Cassie smiled hopefully.

'Yeah, sure.' Adira was pleased to be included.

'Oh, and you'll be wearing this.' Cassie reached up to a shelf, then unfolded a black tunic. On it was written 'The Bath House' in cream, cursive font.

'Hey, that's cool,' approved Adira. 'Very professional.'

'That's me,' laughed Cassie.

The next morning, Adira reported for duty at the Inn nice and early. Cassie had wanted to start posting the flyers first thing, with a view to approaching the shops on the village high street and asking if they'd advertise the hog roast too. It was promising to be a scorcher of a day with a beautiful blue, cloudless sky. Already, the sun had started to shine brightly and it was only going to burn stronger as the day went on.

'Lovely day for it,' Adira smiled, joining Cassie and Lisa at reception.

'It certainly is,' replied Cassie, armed with a pile of flyers. She separated them evenly and gave Adira and Lisa their share. 'Right, we'll start by posting along Fishers Row, then move onto Primrose Lane and carry on till we reach the village green.'

'OK,' nodded Lisa.

'Then, we'll cross the river and finish off along Hope Cottages and Vicar's Close by the church.'

Adira melted at the quaint names and couldn't wait to explore Lilacwell.

'I thought of doing the shops last and having a well-earned break at Puddleduck Cafe?' Cassie suggested.

'Absolutely!' cheered Lisa.

Puddleduck Cafe? *How cute*, thought Adira.

'Right, come on, team, let's go!' Cassie strode out with determination.

Adira strolled slightly behind Cassie and Lisa as they chatted away, wanting to take in the scenery. She'd never come across a prettier village, with its fragrant hawthorn hedgerows, babbling brooks, small humpbacked bridges and the sweetest stone cottages covered in ivy and trailing roses. Picture-postcard, she marvelled. Wild garlic wafted through the warm, still air and the sound of a waterfall deep in the nearby woods created a soothing, calming effect on her. Adira was slowly falling under Lilacwell's spell.

They soon reached Fishers Row and began to scurry up the long paths leading to each front door and hastily pushed through the flyers. Cassie and Lisa moved quickly, eager to get the job done, but Adira couldn't help slowing down a little, appreciating her surroundings. She was used to bustling streets, roads crammed with traffic and plain brick buildings packed with people. She breathed in the fresh, country air and paused to listen to birdsong. It was simply magical.

'Come on, slowcoach!' called Cassie laughingly.

'Nearly done!' Adira replied and hurried along to meet up with them.

They continued as Cassie had instructed until reaching the village green. Here a small team of children were playing cricket, looking very smart in pristine whites.

'It's traditional for Saint Jude's to play the neighbouring village school this time of year,' Cassie explained when they drew to a stop to watch.

'Oh, that's a lovely custom,' replied Adira, watching the children clearly enjoying themselves. Again, her thoughts turned to the inner-city schools, with their caged, Astroturf playgrounds.

After watching a few more runs, the women moved on. Crossing a stone bridge over the river, they carried on posting leaflets through letterboxes until they reached the village high street. Here, artisan shops lined both sides, including a farm shop, bakery, post office, a sweet, little bookshop, as well as a deli and coffee shop. It was exactly the kind of quintessential place Adira had longed to see on her travels, and without a tourist in sight.

As promised, Cassie led them to Puddleduck Cafe and promptly bagged a table by the window.

'This is on the Inn, under Charles' order,' Cassie said, passing them each a menu.

'That's good of him.' Lisa scanned the cakes at the counter with a beady eye.

'It's called team building,' Adira joked, loving being there, with them. Once more, her mind flashed back to knocking back the wine in Mario's, alone. There was no comparison.

Just then, her eye caught Jasper walking head and shoulders above the other pedestrians milling outside on the high street. He was strolling nonchalantly along, not appearing to be in any hurry.

'Oh look, there's Jasper.' Cassie tapped on the window as he passed.

Stopping, he turned and looked inside. With a wide grin, he nodded at Cassie, who was waving unnecessarily vigorously given the man was right in front of them by now. Then his eyes slid over to Adira. She met his gaze full on. There was a slight pause before either of them smiled in acknowledgment, as if both sizing the other up. It wasn't lost on Lisa, and she gave a sideways smirk to Cassie, who was stifling a giggle.

'Come in!' Cassie called, mischief dancing in her eyes.

Adira chewed her bottom lip. She watched Jasper pause to consider, then he shook his head politely.

'Gotta go,' he mouthed back, then waved again before moving on.

'Well, that could have been cosy,' Cassie said, still trying to keep a straight face, whilst Lisa's shoulders were shaking behind her menu.

'What?' Adira asked, staring at them with a frown.

'Nothing, just saying, that's all.' Cassie's hands went up defensively.

After a light lunch and a good chat, the three of them said their goodbyes. Cassie was going to visit each shop with the flyers and Lisa was returning to the Inn. Adira decided to walk back along the riverside, using the route she had taken that morning.

Instead of crossing the humpbacked bridge though, she took her pumps off in an attempt to jump barefoot along the stepping stones in the river. It was getting really hot and she longed to sink her feet in the cool water. On doing so, though, she slipped and missed her footing, sending her tumbling into the shallow stream.

'Agh!'

Her body hit the cold water and the pebbles on the floor of the riverbed. She closed her eyes, shivering.

Suddenly, two strong arms reached out to ease her up. Jolting her head up in shock, she was faced with brown eyes staring down at her.

'Are you OK?' Jasper had seen her fall and rushed down to help.

'Y… y… yes,' she stammered, still shaking.

'Come on, let's get you out.'

Without waiting for her to reply, he lifted her body up and carried her effortlessly to the other side of the river.

'Sorry, you're getting wet through.' Adira was mortified as he waded through the river.

Jasper smiled wryly down at her. 'Not as wet as you,' he half laughed.

It took a moment, but then, seeing the funny side, Adira joined in. She felt safe and secure in his arms, held against his broad chest. She could feel his heart beating against her as she breathed in that bergamot scent of him.

'There you go.' He gently let her down to stand beside him once reaching the side.

'Thanks, Jasper.' She gave a shaky smile, feeling a tad foolish, then bent down to put on her pumps she'd been carrying. Luckily, they were only damp, not drenched.

'I'll escort you, shall I?' he teased, mouth twitching.

'I'm not usually so clumsy,' she tried to make light of the situation. Their eyes met and held. Everything stood still.

'Come on, you need to get into dry clothes,' Jasper quietly told her.

Adira nodded in agreement, unable to speak.

Chapter 16

Adira woke with the sun streaming through the camper van. Stretching lethargically, she contemplated what to do with the whole day to herself. Basking in contentment, she once again reflected on her previous lifestyle, where the alarm clock would shrill her out of a deep sleep. Adira had never been a 'morning' person. Her body clock had never been in tune with the five thirty a.m. starts. She pictured dragging herself out of a warm, comfy bed to wrestle with the early London traffic, then face another day in a dog-eat-dog environment. She grimaced at the memory. Literally feeling a heavy burden had been lifted from her shoulders, she threw back the covers with optimism.

After breakfast, her thoughts turned back to the tombstone she had seen in St Jude's graveyard. Ever since reading its inscription, a spark of inquisitiveness had ignited within her: *Grace Conway, 1891–1941, devoted wife and mother.*

The dates coincided with Edie's lifetime – Adira knew Edie had been a war baby, born in 1941. How sad if Grace Conway *was* in fact a relative, dying the same year that Edie, her possible granddaughter was born. She made a mental note to ring and ask Edie how much she knew about her grandmother. All Adira knew was that her name was also Grace Conway. Hopefully Edie would be able to fill in the blanks. The thought that Adira had landed in Lilacwell, the very village where maybe a family member had lived, once again made her shiver. The whole scenario intrigued her, giving her a sense of validation; like she was meant to be here.

Or was she just being fanciful?

The rational side of her head stepped in, as it always did. Being barrister trained, Adira was programmed to automatically see both sides of an argument and assess the case. And, in order to do that, she had to analyse the evidence, of which she had none yet. Parish records, that's what she needed to look at; written facts, in black and white.

So, armed with pen and paper, she made her way back to the church, this time hoping it would be open.

Walking up the old paving slabs forming a pathway to St Jude's, Adira stopped for a moment to admire the impressive stone structure. It stood, fortress-like, with sturdy stone walls, arched mullion windows, their stained glass twinkling like jewels in the sunlight. A square bell tower rose majestically, ready to give panoramic views of the village.

Adira willed the cast-iron door handle to turn and allow her entrance. To her relief, it did and she quietly pushed the wooden door open with a creak.

An elderly lady polishing the pews looked up at her in surprise.

'Hello,' Adira smiled.

The lady smiled back and continued with her cleaning.

'Excuse me,' Adira approached the lady, 'would it be possible to look at the parish records?'

'Well, you'd have to ask Father Forbes.' The lady nodded towards the vestry. 'He's in there.'

'Thank you.' Adira walked down the aisle towards the vestry at the side of the altar, marvelling at the high vaulted ceiling and the intricate carvings. She heard humming and tapped on the door, which was slightly ajar.

'Hello!' called a cheery voice.

Adira poked her head through.

'Excuse me, but would it be possible to look at the parish records? I... I'd like to learn more about one of your graves.'

The priest grinned. He had a kind, lived-in face, Adira thought.

'I see. Not from these parts then?' His grey eyebrow raised.

'No. I'm on holiday... sort of.' Realising she wasn't being particularly eloquent, she held out her hand, which he shook firmly. 'Adira Summers.'

'Father Edwin Forbes,' he supplied. Adira liked the way he included his Christian name, making him seem more personable.

'I was strolling round the graveyard here and came across a tombstone which I wondered if it belonged to a relation.'

'Really? How interesting.'

'Yes,' she agreed. 'It belongs to a Grace Conway. Conway was my grandmother's maiden name and I know her grandmother was called Grace. The dates on the stone all correspond, you see—'

'And you want to delve further?' interrupted the priest.

'Exactly.'

'Well, come this way, Miss Marple,' he grinned again, causing Adira to warm further to him.

He opened a drawer in a nearby sideboard and took out a small key. Then he turned and walked to the far end of the room, where a row of glass cabinets lined the wall.

'What where the dates on the gravestone?' he asked.

'1891 to 1941,' Adira replied, anticipation building.

'Let me see...' He opened the middle cabinet and pulled out a huge ledger. With care, he opened the faded pages and finally found an entry. Adira had moved to look over his shoulder, her heart had started to thump. 'Here we are, Grace Conway, wife of Timothy Conway, died the first of June 1941. Buried St Jude's, Lilacwell, Forest of Bowland, Lancashire.'

'Timothy? That was my grandmother's father's name,' she stated in surprise. 'Could these be his parents, do you think?' Adira was thinking out loud.

'It is possible. Very often children were named after their father. Especially the first born. Was your Timothy the eldest child, do you know?'

'He was an only child.'

'Well, that could tie in.'

Adira's mind was racing. 'Could we check their marriage record?'

'Of course.' After opening the glass door to another cabinet, the priest began to search for the marriage entry of Grace and Timothy Conway, estimating the years to look for. 'If Grace was born in 1891, we would be looking at roughly—'

'1911 onwards?' Adira instantly responded.

'Yes, on or around that time.' The priest motioned her to help him look. Adira's eyes scanned the lengthy pages. They smelt musty, mottled with damp blotches, their faded black writings meticulously scrolled. Then she saw it.

'There!' Her finger pointed to the centre of the page. 'Timothy James Conway, married to Grace Griffiths, twenty-first of August 1913.' Adira was at fever pitch. She looked excitedly at the priest. 'Can we look for Grace Griffiths' birth record?' she asked eagerly. 'She may have been born here.'

'Of course,' he smiled, enjoying her enthusiasm.

Taking out another ledger marked 'Baptisms', he again leafed through the dusty pages to the year 1891. Adira held her breath in hope. Was she really delving into her own heritage? It was incredible to think she could be.

'Ah, there we are, look, Adira.'

And there she was, Grace Griffiths born 1891 in the village of Lilacwell. She bent down closer to inspect the entry. Grace's parents were named: Michael Griffiths and Edith Mary Griffiths. A small gasp escaped her. Edith, could that be who Edie had been named after? It all became suddenly overwhelming and her eyes began to fill.

'Take a seat,' the priest quietly told her, noting her reaction. 'Would you like a drink of tea?'

'No thanks,' Adira half laughed. 'Sorry, I'm feeling a tad emotional.'

'Not at all, it's an amazing thing, to look back into one's family history.'

'It certainly is.' She looked at him. 'And thank you so much. I really appreciated your help.'

'My pleasure,' he beamed.

Adira took a steady breath. 'Do you mind if I make a few notes and take photos of the entries?' She pulled out her phone, notebook and pen from her bag.

'Be my guest.' Then, sensing she perhaps needed a little time alone, he added, 'I'll be back shortly.'

'Thank you.'

Adira immediately set to work, taking pictures of the ledgers. She made contact notes, the name and address of the church, the priest's name and the reference numbers of all three ledgers used. Then, when she had finished, she went back into the main church, thanked the priest and cleaner again and went to visit Grace Conway's grave; her great-great-grandmother?

That evening, Adira couldn't wait to ring Edie. After explaining the day's events, there was a momentary pause from her grandmother.

'Oh darling,' Edie's voice cracked slightly. 'Yes, my father was born in Lancashire, but I'm not sure of the exact place. And, of course, I've no one to ask now.' There was another pause.

Adira thought about it. 'What about his marriage certificate, or even birth certificate? Could you have them?'

'I'm not sure… There were some papers given to me, as I recall, but I didn't think too much of it at the time. From what I can remember, it was just his will.' Edie was trying her best to think back.

'Can you check?' asked Adira urgently.

'Of course I will! I'm as interested as you, love.'

'Oh Gran, just think, I could be in the place where your dad and grandmother lived.'

'I know, it's quite remarkable. Listen, darling, I'll let you know if I find anything. Sweet dreams.'

'You too, bye.'

Adira's mind was spinning into overdrive. Lilacwell, she was certain, had not been just a chance stop-off point. It held so much more. Not just the present, but the past too.

Chapter 17

Jasper stared out of the coffee shop window. He'd been busy working all morning and had been in need of a break and change of scenery. Deciding against the pub this time, he'd opted to go for a coffee in the village cafe. At least there he wouldn't have any distractions. The Inn at Lilacwell was always filled with locals who were keen to catch up with him. His sudden presence in the village had created attention – busybodies wanting to know his business. And they weren't discreet either. One old farmer had outright asked him if he'd 'come to take over?' Jasper had simply laughed the question away, avoiding a direct answer.

He had been reminded what life was like in Lilacwell – in any village, really, living in such close proximity. Was he ready for it? He'd lived an almost anonymous existence in Dubai. Apart from work colleagues, he'd never had a close network of friends out there. Jasper had chosen to live on the sidelines, not in the hub of action, forming bonds with people. He knew his time in Dubai was temporary, that he was never going to settle there, so he never felt the need to grow real friendships. While he liked most of his colleagues, that's exactly what they remained – just people he happened to work with. He had established one or two acquaintances at his golf club, enjoying a round of golf and a few drinks in the clubhouse, but that was about all. In

Lilacwell, it was the polar opposite. Here, *everybody* knew *everything*.

He smiled to himself at the current whispers in the village. Apparently, he wasn't the only one causing a stir at the moment. Tales of Fletcher's new guest had been circulating thick and fast: the 'new-age traveller' in the camper van with her potions. Some had dubbed her a white witch, others an opportunist, some had even labelled her as Fletcher's long-lost lovechild. At this, Jasper had chuckled to himself. Then again, hadn't his thoughts taken a similar route? One thing was for certain, Adira Summers had most definitely caught the attention of Lilacwell. She'd certainly caught his attention too.

It had slightly unsettled him the way people had taken to her. Jasper had to know a person well before allowing them to befriend him. It was his instinct to suss a new acquaintance out thoroughly, looking for any cracks in their armour, or any signs at all that he didn't like. Yet, try as he might, he couldn't find anything negative at all about Adira, apart from how her popularity niggled him slightly. Was he jealous? No, he concluded, he was just cautious. After all, Fletcher really had taken to her, and all too quickly for his liking.

Jasper laughed into his coffee cup again at the rumours of Adira being Fletcher's lovechild. Then he abruptly stopped. His gaze homed in like a radar, pinpointing the figure walking along the pavement opposite the road. There she was, the very lady on everyone's lips. Adira.

He noticed her slow, composed walk; shoulders back, head held high, occasionally nodding and smiling to those she passed. A beaded bag was slung over her shoulder. She wore a long, tie-died dress with tassels at the hem. Not hard to guess how the 'new-age traveller' label had sprung up. She had poise, he'd give her that. That's not all Jasper wanted to give her, truth be told, but he hated admitting this. It irked him to think she had some kind of power over him, whether she knew it or not. He admired her confidence, her natural self-ease, the way she seemed happy in her own skin. Then suddenly, as if she'd become aware of being watched, Adira turned to face him.

He froze as her eyes looked straight into his. He put his cup down and forced out a smile, trying to look as natural as possible, when inside he was embarrassed to be caught staring.

Was that a playful twitch of her lips? As though knowing exactly what he'd been up to?

Not liking the thought of her having the upper hand, he waved nonchalantly, in a non-committal, fancy-seeing-you-here manner. To which, she openly smirked and mimicked the same cheery wave back. The little minx. Was she laughing at him?

He paused, then a car passed between them, breaking the connection. He watched the back of her as she carried on down the road. Adira Summers, the talk of Lilacwell.

—

The Inn at Lilacwell was heaving. The bar inside was full and the gardens and marquee outside flowed with both locals and people travelling from further afield. All potential customers for the new treatment room, Cassie had reminded the staff at the briefing that morning ahead of the hog roast. Adira had been there, stood in her new uniform of black trousers and The Bath House tunic. She felt a surge of excitement, it was hard not to get swept along with the charged atmosphere. She had been given the job of handing out the spa leaflets and booking as many appointments as possible. It certainly beat having to sit through boring meetings, she thought.

The hog roast was a brilliant success, as queues gathered round and filtered into the marquee, and the folk band were doing a sterling job, having set up at eleven thirty that morning, playing non-stop to an enthusiastic crowd. Adira had also shown off The Bath House to all those wishing to see it. It had been met with such high praise that she couldn't wait to feed back to Cassie.

It was late afternoon. Adira was stood by the stairs leading up to the treatment room feeling a little tired now. She was looking to see if there was anyone else waiting to view The Bath House when she spotted Lilly entering the Inn along with another similar-looking lady. Lilly saw Adira and the two women came over to her.

'Adira! Meet Ruby, my twin sister.'

Adira turned her smile to Lilly's sister, stretching out her hand. 'Hello, Ruby, pleased to meet you.'

'And you too.' The old lady shook her hand and Adira noticed it was gnarled, just like her sister's. Then Ruby leant forward. 'I get the most terrible headaches. What can you do for me?' she asked, looking directly at her. How like Lilly she was.

'Well, Ruby, lavender is good for headaches. Try sprinkling a few drops of lavender oil on your pillow. Or, failing that,' she handed her a leaflet, 'you could book an Indian head massage, I'm sure that would help.'

Ruby examined the price list on the pamphlet.

'At a reduced rate. We're offering discounts for the first week of opening,' Adira informed her.

Ruby smiled. 'Go on then. Book me in for one.' Her eyes sparkled, again just like Lilly's.

While Adira was busy arranging Ruby's appointment, Fletcher and Jasper walked in together, heading straight to the bar. Cassie served them.

'So, Fletcher, will you be booking an all-over body massage?' she teased, exchanging grins with Jasper.

'I don't think so,' he chortled. Then, pointing to Jasper, added, 'This chap could do with one though.'

'Could I?' he replied, his eyebrow raising. Cassie laughed.

'Only the other day, I was telling him to chill out.' Fletcher took a long drink of his pint.

Cassie, never one to miss an opportunity, saw Adira enter the bar.

'Adira!' she called her over.

Adira made her way to them.

'Jasper could do with an all-over body massage.'

Fletcher burst out laughing, while Adira blushed pink. Jasper found it rather endearing.

Her eyes flew to his face. Were his lips twitching? Well, she'd show him.

'Would that be the Swedish massage, or the Aroma massage?' she asked with a sweet smile.

He looked lazily at her. 'Whatever you recommend,' he calmly answered.

'OK. Let's go for the Swedish massage. It'll ease muscular tension and stimulate blood circulation.' She stared back innocently.

'Let's.'

'That's what he's short of,' remarked Fletcher with a wink, making Cassie laugh again.

'Come tomorrow, Jasper, you can be the first to christen the massage bed,' Cassie said, trying desperately to keep a straight face.

Meanwhile, Adira refused to show any embarrassment. 'Two o'clock suit you?' she asked, trying to sound as professional as possible.

'Suits me fine,' he smiled, then watched her leave rather abruptly.

—

Towards the end of the afternoon, after Adira had given the last visit of The Bath House, Cassie caught up with her.

'Smo-king hot!' she hissed.

'Pardon?' Adira frowned.

'Oh, come on, don't give me that,' she nudged her. 'The air between you and Jasper was electric.'

'I don't know what you're talking about,' Adira denied.

'Yeah, right.'

Adira faced her. 'Did he ask for a massage, or was it all a wind-up?'

'Fletcher mentioned it, but Jasper was game… and the way he was looking at you—'

'Enough,' butted in Adira, feeling quite flushed again.

'Just saying,' Cassie spread her hands in surrender.

'He's a client.'

'Of course he is,' she snorted.

Chapter 18

Fletcher had ribbed Jasper relentlessly about his forth-coming massage. He'd taken it in good spirits though and, truth be told, was rather looking forward to it. Who wouldn't want to relax under the soothing touch of Adira? And besides, his uncle had been right, he really was tense and in need of 'chilling out'.

The way Adira had blushed had both surprised and touched him. It also gave him food for thought. Why should she be embarrassed? Did she find him as attractive as he found her? Because Jasper couldn't deny the fire which had sparked since the moment he saw her in the stream. He'd tried to, wanting his sceptical, rational inner self to bring him to his senses; but he couldn't. He knew the pull she had on him was real, and her acting flustered over massaging him told him something – she might feel the same way. Flashbacks of her bathing had tortured his mind and awoken a desire deep inside him. Perhaps his toned body would have a similar effect on her? Although he worked behind a desk, he regularly attended a gym and used the rooftop pool of his apartment. He knew he was in good shape and now more than ever he was keen to impress.

So, with a spring in his step, he walked through the entrance to the Inn to be instantly greeted by Cassie.

'Ah, Jasper, there you are.' She held a camera. 'I'd like to take a few promotional shots, you being the first customer of The Bath House.'

Jasper's eyes widened, making Cassie laugh.

'Not of you stripped down to a towel,' she explained, 'just a few of you and Adira in the treatment room before your massage.'

'Fine by me.' He looked a touch relieved, to Cassie's amused eye.

'Great. Adira's just preparing the room, let's go up.'

Adira had lit the scented candles and put on the tranquil background music. The lighting was subtle, creating a soft, comforting ambience. Despite her initial reservations, she was actually eager to make a good impression – it had been a while since she'd given a massage and wanted it to go well. She hoped Jasper would feel the benefit and recommend her. In a way, she was going to enjoy watching him let go of his inhibitions. It would make a pleasant change to the serious businessman, carrying the worries of his family. Only once had she seen him semi-relaxed: the evening he had visited her with a bottle of wine. Well, perhaps she was about to see that side of Jasper again.

All the essential oils had been prepared and fresh towels lay on the bed. Adira heard the sound of voices coming up the stairs. She took a quick glance at her reflection in the mirror. She'd taken great care of her appearance, and not just because of the promotional photographs Cassie wanted to take. Her hair was freshly washed and tied back into a low ponytail. Her complexion was naturally sun-kissed and a touch of lipstick and mascara finished the natural effect nicely.

She met Cassie and Jasper with a bright smile.

'Adira, can we take a photo of you by the massage bed first?' Cassie asked.

'Sure,' she agreed.

'And, Jasper, if you can sit on it?'

'OK.' He casually sat down on the edge, crossing his legs, looking totally at ease.

'Great!' Cassie clicked away. 'Adira, maybe you sit next to Jasper?'

Adira did as she was told.

'Closer please,' urged Cassie, still clicking.

Adira felt his shoulders graze hers and that electric volt shot through her again.

'Right, all done, thanks.' Cassie gave a wide smile. 'I'll leave you to it.' The humour in her voice was evident, as were the stifled giggles on the stairs. Adira tried hard to ignore them.

'Jasper, I'll need your arms, legs and chest bare, so I'll nip out and let you get comfortable under the towels. If you can lay face down to begin with.'

He calmly looked at her. 'No problem.'

Adira left the room and waited outside. After a few minutes, she knocked quietly on the door. 'Ready,' she heard him say.

She instantly noticed how Jasper's body covered the massage bed. His long, lean legs reached the end and his shoulders filled the width, with his muscular arms only just managing to fit closely at the sides. She reached for the oils and smeared her hands. Then, in slow, sweeping movements began to rub his neck and shoulders. He felt very firm and toned. *Obviously exercises regularly*, she thought, whilst trying to keep a professional distance. It was rather difficult though, given the good shape he was in. There wasn't an ounce of fat on him. *Concentrate, Adira,* she told herself. Then she became aware of a rough edge in the middle of his right shoulder, it was a scar that ran down towards his collarbone. Adira wondered how he got it.

Jasper was in heaven. The rhythmic strokes soothed his aching muscles and he could feel all the tension ooze from him. The more her hands kneaded his shoulders, the more he fell into a deep, restful state. The air smelt clean and fresh and the sound of lapping water gave him a sense of peace. Then her hands travelled down his spine, spreading her fingers out to press against the knots in his back. This was bliss.

Her hands lowered again to rest on his hip bones. He caught his breath. Slowly she circled over them, the circular movements continuing down one thigh, then the other until she reached his ankles. Even the soles of his feet came alive under her touch.

Then his arms received the same treatment as she worked the oil into his biceps right down to his hands and between his fingers. He resisted the impulse to curl them round hers.

'I need you to turn over now, Jasper,' she whispered.

'Right,' he croaked, then rolled over and closed his eyes again.

Adira covered her hands with more oil and worked on his chest, digging the palms of her hands against him. He sneaked a glimpse of her through slitted eyes. She was deep in concentration. She moved and stood at the top of the bed. Her fingers rubbed the sides of his head, then over his scalp, to finally rest over his eyes. He'd never felt so revived.

'I'll leave you to get dressed, Jasper,' her voice spoke softly in the distance.

'Stay,' he half groaned, not wanting the sensation to stop. Then, realising what he'd said, he opened his eyes to see her looking down at him.

Adira slowly bent her head to meet his lips. Instinctively, he reached up and put his hands either side of her face. Her mouth was soft and inviting. He ran his tongue against it and felt her jolt.

'Thank you,' he whispered thickly.

Adira had never felt so roused. Her nerves prickled with emotion and her heart thumped uncontrollably. Without another word, she eased herself up and quietly left the room.

She lent on the door, shaking. Did that really happen? Had she and Jasper just kissed? The tingling of her mouth told her it had. She'd never experienced such a connection with a client and it un-nerved her. She closed her eyes and replayed how his lips had felt against hers, warm and gently insistent.

Taking deep breaths, Adira tried to steady herself. That body, his lean, muscular flesh beneath her hands was intoxicating and it had been a pleasure to explore it, feeling the smooth firmness of him.

Her heart was still hammering; she needed space to simmer down. Deciding not to face any more teasing from Cassie, Adira made her way back home to the camper van, sending Cassie a quick text so the woman wouldn't worry at her sudden disappearance.

Jasper, now fully dressed, made his way back downstairs. Cassie was talking to the receptionist before turning to face him.

'How did it go?' she asked with a grin.

'Fantastic. I'd highly recommend it,' he replied. Then, looking around, enquired, 'Where is Adira?'

'Is she not upstairs? I haven't seen her come down.'

'No sign of her upstairs.' Hell, she didn't regret kissing him, did she?

Cassie was looking pensively at him.

'I need to pay,' he said, suddenly feeling scrutinised.

'You can pay here, no problem,' she replied, still looking thoughtfully at him.

Chapter 19

Zara leafed through the mail on her desk. To her disappointment, none of it was particularly pressing. An urgent query from a letter or email would have provided the ideal excuse to ring Jasper, but instead, all was quiet. He'd made sure he was fully up to date before leaving the office. Typical.

With a sigh, she opened the last envelope. It was the routine yearly service for Jasper's company car, but Zara spotted an opportunity. She quickly glanced at the office clock and calculated the time in England – approximately one p.m. Picking up the phone, she dialled the number he had previously contacted her on. It was answered immediately.

'Hello, Zara. Is everything OK?'

'Hello, Jasper. Just a quick call. Your car's due its service.'

'Right. I'll need you to take it in for me,' replied Jasper.

'No problem. Where are the keys?'

'There's a spare set in the top drawer of my desk.'

'Leave it with me,' Zara answered, more than happy to assist.

'Right, thanks. Anything else?'

Zara paused, desperately trying to think of something else to keep him on the line but unable to come up with anything. 'No, nothing else.'

'Bye.' Down went the phone. Conversation over, apparently.

Zara made her way to Jasper's desk and opened the draw to find a set of keys.

Hmm, this was interesting, there wasn't just the car key on the ring, but a door key and fob too. Was this for his apartment? Most probably. Well, there was only one way to find out. She smiled smugly.

The fact that what she was about to do was actually a criminal offence didn't deter Zara in the slightest. She was on a mission and felt compelled to go ahead with entering Jasper's apartment. The frightening thing was, in Zara's mind, she had a *right* to step inside Jasper's home. She wanted to have a good look round, check out the decor, his possessions, his taste; to see how he lived, where he ate, where he slept, so that, when they were together at last, she would know how to please him. So, it was in his interest really.

Driving through DAMAC Hills, she admired Jasper's neighbourhood. Very tasteful, she thought, taking in the collection of luxurious villas and apartments in the prestigious development. It was surrounded by the lush fairways of an international golf club. She deliberately chose to drive Jasper's car, knowing that the secure car park for residents would automatically record his number plate and allow entry.

With ease, she drove through the underground entrance belonging to the apartment block and parked his car. Then she entered the lift, which took her up to the main lobby. There was a large reception desk, where a twenty-four-hour concierge service operated.

Zara quickly put on her sunglasses, not wanting to be spotted as a non-resident. She walked with confident strides, shoulders back, head held high, and made for the stairs. Nobody would have suspected she was an intruder.

Jasper's keyring had the number *2-18* engraved on it. She assumed the 2 meant second floor, so she wouldn't have far to climb. Usually the stairs were only used by the staff, so she shouldn't be seen by anyone else.

Slightly out of breath, Zara soon reached the second floor. Tapping the fob from the borrowed key ring against the door's access pad, she held her breath. With a beep, the light flashed green and she heard the quiet clunk of the door unlocking, giving her access to the second floor.

Nearly giddy with relief and excitement, she walked down the plush-carpeted corridor, her eyes quickly scanning each door until she found number 18. With cool, steady hands, she took the small, silver key and slotted it into the door latch. It fitted perfectly. Zara smoothly twisted it to unlock the door and her heart gave a leap of joy. A sigh of satisfaction escaped her.

Stepping inside, she instantly caught the minimalist, masculine feel. The apartment was spacious and open plan, filled with black sofas, a large TV screen and a long, glass coffee table. Dotted about were framed photographs, mainly of Jasper and another elderly couple she assumed were his parents, and another of some other old man. Good, no women. The marble tiled floor led to a balcony overlooking the beach. Zara moved towards it and pictured herself and Jasper sat together, hand in hand, taking in the beautiful view. Yes, she could happily live here.

The kitchen area was spotless, with white, gloss units and chrome accessories, including a state-of-the-art coffee machine. However tasteful, this wasn't what interested Zara. After having a quick look inside his cupboards, she peeked inside an opened envelope that was sitting on the worktop. Nothing interesting though, she thought, disappointed; just a utility bill. She noticed a calendar hanging by the fridge and flicked through the months for any appointments he had. But again, nothing earth-shattering, just meetings and golf tournaments marked up. Taking in all her surroundings, she went across the hallway and into Jasper's bedroom.

She stood for a moment and took a deep breath. Her eyes homed in on the huge king-size bed standing majestically in the centre of the room. An image of her and Jasper in it suddenly shot through her mind, their naked bodies entwined. Taking off her high heels, she moved towards it, gently lying down and stretching out her arms and legs. She turned over to breathe in the smell of his pillow and saw his bedside table.

She hesitated. Should she? She'd made it this far, so why not?

Zara opened the drawer but was rather disappointed only to find a packet of headache tablets and the latest crime fiction from Anthony Horowitz.

She got up and carefully pulled the covers straight, then opened his wardrobe doors. Dozens of immaculate suits hung before her, most of which she recognised. Her eyes looked down to the shelves, where his folded boxer shorts lay, she couldn't resist holding a pair, then grinned wryly at the label inside – just as she thought, size L. She made sure they were put back in the exact same position. Then she made her way into his bathroom.

Again, it was pristine, all white tiles and fittings. Pulling the handle of the mirrored cabinet above the sink, she peered inside and found just what she expected – his after-shave, shower gels, shaving brushes, moisturising cream and… Oh, a packet of condoms. She paused; it had been opened. Zara quickly seized it to find how many were left. Huh, only one. *So who were the others used on?* she bitterly asked herself. A splinter of jealousy jabbed her hard. She put the packet back and slammed the cabinet door shut. Time to go. She'd seen enough.

Just then she heard the apartment door open and shut. Zara froze. Someone had come in through the front door. A cleaner perhaps?

Quietly stepping into the bath, she drew the shower curtain across a little to conceal herself. All the time, her heart was beating uncontrollably. Her ears strained to hear the sounds of cupboard doors opening and shutting, then water running, followed by a squelching noise. Mopping – the cleaner must be mopping the tiled floor.

Zara's pulse raced. A layer of perspiration covered her body and she began to shake. Gulping, she stood as still as a statue and tried to gauge where in the apartment the cleaner was. Then, to her utter relief, she heard the balcony doors slide open. If the cleaner was about to mop the balcony floor, she could escape out of the apartment without being seen.

Seizing her opportunity, Zara climbed out of the bath and tentatively peeped behind the bathroom door. Thankfully, the cleaner had her back to her. Without any hesitation, Zara scurried silently through the kitchen, lounge area and straight to the door. She opened it as quickly as she could and got out fast. Very gently she closed it, hardly making a sound, and looked each way, up and down the corridor. There was nobody about, all she could see were the cleaners' trollies parked halfway down. Zara's chest heaved with nervous exhaustion.

Steadying herself, she took a deep breath and walked back to the stairs. Once through the secure door, her heart rate gradually slowed down and she soon regained composure. Slowly she descended the stairs, still keen to avoid using the lifts.

That had been a close shave, but it had been worth it. Zara was pleased with herself – she had successfully managed to infiltrate a part of Jasper and now knew more about the man, what he liked, what made him tick. Even seeing what was in his bathroom cabinet didn't deter her. He was only flesh and blood after all, and once they were together, she would more than satisfy his every need.

She reached the bottom of the stairs and went back out into the main lobby area. It was busy now, with various people milling about, stood at the reception desk, or collecting post from the pigeonholes. Zara breezed her way through without a care in the world.

Chapter 20

Adira was making good progress on The Laurels. The downstairs was completed, with floors having been polished to a shiny finish, sparkling windows, rooms now dust-free, and a kitchen that was fresh, clean and organised. She had filled vases with bright flowers to add a touch of colour and just sliding up the sash windows and letting in the summer breeze had made a difference, injecting life into the place.

Adira had also arranged for all the chimneys to be swept and had winced at the amount of debris which had been collected. Gone was the slight whiff of damp and now the air was filled with the scent of roses, lilies, peonies and stocks. The beams of sun blasting through the windows no longer illuminated all the dust, but made the cut glass and chandeliers twinkle cheerfully. The rugs looked new, having been vacuumed and washed and all the cabinets and wooden mahogany panelling shone.

Now for the second floor. Adira stood at the bottom of the stairs contemplating where to start. Probably Fletcher's bedroom. She had already cleaned the family bathrooms, but all the bedrooms and the landing needed bottoming. This was a little trickier than downstairs; bedrooms were personal after all, and she wanted to run a few things past Fletcher first, plus Jasper, as he was using the eaves bedroom and she had thought of leaving that till last. Possibly after he had returned to Dubai.

Although she was reluctant to acknowledge it, the thought of Jasper's eventual departure left her feeling somewhat empty. Since his kiss, they had only exchanged pleasantries, bright smiles, cheery hellos and plenty of compliments for the hard work she had done on The Laurels – but nothing else. Which left Adira thinking maybe Jasper didn't recall what had happened in the massage parlour. Had he been in such a state of relaxed oblivion that he hadn't been conscious of reaching out and lowering her face to his? Did he remember how his lips had sought hers and how his tongue had sensuously probed? Because she certainly did.

Her face flushed at the memory of it. And yet, for Jasper it seemed to be business as usual, as though he'd been totally unaffected by the whole incident. Adira decided to follow his lead. If pretending the kiss had never happened, so be it. She would be as composed as he.

Overhearing him on the phone in the library told her he was definitely preoccupied with the estate. He was certainly keeping Colin on his toes. The broken windowpanes had been replaced and the whole of the roof was being inspected within the next few days, which meant scaffolding was due to be erected. The Laurels had never seen such industrious activity.

Fletcher was in his element, sitting back and letting it all go on around him, very much the embodiment of the lord of the manor. Even Lilly was rather enjoying her 'tea breaks', which meant once the odd bit of ironing had been done, she would join Fletcher for afternoon tea. As promised, Jasper's coffee machine had been delivered and all of them had delighted in the cappuccinos and lattes which it bubbled and hissed to produce. The four of them rubbed along quite happily, each going about their business in The Laurels.

Now and again, the experience was tinged with a wave of sadness for Fletcher, knowing it wouldn't always be this way. Soon Jasper would return to Dubai and Adira would move on. It struck him as such a waste; he was convinced the pair made a good couple. He'd seen the way they looked at each other, at pains to be discreet, yet the attraction was glaringly obvious to him. He felt like shaking some sense into Jasper, but this wasn't the way. Fletcher knew more than most how restricting affairs of the heart could be. Hadn't it been the same for him many years ago?

Faded memories of a beautiful face with a kind smile passed through his mind; of a delicate, lithe body dancing on his lawn in a lemon taffeta silk dress, her dark hair smoothed up in an elegant chignon. How he had longed for her... and how forbidden she still was. His heart had been broken, his desire locked captive in a cage. Only once had it been released and he would treasure the utter bliss forever. But this had also been Fletcher's downfall. For as glorious as the moment had been, it had also set the bar – way too high. Nobody was ever going to compare to her, not ever; and as a result, Fletcher had remained alone. His eyes filled at the sadness of it all when Lilly entered the drawing room carrying a tray.

'Time for our tea break, Fletcher.'

'Ah, yes, very good.' He sat up and rubbed his hands together, shaking himself out of his reverie.

Meanwhile, Adira had made herself a cappuccino and was at the kitchen table with her laptop. She wanted new bedding and towels to replace the old, rather worn ones and was going to ask Jasper to order them, when in he came.

'Jasper, I was going to suggest we buy new bedding and towels. What do you think?'

He ducked down to see the items she had chosen. Adira inhaled his tangy, citrus aroma and could feel his breath on the back of her neck.

'Looks fine to me. Order it now, on my credit card.' He made a coffee, then sat down next to her and reached into his back pocket for his wallet. She could feel him watching her as she typed in the order.

My God, she was pretty. Seeing how she chewed her bottom lip in concentration, his mind flashed back to how he had explored her mouth. His pulse quickened.

'There you go.' She turned the laptop to face him. He tapped in his credit card details and turned it back to her.

'All done,' he smiled.

There was a slight pause as each waited for the other to speak.

Jasper broke the silence. 'You've done an amazing job here.'

'I haven't finished yet,' she breezed, feeling a tad self-conscious.

'But what you have done so far is incredible. It's made a huge difference to Fletcher.' For all his initial reservations about Adira, Jasper was actually quite moved to learn that she had refused to take a penny, even though her hard work far outweighed the free rent and use of utilities Fletcher was supplying.

'You're making a huge difference too.' She returned his gaze and felt a lump form in her throat; she was suddenly feeling rather emotional.

'Let me take you out for dinner, as a thank you.'

How could she resist those gorgeous brown eyes? She tried to speak, but her mouth had gone dry.

'Tonight?' he pressed.

'Yes… OK. Thank you.'

'Good. I'll pick you up at seven.'

He took his coffee and went back to the library. Adira's head spun.

It's just a thank you meal, no need to read too much into it, she tried to convince herself.

Adira's mind was still buzzing as she tried to decide what to wear that evening. Where was he taking her? Should she dress sophisticated, as in the little black dress she had debated packing, or smart but casual, as in the strappy red sundress? No – he'd already seen her in that the first evening she'd met him at The Laurels. In the end, she opted for cute black Capri pants and an amber off-the-shoulder top which flattered her tan and highlighted hair.

After showering and rubbing in her favourite freesia body lotion, applying the minimum of make-up and brushing her long hair to fall silkily past her shoulders, she was ready and waiting.

Jasper arrived promptly with a tap at the camper van door. Adira opened it and caught her breath. There he stood, looking tall and utterly handsome in dark trousers and an olive linen shirt. She could see the top of his chest through the open neck and was reminded of how her palms had run across it; it was a strange sensation, knowing his body so well, yet not as his lover.

Jasper was having similar thoughts as he swept up and down Adira's svelte, curvaceous figure. His eyes rested on her graceful neck and shoulders, then below to her heavenly cleavage dusted with freckles.

'Ready?' he smiled.

'Yes,' she smiled back, locking the door behind her.

Jasper had parked Fletcher's Range Rover on the road, by the open gated entrance. Adira was impressed to see he had cleaned the car, being used to seeing it covered with dried mud. Inside looked pretty tidy too.

'I thought we'd go out of Lilacwell and into Clitheroe for a change. It's the nearest town.'

'Great. It'd be nice to see the surrounding area.'

He laughed. 'So much for your exploring with Sheila,' he grinned ruefully at her.

'I know,' she agreed. 'Not the best of starts having a broken fuel pump, but there's plenty of time yet. To be honest, I've really grown attached to Lilacwell.'

'I rather think Lilacwell's grown attached to you,' he replied in a quiet voice, making Adira turn her head sharply, but Jasper was simply looking ahead.

He started the engine and was soon pointing out places of interest along the way to Clitheroe.

'You obviously know this area well, but where did you live as a child?' Adira asked.

'Not too far away in North Cumbria.'

Immediately, she pictured him growing up amongst the Lakeland hills and crystal-clear waters, ruddy-faced from the elements, in check shirts and hiking boots. All that fresh air and countryside made her envious, compared to the upbringing she'd had. 'Must have been heaven.'

'It was, but being with Fletcher was better,' he replied, taking a road which led into the town centre.

Adira turned to look at him. 'Why's that?'

'Fletcher had time for me, took a real interest. Dad was always preoccupied and Mum, well, as lovely as she is, I think having a daughter would have somehow suited her better, rather than a boisterous tearaway like me.'

'Boisterous tearaway?' she laughed, imagining him to be anything but.

Jasper shook his head. 'I wasn't always this grown up and sensible, you know,' he half-smiled wryly.

Was he being serious? It was hard to tell. Then she remembered the scar on his shoulder – could that have come from a fight of some sort? Not for the first time, he left Adira feeling very intrigued.

On entering Clitheroe, Adira was impressed by the market town, particularly the ruins of a medieval castle standing high on a hill, overlooking the many shops. Jasper parked along the high street, near to a small Italian restaurant.

'I've booked a table, it's supposed to be good here.' He held the door open and led her into The Italian Garden. It was quaint, with small tables covered in red and white gingham tablecloths and lit candles. Italian music gently played in the background. They were seated outside on the balcony at the back, overlooking a courtyard garden filled with terracotta pots overflowing with rich, vibrant flowers and surrounded by a stone wall wrapped with trailing clematis.

'How sweet,' remarked Adira.

'Glad you like it.' Jasper opened the wine menu and, after asking Adira what she'd prefer, ordered them a bottle when the waiter returned. Within minutes, they were sipping cool Sauvignon Blanc and choosing their main course.

'Thanks for this, Jasper. It's wonderful to have a meal out for a change.' Adira couldn't remember the last time she had eaten out in company. Having the sneaky glass of lunchtime wine at Mario's hardly counted. For a moment, she pictured Goldgate Square with its sweet little wine bar, deli and artisan shops. She didn't miss it. In fact, it seemed like a lifetime ago now.

'Penny for them?' Jasper was looking at her, head tilted to one side.

'Oh, just thinking about my old life, you know, before I bought Sheila.'

'Do you think you'll go back to it?'

'No,' she answered instantly, surprising herself at the speed of her response. 'Well, not to London anyway.'

'You've been bitten by the country bug then?' he grinned, taking a sip of his wine.

'I think I have.' Then, after a pause, added, 'But not you?'

He suddenly looked serious and Adira hoped she hadn't ruined the mood. A few seconds passed, then he answered.

'I've some serious decisions to make.'

He didn't elaborate and she had the intuition not to press any further, instead leading the conversation towards a lighter tone, talking about his work on the estate and hers at The Bath House.

'Most of the bookings only start from next week, so Cassie had chance to hire another therapist.' She gave a smirk. 'I think it was her idea of fun to have you first in to christen the massage bed.'

'Well, I'd certainly recommend your massages,' he winked. It was pleasant seeing this playful side of Jasper. He suddenly reminded her of Fletcher and she could picture exactly how the two would have been like peas in a pod during Jasper's summers at The Laurels.

'That's good to know,' she laughed. 'Anytime.'

There was a pregnant pause as they both locked eyes. They swiftly read each other and for the first time neither had any doubt about the other's attraction. The pull between them was too strong.

Instinctively, they leant forward and their lips met. It was tender, the most natural kiss, yet loaded. Adira's heart thumped in her chest. Jasper's hand covered hers on the table, warm, strong and comforting. They were interrupted by the waiter and both giggled in embarrassment, feeling like teenagers.

After a delicious meal of rich, creamy lasagne and spicy Bolognese, followed by tiramisu and coffee, they travelled home and continued to chat comfortably, trading work stories of pompous clients and even more pompous colleagues, as well as comparing notes on their experiences of London where Jasper had lived before moving out to Dubai. Once Jasper had pulled up by the camper van, Adira faced him. She had no hesitation inviting him in for a drink, not wanting the evening to end. Jasper was only too happy to follow her into the camper van's snug interior. He completely dwarfed the van, looking somewhat comical.

'I don't think the travelling life would suit you,' she giggled as his head almost hit the roof.

'No, I'll sit down before I knock myself out,' he grinned.

As Adira made coffee, he sat back and admired the view. Those trousers really did show off her slim hips and pert bottom.

She turned, putting the two mugs on the table, and sat next to him. There was only just enough room for the two of them and his arm naturally stretched out across the top cushion alongside her back. She loved the comfortable feel of it. Again, that hint of bergamot she'd grown to love drifted past her. Their eyes locked once more. Without another word, Jasper pulled her into him and bent his head to kiss her. Adira's lips met his, sparking an energy within her. She wrapped her arms round his waist and moved closer.

The kiss grew hot and urgent. She felt the hard muscles in his back tighten as he leant further into her, trailing kisses down her neck to her exposed shoulders. Adira struggled for breath as his lips hovered over the swell of her breasts.

'Jasper,' she whispered, running her hands through his dark hair, soft and glossy. His touch was gentle, caressing and tantalising, sending waves of pleasure through her. Then a loud thud from above made her jump.

Abruptly stopping, Jasper raised his head.

'What was that?' hissed Adira, alarmed.

He got up quickly. 'Stay there,' he told her and went outside the camper van to investigate.

Adira sat still, waiting silently for him to return.

Moments later, he stuck his head round the door. 'There's an owl on your roof.'

'An owl?' She went to join him. Sure enough, there it was, sat proudly on the top of Sheila, hooting into the clear, starry night sky. They both laughed. 'Well, that's never happened before,' Adira said, staring at the beauty of the magnificent bird. Suddenly it took off, wings flapping elegantly as it soared into the trees.

Jasper put his arm around her. 'I better get going.'

Though she knew he would have to leave eventually, she couldn't prevent the brief burst of disappointment at his announcement. 'Thanks for a lovely evening, Jasper.'

She turned into his arm, looking up at his face with the glow of the light from Sheila's windows.

'My pleasure.' He gave a knowing look, making her insides melt.

Chapter 21

Zara was not happy. Still there had been no word from Jasper, not directly anyway. She knew he had contacted the other directors from overhearing conversations – well, eavesdropping telephone conferences actually, which she should have vacated after connecting everyone. Once or twice, she had been copied into emails, which told her Jasper would be back soon, but *when* exactly? She was at fever pitch to see him, feeling despondent and unaccustomed to being kept in the dark. It was pointless being sat at her desk with hardly anything to do. Normally Jasper would keep her busy, but without him there and having fully caught up with all his projects, there was a temporary lull in the office. The sensible action to take would be to offer her services elsewhere in the building, but the fear of another director becoming familiarised with her efficiency and snaffling her as their PA in Jasper's absence gripped her. What if it was decided to move her permanently, leaving another to fill her place? No way. So, Zara kept up the pretence that she had been given enough work to keep her busy, when in fact she was bored and restless.

Sighing, she got up from her desk and walked into the corridor to the water machine. On doing so, she passed Abbas, a senior company director.

'Zara, I need a copy of Jasper's report, for the Global Petroleum Group.'

'Certainly, I'll email it you immediately.' She gave her sweetest smile.

Back in the office, she forwarded on the report to Abbas, then sat back with another sigh. That restless itch started to niggle her once more. Where exactly was Jasper anyway? She knew he'd gone to visit family in Lancashire, but that was about all. Having sent various parcels on his behalf over the years to his parents in Cumbria, she could deduce that he wasn't staying there with them. Then she remembered a photograph of another elderly man in his apartment. Could Jasper be with him? He had referred to an uncle he was close to once and mentioned the village where he'd often stayed as a child. It had a quaint, quintessentially English ring to it, she'd thought at the time. What was it? She was sure it had some sort of colour in it... something Belle. Whitebelle? No, Lilac; was it Lilacbelle?

Frowning, she typed the name into her computer and searched – 'Lilacbelle, Lancashire, England'. Several results flashed up before her, but no Lilacbelle. Then her eyes caught the name Lilacwell. Yes! That was it, Lilacwell. Zara clapped her hands in glee, then clicked onto the website.

> *Lilacwell is a hamlet within the civil parish of Bowland Forest Low and Ribble Valley borough of Lancashire, England. It is in the Forest of Bowland Area of Outstanding Natural Beauty. The River Hodder winds its way along the wooded valley. A church, an inn and a few cottages grace this very pretty spot. The manor, now known as The Inn at Lilacwell, used to be the location for a thriving market, which was held on the forecourt. Aged old village customs are still an integral way of life for the local community.*

How utterly charming it looked, she thought, with its cute stone cottages covered with ivy and climbing roses. Pictures of humpbacked bridges, babbling brooks, lush green forests and cobbled streets filled the screen. It seemed a friendly, homely place, with photographs of families picnicking along the riverside, enjoying local traditions such as May Day, with children skipping round a maypole holding reams of ribbon. Zara chuckled to herself at the 'Morris Men' dancing in funny-looking wooden shoes and peculiar outfits, carrying sticks with bells on; how eccentric the English could be.

She then clicked on a link to the local pub, The Inn at Lilacwell. What an impressive place this was, characteristically British with its country decor and long, wooden bar with handpumps. Even the large blackboard displaying the specials made her smile. All so timeless, not a TV screen in sight. Would Jasper visit this place? she wondered, scrolling down the webpage. Then she saw further pictures of the villagers enjoying the 'Hog Roast Day'. She read on, trying to get a feel for the place. The event was to celebrate the opening of a new spa room apparently.

She stopped short. There, staring out at her, was Jasper himself, smiling nonchalantly on… She sat forward with slit eyes – a *massage bed*! Next to him was a woman. A slow, hot fury began to burn inside Zara.

Reading on, she learnt that: *'Jasper Hendricks was the very first customer of The Bath House and was about to enjoy a full Swedish body massage, from the Inn's therapist, Adira Summers.'*

Oh, *was* he? That fury boiled over, sending Zara into an outright rage. She glared at Adira, nostrils flaring, shaking with anger. How dare she touch him? Not that he looked at all perturbed at the prospect of being groped by her.

There was another picture – they were sitting much closer now, smiling openly to the camera. That empty packet of condoms suddenly shot into Zara's mind, sending her into orbit. Here was she, a loyal PA serving his every need… and there he was with some… common English prostitute.

Enough was enough, it was time to bring Jasper back.

Chapter 22

Adira had just finished preparing the treatment room for the next appointment. Lilly's sister, Ruby, was due to arrive for her Indian head massage. There was a slight knock at the door.

'Come in!' called Adira.

A grey, curly head popped round the door.

'Hi, Ruby.'

'Hello, Adira. I've been looking forward to this.' Ruby shuffled into the room, giving Adira a warm smile.

'Still getting the headaches?'

'Hmm, afraid so.'

'You sit here, Ruby,' Adira patted the chair in front of her. 'If you could remove your jacket, so your neck's bare.'

Ruby did as she was told and sat still in the chair.

'Just relax.' Her shoulders immediately sank. 'That's it. I'm going to start here, at the nape.' Adira's hands gently rubbed the tender area, which was stiff with tension.

Slowly, the muscles started to soften, and she carried on in the same slow motion up to Ruby's skull, gradually working her way round her whole head, taking particular attention to the temple area.

'Oh that feels better already,' sighed Ruby, closing her eyes.

No wonder she'd been having headaches, thought Adira, feeling the tightness in her scalp and neck. The oil she used contained lavender for soothing the senses, and after twenty minutes, Ruby was practically asleep.

'There you go, all finished,' murmured Adira.

Ruby's eyelids fluttered open with obvious reluctance. 'Lovely, thank you, dear,' she murmured.

Adira smiled; she was so like her twin sister, Lilly. She pictured them as little girls together, then imagined Fletcher growing up with them; the older influence, always looking out for them like an older brother.

As if reading her mind, Ruby commented, 'You've made big improvements at Fletcher's house, I believe.' Her eyes had the same twinkle as her sister's. 'Lilly sings your praises.'

'Does she?' laughed Adira. 'Lilly has helped too.'

Ruby chortled. 'Lilly would do anything for Fletcher. She adores him. Always has.'

'Really?' Adira was surprised, it had never occurred to her that Lilly could harbour romantic feelings towards Fletcher. But why not? She'd known him all her life and he had obviously been quite a catch in his day. It wasn't hard to envisage how handsome he would have been – *just like Jasper*, she thought.

'Oh yes,' replied Ruby with conviction, 'but Fletcher never saw it.'

'Oh.' Adira felt her heart sadden a little, knowing how Lilly must have spent all those years pining for a man who was oblivious to her feelings.

'Too busy with his eye on someone else.' Ruby looked wistfully into the distance, deep in thought.

Adira frowned, puzzled by the statement.

There was a pause, as if Ruby wanted to divulge more but wasn't sure if she should. 'Typical Fletcher, to fall for someone out of bounds.' She shook her head. 'He always did make life difficult.'

Adira's inquisitiveness rose. Who was Ruby talking about? She had often speculated why Fletcher had never married, especially when he clearly had so much going for him — good looks, personality, country estate. So it seemed unrequited love was the reason, or at least prohibited love. How desperately sad. Poor Fletcher.

'Now don't go feeling sorry for him,' warned Ruby, her eyes cold and unforgiving as the winter frost. 'If Fletcher had woke up and seen sense, he could have had the love of a good woman in Lilly,' she nodded her head firmly. 'And been happy,' she added with force.

Adira was a little taken aback. The subject was evidently an emotional one for Ruby who had, first-hand, seen the hurt and upset Lilly must have suffered over the years.

Not really knowing what to say, Adira awkwardly looked towards the tiled flooring.

'Right,' said Ruby, 'I'd better be on my way and thank you, dear. I feel so much better.'

'You're welcome, Ruby,' smiled Adira.

As the petite old lady left, Adira couldn't help but wonder if it was the head massage or spilling her emotions which had made Ruby feel better.

—

Jasper was busy at his desk in the library, leafing through the paperwork which Colin had given him. He was deciding which of the crumbling old outbuildings were worth salvaging and was still considering how best to utilise the fields. Having Adira's camper van on site had given him the kernel of an idea. Camping, or rather glamping, was all the rage these days. In his mind's eye, he could see twee shepherds' huts and maybe a few yurts in the fields nearest the stream. It would be an ideal spot – Adira had certainly thought so, he grinned to himself. The thought of her heated his blood.

Back to business, he sternly told himself. Yes, a glamping site could be a good solution to the land just standing empty and the outbuilding nearest to them could easily be renovated into a shower and utility block. Without knowing it, Adira had inadvertently given him an idea which had the potential to really take off and keep The Laurels running in modern times.

His phone rang, interrupting his thoughts on what else they would need to turn the land into an attractive glamping prospect. It was Zara.

'Hello, Jasper.'

'Hello, Zara. Everything OK?'

'Well…'

Jasper sat up abruptly at Zara's hesitant tone.

'Abbas has asked to see your report.'

He frowned. 'And?'

'I just get the feeling something's…' Zara stalled with deliberate uncertainty.

'What?' snapped Jasper, not liking the sound of this.

'Not quite right,' she finished, supposedly at pains to disclose it.

'How do you mean?' asked Jasper tightly. Abbas certainly hadn't mentioned anything to him last time they had spoken.

'Sorry, I shouldn't have bothered you.' Zara sounded apologetic now.

She only just managed to keep the glee from her voice; she had obviously rattled Jasper enough. Mission accomplished.

'I just thought I should warn you, in case something was amiss.'

'Amiss? Such as what?' Jasper was beginning to grow impatient with Zara's elusiveness.

'It's probably nothing. Sorry, I shouldn't have contacted you.'

Then why did you? thought Jasper in annoyance. Deciding to end the call, which he deemed pointless, he curtly said his goodbyes.

Minutes later though, Zara's attempts to unsettle Jasper had succeeded. He kept replaying the ambiguity in Zara's voice. It was unlike her to sound so unsure, which then prompted the question, *could* her instincts be a forewarning? But what could be wrong? The report he'd written was concise yet packed with relevant detail and good advice. The more he considered it, the more it played on his mind. He'd ring Abbas.

Then again, what if Zara was mistaken? How would it look for him to call with concerns – like he had something to hide? The best solution, his head was telling him, was to return to Dubai and face the inevitable decision he was avoiding. He couldn't keep putting it off. Logically, now would be a good time to go back, for a while at least. The Laurels was in good shape, thanks to Adira, and the estate was under far more control now. Jasper would decide how to go forward with the outbuildings before he left and get Colin to make a start with the renovations. Once he returned, he would continue with the glamping site project.

He looked out of the library window; the scaffolding for The Laurel's roof was now up and he'd already given instructions for the builders to replace or completely retile where necessary. A sudden reluctance to leave spread through him, reminiscent of his younger self, when a sad little boy was made to pack his suitcase and bid farewell to uncle Fletcher. How he'd hated those goodbyes, seeing Fletcher's eyes mist over as he clung tightly to his big, burly frame.

In that instant, Jasper made his choice.

It was no use convincing himself he'd be able to oversee operations from Dubai. He needed to be here, on site. It was time to come back to The Laurels for good. This was his home and where he belonged.

Once Jasper had made the ultimate decision, his mind became clear and focused. No longer clouded with uncertainty, he was able to put the necessary motions in place.

Emailing the company directors to inform them of his imminent return, he sent a separate message to Abbas, asking him to meet the first day back. Jasper intended to hand in his notice, explaining the situation he was in. He had reread and scrutinised the contract he'd signed and the get-out clause of 'exceptional circumstances' ought to cover his resignation. They were exceptional circumstances – his uncle desperately needed him. He had an obligation, a duty to take care of him and the family home that was to become his.

Jasper paused and sat back in his chair for a moment, contemplating the day he would hand The Laurels on to his child. For the first time, the liability dawned on him. Fletcher's words echoed in his ears, *'It's time to pass on the baton.'* Jasper felt like he'd aged overnight, from being a young, free and single man living it up in Dubai to a responsible nephew with commitments to fulfil. The estate was running and there were people who depended heavily on it. The Laurels supplied livelihoods, homes and produce for local businesses and was an integral part of the village. The Hendricks family had always lived in The Laurels and Fletcher was right, it was a part of who they were.

And now the burden had landed well and truly on Jasper's shoulders.

It could be daunting to some, but not Jasper. He knew what needed doing and he was more than prepared to do it. Unlike Fletcher, he wasn't going to bury his head in the sand but would face the challenge full on. Nobody was going to take advantage. The difference in the estate manager and the now up-to-date rent from every tenant proved this. He'd been reluctant to let Colin go, as the man had been working on the estate for years and had experience. He suspected that all Colin had needed was a sharp wake-up call. Plus, Jasper really didn't want to have to advertise for a new estate manager at the moment – he had enough on his plate as it was.

He would make it clear to Fletcher and Colin that his going back to Dubai was only a temporary measure. The last thing he needed was a lapse back into old ways.

Then his thoughts turned to Adira. Would she still be here when he returned to Lilacwell? He knew her plans were to travel and he couldn't expect her to wait for him – if indeed she wanted to. He would have to work a month's notice and a lot could happen in a month – look at all that had happened since his arrival. The Laurels had been transformed, the estate was undergoing big changes, Fletcher was a different man, and... Adira. From the moment he had seen that heavenly body bathing in the river, she had got under Jasper's skin – her smile, her laughter, her caring nature, how she'd helped Fletcher with the house and all the locals with her knowledge of natural medicine. Adira was intelligent, she spoke sense without sounding judgemental. He admired her courage to ditch the rat race and her quest for travelling. She was a free spirit. And free spirits shouldn't be confined. He had to explain his actions and let her make her own decisions. It was unfair to ask anything from her, no matter how much he wanted to.

With a heavy heart, he booked his flight.

That evening over dinner, Jasper broke the news to Fletcher. At first, his uncle's face had dropped with disappointment, but as he quickly outlined his full plans, Fletcher had nodded sagely, understanding the circumstances. It was only for a month, then his nephew would be back for good.

The relief Fletcher felt was immense. Finally, it was time to hand it all over, and with a clear conscience. He'd held it together for as long as possible, he was eighty-five after all.

'Will you miss Dubai?' Fletcher asked quietly, assessing Jasper from the rim of his whisky tumbler.

'No,' came the firm reply. 'I've enjoyed my time out there, but it's time to come home.' He looked levelly at his uncle. 'I want to be here.'

'Good, good.' He threw back his whisky. 'When do you fly back?'

'In two days' time. Don't worry, I'll brief Colin before I go. Everything's in safe hands.'

'I don't doubt it.' Fletcher paused. 'Have you told Adira yet?'

'No.'

Fletcher stared him in the eye, somewhat accusingly, thought Jasper.

'I'll tell her tomorrow,' he added lamely.

Fletcher raised an eyebrow. 'I suggest you tell her tonight,' he replied in an even tone, which Jasper had never heard before.

He coughed and shifted uncomfortably.

'Perhaps you're right,' he finally replied.

Chapter 23

Adira had finished a full afternoon at The Bath House and enjoyed an evening meal at the Inn before coming back to the camper van. She was relaxing with a cup of tea when she saw Jasper through the window, heading towards the van. Her heart instantly skipped a beat.

'Hi,' she smiled, opening the door. Was it her imagination or did Jasper look rather serious?

'I need to talk to you,' he replied, his eyes looking intense, making her stomach contract. What was the matter?

He came inside the van and sat down, and she followed, sitting opposite him.

Running his hand through his hair he turned to face her. 'I'm going back to Dubai in two days' time.'

Adira felt like she'd been slapped in the face. She blinked and stared at him, speechless.

He carried on. 'It's just for a month. I'm going to hand in my resignation, but I'll have to work a month's notice.' His eyes searched her face, willing her to understand. Still she said nothing. 'I… Something's come up and I need to sort it out… but it's made me realise what I want. Where my future lies,' he finished, wishing she'd at least say something.

After the initial shock, Adira's face remained calm.

'I see,' she croaked, a huge lump was forming in her throat. Quickly she swallowed, anxious to retain composure. *Don't lose it*, she told herself, *you always knew he was going back.*

And what about your plans? a voice inside asked.

What had happened to that wanderlust spirit that had empowered her? Suddenly it all seemed futile now. In that instant, she realised just what Lilacwell and Jasper had come to mean to her. Lilacwell had worked its magic on her, she'd fallen under its spell and, if she was honest with herself, she had fallen for Jasper too. It was all well and good pretending to carry on, business as usual, with future travels on the horizon; but it wasn't as simple as that now. She'd discovered Lilacwell. She'd met Jasper. And she couldn't put them behind her to wander off to another destination. In a nutshell, she'd found what she wanted.

A sad, empty feeling took over. Blinking back the tears that threatened to fall, she got up. 'Would you like a drink?'

She couldn't look at him. She stood at the stove with her back to him.

'No, thanks.' There was a pause. 'Listen Adira, I...' Then he broke off as he saw her wipe her face. Was she crying? He shot up and moved to stand behind her. 'Adira,' his voice was thick with emotion as he reached out and folded his arms around her. He kissed her neck, then ran his lips lightly up to kiss her tear-stained cheek. 'It's only for a month,' he whispered. The depth of his feelings amazed him. Never had he felt this way before, especially in such a short space of time. Intuition told him that Adira felt exactly the same.

'I know... sorry,' she eventually managed to stammer. 'We both knew each of us would be leaving at some point.'

Jasper stilled. What did she mean? Was she about to go off travelling now? Would she be here for him when he got back? He took a deep breath, not able to bear the thought of her camper van driving off into the sunset forever.

Say something, man! he heard Fletcher's voice inside his head. But he couldn't. He'd already reasoned with himself it was unfair to do so. Adira was her own woman, with her own choices to make. He'd made it clear where he would be in a month's time.

But where would she *be?* he dully asked himself.

–

The next morning, Adira woke with a thumping head-ache. Hardly surprising, given the fact she'd spent most of the night twisting and turning, her mind in complete turmoil. Half of her – the sensible, logical side – told her that Jasper's going was inevitable, while the other half – her heart and emotions – screamed 'no!'. But what could she do? She had no say. Jasper had a job in Dubai and work his notice he must – thousands of miles away.

Staring up at the camper van ceiling, she contemplated the timing. Technically, she was ready to go too. The fuel pump had been replaced so the camper van was ready now. Cassie had the other masseuse set up at the Inn to continue treatments. Practically, she had no excuses to stay. Was this a sign? Had both their departures meant to be in unison?

With deep reluctance, she pulled the covers back. She was due at The Laurels today. Adira bleakly realised that her work there was almost complete, another sign to move on. She only had three more bedrooms to clean – one of them being Jasper's. Her chin wobbled thinking about his empty bed, all his possessions packed up, winging their way back to his apartment in Dubai.

Get a grip, she reprimanded herself, *stop behaving like a big baby*. A touch of embarrassment entered her at the memory of last night. Why did she have to cry in front of him? What must he have thought?

Sighing, she tried to motivate herself. She got up, got dressed and skipped breakfast. Her appetite had vanished, to be replaced with a heavy, sickly sensation.

Adira was greeted by Lilly in the kitchen at The Laurels.

'Hello, dear,' the housekeeper chirped, pouring herself a cup of tea. Adira noticed how her hands seemed more supple these days. Where once they appeared twisted and gnarled, making Lilly wince in pain, now they seemed a touch looser and Lilly's face didn't indicate any discomfort. Her recommendation of turmeric must be helping. Then she thought of Ruby and how much better she'd appeared after her head massage, and Adira wondered how Lisa was doing after her advice. A wave of gloom over came her. How attached she had grown to Lilacwell and its idiosyncratic, loveable residents. As if on cue, in walked Fletcher.

'Morning, Adira.' He eyed her carefully.

She knew he was assessing her. Resolute to put on a brave front, she replied cheerily, 'Morning, Fletcher. I'm going to do the rest of the bedrooms today.'

'Righto.'

'Then, I've finished. Job done,' she said with finality, making Fletcher sharply turn his head towards her.

'You mean, that's it? You're—'

'Moving on,' she interrupted with a forced smile that was in danger of cracking any second.

'Oh,' came the flat reply.

'But—' Lilly attempted to intervene.

'No really, it's time to go,' Adira turned to Lilly, her crestfallen face nearly killing her. She swallowed. 'Poor Sheila's been parked up long enough.' The attempt at humour fell flat. A leaden silence hung in the air like a thundercloud.

Fletcher opened his mouth, then shut it tight, fighting the urge to say something. He was literally biting his tongue. This was bloody madness – a feeling of déjà vu crawled into him, taunting his senses.

'Right,' said Adira with a strained bravado which didn't meet her eyes, 'I'll make a start.'

Fletcher and Lilly exchanged glances, but neither spoke.

Adira collected her cleaning tray and went through the hall, passing the library on the way. She glimpsed Jasper's profile, working at his desk by the window. He hadn't noticed her, so she quickly continued up the stairs.

She vacuumed and dusted the bedroom next to Fletcher's, which contained only a single bed and wardrobe, so didn't take long. Then she came to the bedroom opposite on the landing. Turning the handle, the door wouldn't move. Adira tried again, ever so slightly forcing her weight against it. But still it wouldn't budge. She frowned. It must be locked. Only having Jasper's bedroom to clean, which she wasn't going to do till he'd left, she went back downstairs. Fletcher and Lilly were in the drawing room with their mid-morning tea and she saw that the library was now empty. Deciding to have a drink herself, she went into the kitchen. Jasper was standing by the coffee machine staring out of the window. From the set of his shoulders, Adira thought he looked tense. She longed to put her arms round him.

He turned at seeing her. 'Hey,' he smiled, but couldn't quite meet her eye. He didn't trust himself to speak. For the first time ever, he was torn between work and pleasure. He had work commitments to fulfil and had to go to Dubai, but that was the last thing he wanted to do. His mind wasn't on the job. He longed to stay here, at home, with Adira. Never before had he allowed his personal life to interfere with his professional life. But inside now he was breaking. Ridiculous, he told himself.

Adira sensed the awkwardness, finding it strange seeing the usual quietly confident Jasper ill at ease.

'All packed?' she said lightly, trying to fill the stillness. Then immediately cursed herself at seeing the anguish shoot across his face. It must be hard leaving Fletcher, even if it was temporarily. His uncle wasn't getting any younger after all; time was precious. Mortified, she could feel her eyes swilling with tears again.

'Come here,' Jasper said gruffly, holding out his arms.

Without hesitation, she went straight into them. She buried her head in his shoulder and breathed in that manly, citrussy scent.

For a split second, Jasper considered asking her to go with him, but then instantly dismissed it. Dubai was *business*, he had things to do there, not spend time in the sun with Adira. He sighed heavily. Adira looked up at him.

'We will stay in touch?' Her eyes searched his.

'Of course,' he answered incredulously. 'Here,' he reached for his phone in his back pocket, 'take my office number.' They'd already exchanged mobile numbers, but he wanted her to have his work number as back-up. Adira tapped the details into her phone.

Fletcher had witnessed the exchange from the hallway and had kept a discreet distance. He so wanted to go in there and bash their heads together. *Definite bloody plans*, that's what Jasper should be insisting on, not ifs, buts and half-hearted 'keep-in-touch's! The frustration was killing him. Then, deciding to take matters into his own hands, he marched into the kitchen.

'Right, tonight we're having a farewell – no, not farewell,' he corrected himself swiftly, 'a bon voyage dinner.' He turned to Adira, 'I want you here in your glad rags,' then looked pointedly at Jasper, 'and you too, black tie and dinner suit—'

'I haven't got—' Jasper started to say.

'I've one you can wear,' Fletcher spoke over him. He was on a mission. 'This is a special occasion, *time to make an effort*,' he said with force, looking at them both.

Jasper grinned wryly to himself. The sentiment wasn't lost on him. He knew what Fletcher was implying and Adira also smiled, knowing Fletcher meant well. Then she suddenly remembered the bedroom she couldn't gain access to.

'Oh, Fletcher, I couldn't clean the bedroom opposite yours. The door's locked.'

Fletcher's face turned sombre. 'Leave that room,' he answered.

'But—'

'I said leave it, Adira,' he replied sternly, before walking away.

Adira turned to Jasper, with her hands open. 'What was that about?'

Jasper shook his head frowning. 'No idea.'

The two exchange'd puzzled looks.

Chapter 24

Zara sat back in utter satisfaction with a gleeful smirk spread across her face. At last, the email she had yearned for, telling her Jasper was returning, appeared there on her screen. Albeit the words read concise and business-like, with no warmth whatsoever. Yet still, the message informed her he would very shortly be back in the office. In fact, his plane would be landing at seven p.m. the next evening to be precise, she eagerly thought. Should she offer to meet him at the airport? No, knowing Jasper, he would already have arranged transport.

She knew she'd disturbed him because he had made enquires in his email for any feedback regarding his report. Of course there wasn't any. Abbas hadn't even mentioned it since asking for a copy. Still, her phone call had been enough to sow the seed of doubt and get him scuttling back. The corners of her mouth twisted with content-ment. Perhaps she could control him after all?

She hummed cheerfully as her hands ran across his now empty desk. Zara had cleared every single piece of paper and item on it, emptied his in-tray and wiped over the keyboard and monitor. There, everything clean and tidy for his return. How he'd realise what a gem he had for a PA, and hopefully more.

She had bought a new outfit to wear for the day of his arrival – a fitted black dress, which enhanced her figure whilst still complying with the professional dress code. Zara had also managed to source the coffee he liked, having seen the brand in his kitchen, and had arranged for his car to be valeted. So yes, she was more than prepared for his return. All she needed was to see those rich brown eyes gaze into hers.

A hot rush flew up her. She'd never experienced such a craving. The saying *absence makes the heart grow fonder* was an understatement in Zara's case. Jasper had become an obsession to her. So desperate was she to see his face, she had scoured the company's website and downloaded any photograph of him. She'd been reduced to printing them out and making a collage of him for her bedroom wall, though she blankly refused to include any photographs of him in that ridiculous massage parlour.

Having reviewed her progress – or rather lack of progress – on the romantic front with Jasper, Zara had decided to up her game. Perhaps he was the type of man that needed a little encouragement? Yes, she convinced herself, that's where she was going wrong; she hadn't made her intentions clear. All it required was a touch of support to get the ball rolling. Zara was a master of manipulation, she'd grown up knowing how to wheedle her way round men, how to twist them round her little finger. From an early age, she had seen how her mother had very easily manipulated her father. Good looks counted for a lot, she had discovered. Beautiful people got attention; they also got their own way. Being the youngest, and the only girl at that, had got Zara even more. Look at how her father idolised her. Although she had had a strict upbringing, her father had always had a soft spot for his only daughter. Arun Kassis was born and bred in the UAE, her mother was western, having met her husband in similar circumstances to Zara and Jasper (another fact persuading Zara it was fate). Deborah Mercer had landed a plum job as a personal secretary to the head of a thriving oil business – it was one of the founder groups which had joined forces to form the present company which had provided Zara with a position. There had been a few raised eyebrows within the Kassis family when Arun had announced his engagement to the pretty blonde-haired, blue-eyed secretary from Kensington, London. This wasn't what his parents had envisaged for their youngest son. Still, as Arun had been forty-five and not showing any sign of a partner so far, they were just relieved that he had finally chosen a woman, even if she was western. Granted, she was extremely attractive, and wasn't Kensington in the Royal Borough? Well, she was practically regal; that was the party line anyway, trotted out at dinner parties and business events.

When the pretty secretary had provided Arun with four strong boys, all the image of their father, she had exceeded all expectations. Then, a touch later, and to everyone's surprise, out popped a daughter, still with dark eyes and jet-black hair like her daddy, but every inch as beautiful as her mother. Zara had been the ultimate blessing; the cherry on the cake to her parents, grandparents and brothers. She was adored, pampered by a string of nannies and worshipped by the whole family. Her every whim, wish or desire was granted. Zara had persuaded her father, despite his strong reservations, that working as a PA would be the making of her. To her credit, she *was* a good assistant. But her diligence was more due to her attraction to Jasper, than anything else.

In short, Zara had always got what she wanted. And now she wanted Jasper.

Chapter 25

That evening, Adira didn't have a quandary deciding what to wear. Under strict orders from Fletcher, she pulled out her little black dress from the tiny built-in wardrobe, remembering the last time she had worn it. It had been at the Law Society dinner, full of ambitious social climbers, frantically attempting to rub shoulders with the upper echelons. She pictured the Hooray Henrys in stiff, white shirts and black ties, guffawing with false joviality and the horsey-set women donning flamboyant evening gowns, always with an eye on who to sidle up to, whether their quarry be husband material or a potential rung up the professional ladder. Adira hated it, truly abhorring the whole sorry set-up. She simply didn't belong and she never had.

'Fish out of water, eh?' Rory had nudged her, accurately interpreting the look of despair in her face.

'You know the feeling then?' she'd replied, smothering a smile as she saw the Head of Chambers catch their exchange from the corner of her eye. Although she wasn't happy in her job, it would be foolish to make waves. Career suicide, that was for certain. Adira had seen first-hand the treatment of any barrister refusing to conform. Nigel Kerfoot took it upon himself to scrutinise all the barristers who he deemed fortunate enough to grace his chambers, including both their professional and, inappropriately, personal life. He liked to think it 'thorough' and in the chamber's best interests, when in fact 'intrusive' was more the word. His 'thoroughness' knew no bounds, often taking to following newly appointed barristers, especially the young, pretty ones, to get a feel for their tastes and whereabouts. Nigel was paranoid about upholding the excellent reputation of Goldgate Chambers, to the point of fixation. It wouldn't do to have a colleague sully the name in any way, shape or form. Adira had once or twice seen him whilst out and about – always he would make himself known, whether with a cherry hello, or a bottle of wine sent to her table, making sure his presence was acknowledged. She found it creepy. It was creepy.

She shuddered at the memory and thanked her lucky stars she was out of all that. Her black dress was coming out this evening for a *positive* event, she counselled herself. She was spending time with genuine, caring people. Her chin wobbled.

Stop it. She took a shaky breath and willed herself to stay calm.

'Cool and composed,' she repeated the words in the mirror, as though saying them out loud would have the desired effect. The sharp, logical side of her brain kicked in, as it often had at work, particularly whilst in court. Any hint of feeling vulnerable or exposed and Adira would retaliate. It was a coping mechanism, self-preservation. As a barrister, she had often come under fire in court and had to retain a hard exterior, ready to retaliate. To show any chink in her armour would be a weakness. She *would* be strong. Adira reminded herself of the reason why she was in Lilacwell in the first place; for a new way of life.

It wasn't to feel unsettled or subdued. She couldn't fall at the first hurdle!

–

Jasper too was staring at his reflection, fiddling with his dicky bow. It seemed a touch bizarre to be going to these lengths, just to have another dinner at The Laurels. But, as Fletcher insisted, it was to give 'a sense of occasion' and he respected his gusto. Fletcher clearly approved of Adira, knowing this only cemented his already strong feelings for her. What troubled Jasper was how deep *her* feelings were for him. Granted, she had shown them by responding the way she had to his advances and there was no denying her upset about his return to Dubai, but how would she be feeling in a month's time? Would it be a case of out of sight, out of mind? They'd both be busy after all: he with his work, only having a month to wrap it all up, and she with her travels, exploring new-found places. He half envied her and once more admired her spirit.

Who else would admire her? a voice whispered inside him. People like Adira didn't go unnoticed. Look how well she had stood out in Lilacwell.

A dark foreboding punched into his stomach. Was he about to lose something special?

No, common sense intervened. If it was right, if he and Adira were meant for something more, then a month apart wouldn't make any difference. If anything, it should make them stronger, he persuaded himself. First, though, he needed to confirm with Adira that they were on the same page about there being a 'them'.

There, he'd finally fixed his tie. Not bad, he thought, considering he was wearing his uncle's clothes. Typical of

Fletcher to have a wardrobe full of formal evening wear, but then again, he always did like to dress up for his parties. Jasper vaguely recollected his uncle's descriptions of them, particularly the last midsummer ball. He recalled how Fletcher's face would light up, his eyes shining, reminiscing all the details; what music was played – ragtime and quickstep to graceful waltzes – the colourful silk gowns which floated across the lawn, the dark velvet sky, dusted with pinpricked stars, the fragrance of fresh cut grass and limoncello candles, the tinkle of chat and laughter spilling out from the orangery… Yes, he'd painted a magical scene, one which a young boy could only imagine with awe.

Now, as an adult, Jasper had wondered why the parties had suddenly ceased. Before he'd been born, in fact. Why, when they'd all still been so young to enjoy them – Fletcher, his parents, Lilly and all the other guests?

His thoughts were interrupted by a knock at the bedroom door. It was Lilly.

'Fletcher wants to know how the suit fits,' she entered the room, smiling at Jasper. 'What a dashing figure you cut.'

'You don't look so bad yourself, Lilly,' he replied, turning to look at her. 'Very nice,' he added with a grin.

'Oh stop,' she waved him away, however pleased she was with the compliment. And well deserved it was too, with her silver hair in a neat French plait, coral layered dress and string of pearls.

'Pre-dinner drinks!' roared Fletcher from downstairs, making them both jump.

'I'm surprised he hasn't a dinner gong,' said Jasper in a dry tone, which made Lilly giggle. He was pleased to see her enter into the spirit of things. Then he heard

Fletcher welcome Adira, who must have come in through the kitchen door.

'Ah Adira, what a picture you look,' Fletcher crowed. Then added, somewhat clumsily, 'Jasper! Get yourself down here!'

Jasper shook his head in disbelief. How many pre-dinner drinks had the old boy already had?

On entering the drawing room, Jasper's eyes widened at the beautiful creature stood before him. Their eyes locked, and he was speechless. Her golden hair was piled in curls set to the top with waves cascading down – like a Greek goddess, he thought. She looked slim and curvy in a classy black dress which showcased her long, tanned legs. The strappy high-heeled sandals and thick, silver jewellery finished off the look strikingly.

'Adira…' he stumbled. She stared back, hardly moving.

'Right,' Fletcher slapped his hands together loudly, breaking the moment. 'What'll we have?' He turned towards the drinks cabinet.

'Just a small one for me please,' said Lilly, following him.

'You look stunning,' Jasper whispered in Adira's ear, having crossed the space dividing them so he could take her hands in his, unable to resist touching her.

'So do you.' Her eyes slowly looked him up and down, seductively, making his blood pump. For two pins, he'd pick her up and carry her delicious body all the way upstairs to his bedroom.

'Sorry to interrupt,' cut in Fletcher with a sly grin, 'but would either of you two lovebirds like a drink?'

Jasper rolled his eyes and Adira laughed.

'Yes, Fletcher, two stiff gin and tonics,' Jasper said, then leaned into her and said sotto voce, 'I think we're going to need them.' It was blatantly clear how his uncle so wished the pair to underpin their relationship before they separated for a month. In fairness to Fletcher, he just wanted to see them both happy, with cast-iron plans, rather than leaving things untied.

The dinner reminded Adira of the first time she had visited The Laurels, with easy banter batting back and forth, much to the delight of Lilly, who was thoroughly enjoying herself, pleased that her rack of lamb was going down a treat. Adira thought of what Ruby had told her about Lilly's adoration for Fletcher, and she felt a rush of sympathy. Seeing how the old lady hung on Fletcher's every word, she couldn't help but wonder what might have been for Lilly.

Jasper caught her pensive expression and frowned. What was she thinking? He'd thought tonight was going extremely well, so much so that he didn't want to think about leaving for the airport in the morning. Neither did Fletcher by the looks of it, as he proposed toast after toast, to 'safe journeys,' 'welcome reunions' and 'happy-ever-afters,' almost making Jasper choke on his champagne, such was his uncle's subtlety. Adira had seemed to take it all in good humour, her cheeks rosy with a combination of alcohol and happiness.

By the end of the evening, however, Fletcher did show some discretion and after a pleasant, entertaining meal, bid them goodnight. Both he and Lilly, who was staying in one of the spare bedrooms, quietly made their way upstairs, leaving Jasper and Adira alone.

'I'll walk you back,' he said, and for a charged moment they looked into each other's eyes.

'Thanks,' she smiled.

Together they walked hand in hand in a comfortable silence under the pale moonlight. When they reached the camper van, he turned her towards him and kissed her gently. Adira held onto him, not wanting to let go. Finally he released her.

'Let me know when you land safely,' she choked, battling to keep her tears at bay.

'I will.' He gave her another squeeze. 'Now off you go and have a wonderful time travelling.' He planted a hard kiss on her lips, then turned and walked away, only glancing round once. She'd gone, locked inside the camper van, leaning against the door in tears.

Chapter 26

Jasper watched the raindrops dribble down the airplane window. The weather had changed, matching his mood. He closed his eyes. He was tired, not having slept a wink last night. No matter how hard he tried, Adira's face constantly flashed before him. It was unnerving how much she was affecting him and he was beginning to worry about concentrating on his work, at a time when he really needed to. Now more than ever, he had to stay focused; it was imperative he completed his latest project and gave word on the future ones lined up for him so he could return to Lilacwell as soon as possible.

Since making his decision and knowing where he was heading, the impending meeting with Abbas didn't faze him. He was going, and that was that. He did, however, want to uphold his good name and complete all that was needed of him, professionally as well as speedily. Although he'd enjoyed his time in Dubai, he'd always known it wasn't forever. It wasn't the place to set down real roots. Deep down, Lilacwell had been ingrained in him and from childhood he had grown up knowing that The Laurels would one day be his home, his responsibility. In a way, he relished the idea of being master of all he surveyed, so to speak. After years of company regulations, deadlines, laborious meetings and tight schedules, it was almost time to close the door and re-emerge as his own boss. He would comply to his own timetables, set his own rules, and the notion pleased him.

A part of him wondered why he hadn't thought this way before, and then he dully realised it was because Fletcher hadn't needed him as badly. He dreaded to think how it would have all panned out, had he not made that phone call. What if Lilly hadn't warned him of Fletcher's health? He sank further into his seat, imagining his poor, elderly uncle sat all alone in The Laurels. Then he snapped himself out of it. He *did* make the call, Lilly *had* warned him and he'd responded. He had come to the rescue and taken over, and he was going back for good. But would Adira be there when he returned?

'Drink, sir?' asked the stewardess politely.

'A large gin and tonic,' he smiled back. So what if it was only ten in the morning? He needed a drink.

–

Adira languidly made her way up the stairs to complete the last task of her cleaning The Laurels – Jasper's bedroom. She opened the door to the small attic room tucked in the eaves. For a moment, she wondered why he chose to stay in this, the smallest of the bedrooms. It must be for sentimental reasons, she concluded, taking in the tiny, cast-iron fireplace, the quaint leaded window in the rooftop and the window seat beyond, with an old teddy bear sitting there. There was even a wooden train set on top of the bookcase.

She turned to the bed, perfectly made, and pictured Jasper as a little boy sleeping there. Adira gave a deep sigh and got on with the job in hand.

Fletcher was in the kitchen endeavouring to make sense of the coffee machine.

'Bloody thing,' he grumbled, then flinched as it let out a loud hiss. 'Oh, blow it.' He switched it off and filled the kettle. He'd make do with plain old instant instead.

When sat at the table sipping from his mug, the silence smacked into him. How depressing; no banter with Jasper, Lilly was still asleep and Adira was on the verge of leaving. The only sound was the distant tick of the grandfather clock in the hall.

Just get through this month, he told himself firmly. In a few weeks, Jasper would be back for good and all would be well, wouldn't it?

Lilly emerged from her slumber, slightly bleary-eyed. Yawning, she flicked the coffee machine on.

'Good luck with that blasted thing,' he muttered.

'It's easy when you get the hang of it,' she replied, delving in heaped spoons of dark ground beans.

'Hmm,' he grunted back.

Lilly turned and looked at his scowling face. 'Is this how you're going to be until Jasper gets back?' she asked, tight-lipped.

Fletcher looked up surprised. It was most unlike Lilly to be so sharp.

'Because if it is, I'm not coming here again.'

Fletcher's eyebrows shot up. 'What?'

'I said,' Lilly said calmly, 'you buck up, or I'll go.'

His jaw dropped. Stunned, he gaped at her in disbelief.

Lilly was rather enjoying his reaction and realised this is what he was short of – straight talking. She stared directly at him. 'So, what will it be, Fletcher?'

Fletcher blinked, still not quite believing his ears. No Lilly? It was inconceivable. Lilly was always here, bobbing about in the background, pleasantly chirping away, keeping him company. Where would he be without her? He gulped and, after a few seconds, cleared his throat.

'I… I'll buck up,' he said faintly, like a naughty schoolboy in the headmistress' office.

'Good,' she nodded. 'Now get up from that table, stop feeling sorry for yourself and I'll show you how to work this machine.'

Fletcher put down his mug and did as he was told.

If only she'd been this assertive years ago, she cursed herself.

–

It was dusk by the time the airplane started its descent. Gradually swooping down, Jasper's anticipation refused to spark as it normally would at seeing the whole of Dubai lit up, looking exotic and inviting. Instead, a flat sensation loomed, as though he was merely going through the motions on autopilot. He heard one or two gasps of relief at the safe landing from overexcited holidaymakers, understanding their enthusiasm even if he couldn't match it. Hadn't he once reacted in the same way? Now Dubai was a workplace, a tie that he needed to unknot and release.

Sitting patiently whilst those around him fussed and fidgeted, he reflected that at times like this it was easy to spot the more practised travellers, who just waited calmly as par for the course.

Finally, he exited the plane, his feet touching solid ground, and he slung his rucksack over a shoulder. He dutifully stood in the long queue, showed his passport, then got in one of the taxis lining up outside the airport. Dry, warm air filled his lungs, a far cry from the dewy mist he'd inhaled that morning.

'Jumeirah, Tiara apartments please,' he informed the driver and sat back, staring out of the window. Tarmac and sand, with a skyscraper backdrop. For the first time, he wondered what all the fuss was about. Perhaps it was because of the comparison to the lush, green hills and verdant forest of Lilacwell.

Character, he thought, the Forest of Bowland had real earthy character, whereas Dubai was… superficial, manmade.

Within half an hour, the taxi was pulling up outside his apartment. With weary effort, Jasper paid the driver and made his way in. The last time, he promised himself. This would be the very last time he'd have to make this trip. Then he pulled out his mobile and texted Adira. He kept it short and sweet, 'Back safely'.

Chapter 27

Zara was at fever pitch, paying meticulous attention to her beauty regime. She'd thought long and hard over which perfume, hairstyle and accessories to wear. The new dress was perfect. Whilst black and formal, it still hinted at a touch of hidden promise beneath the soft, silky material. Finally, she opted for Black Opium, her hair down – falling rather sexily, she thought, past her shoulders – and the thick gold chain necklace and matching bracelet her father had presented on her last birthday. She smirked with intention at the large, lit mirror. How could he resist?

–

Jasper woke with a dull, throbbing headache. Reaching for the glass of water on his bedside table, he frowned, noticing the drawer wasn't fully shut. It was unlike his cleaner to leave a drawer partially open. His frown deepened. Why would she even need to go in it?

Leaning back against his pillow, he took a long drink and contemplated the day ahead of him. Out of the corner of his eye, he saw a long, black hair on the bed's pristine, white sheet. Where had that come from? An uneasy sensation edged inside him. He pictured his cleaner in the brown uniform and bandana she always wore, constraining her grey hair. She'd never let a hair stray out of place, such was her attention to detail; Nesima was a perfectionist, not to mention trustworthy, which was why he could rely on her not to nosey in his drawers. His eyes narrowed in thought.

—

Zara arrived at the office early. She made sure the coffee she had recently bought was brewing, ready for Jasper's entrance. As she heard the door open, she whipped round with a huge, beaming smile on her face.

'Jasper, good to see you.' She wanted to sound professional, yet warm.

'Zara,' he nodded and sat down at his desk.

OK, not quite the welcome she'd expected.

'Good holiday?' she tentatively enquired.

He didn't appear to hear her, as he fired up his computer.

Never mind, he's obviously tired, she placated herself. Then she quickly made his coffee and placed it at the side of him. 'It's your favourite,' she said, almost gloating.

Jasper looked down at the white cup and saucer, then his gaze turned on her. Her heart leaped at seeing those deep brown eyes, pulling her in.

'How do you know what my favourite coffee is?' he asked impassively.

Zara stalled. 'Err… I remember you ordering it once,' she stumbled, thrown completely off guard. This wasn't going according to plan at all.

Jasper had clocked the way she had leant over to put his coffee down, ensuring he'd catch a glimpse of her cleavage, and he found it rather vulgar. He couldn't help but inhale her potent aroma, which was practically stinging his eyes, as was the brash bling of her jewellery. Sighing wearily, he swivelled his back to her and looked out of the window to the panoramic view before him. Still, even this couldn't raise his spirits.

'I've arranged to speak to Abbas,' he told her. 'Could you let him know I'm here?' It was more an order than a request.

'Certainly,' she replied primly, feeling well and truly affronted.

The rest of the morning was spent in silence as Jasper pored over his emails. Clearly Zara hadn't been privy to many of them, which further niggled her. And why did he need to see Abbas so urgently? Her vexation started to build – first not seeing him for weeks, then being brushed to one side and excluded.

At midday, Abbas called the office to summon him. Jasper walked through the smoked-glass walled corridor and knocked quietly at the office door. Abbas was sat behind a huge desk covered in open files.

'Hello, Jasper,' he smiled. 'Take a seat.'

Jasper noticed the chair was slightly lower than Abbas's. Was this deliberate, reminding the visitor of their status?

Abbas clasped his hands together and sat ready for Jasper to speak.

'I'll get straight to the point. I want to hand in my resignation.'

Abbas continued to look calmly at him, waiting for Jasper to elaborate.

'I know I signed an extended contract, but my uncle needs me, Abbas, he's eighty-five, in failing health and I have to run his estate. He cannot manage without me.' There, he'd said it.

There was a brief pause before Abbas replied.

'Did you not think of this before signing the contract?' His tone was neutral, not accusing.

'To my shame, no.' Jasper looked downwards in guilt. 'My uncle always gave the impression he was coping. I realise now I should have been more diligent towards his care.'

This must have resonated with Abbas as he nodded in agreement. 'Yes, family is important Jasper.' He looked directly at him, making his guilt soar.

'It is, which is why I want to put things right, as soon as possible,' he replied forcefully.

Again, Abbas gave a wise nod. 'Then you must do so. Together we will make all the necessary arrangements.'

Relief surged through Jasper. A weight had lifted from his shoulders knowing he had Abbas's approval. 'Thank you, Abbas.' Jasper stood and they shook hands.

'I've read your report,' Abbas called as Jasper was leaving. He stopped and turned. 'Good work, Jasper, I'm impressed.'

'Thank you,' he smiled.

Walking back to the office, Jasper pondered over Zara's phone call. So much for there being a potential problem. That uneasy sensation edged further into him. On his return, he found Zara hovering over his desk. She hastily picked up his cup and saucer and smiled sweetly. Jasper eyed her suspiciously. Had she been touching his mobile phone? He moved swiftly to retrieve it and put it in his jacket pocket.

Zara pretended to look occupied, whilst inside she was cursing herself for nearly getting caught. Still, it had proved worthwhile.

Chapter 28

Storm clouds gathered threateningly over Lilacwell, breaking the glorious spell of sunshine. Adira looked gloomily out of the kitchen window of The Laurels. She didn't really fancy driving in this weather, but she worried that if she didn't leave today, she'd simply find excuse after excuse to stay. That said, she *did* have a bona fide reason for being in Lilacwell. Grace Conway. Despite all Adira's emotional turmoil, Lilacwell could well be the place where her ancestors had lived. She could have a genuine connection to the place, regardless of what was currently happening in her life.

Glancing at the clock, she worked out the time in Dubai, late afternoon by now. Two words, that's all she'd got from Jasper: 'back safely'. Well, what more did she need to know? she thought rationally. He told her he'd let her know he was back safely and that's precisely what he'd done, her head told her; but her heart wanted to hear far more.

Don't be ridiculous, you've taken a year out to enjoy travelling, she reminded herself, making a mental note to get out the map and start plotting her next move when she got back to the camper van. But first, she had to say her goodbyes. She poked her head round the drawing room door, where Fletcher and Lilly sat drinking tea.

'I'm just going to the Inn to say goodbye to everyone there.'

'Oh.' Fletcher's face fell. Lilly looked away. Neither of them were making this easy for her.

The pub was jostling with customers when Adira entered. Cassie waved to her from behind the bar.

'So, this is it then, you're off,' she gave a half sad smile. Cassie had been gutted when Adira had told her she was leaving. They'd bonded and become such good friends. It hurt to see her go.

'Yep, time to go.' Adira swallowed the lump in her throat. She was so going to miss this place. It astonished her just how much at home she felt in this quaint, little village, and how well she had seamlessly fit in. The locals had welcomed her with open arms, almost to the point of not wanting to let go.

'Well, if ever you need a job, there's always one here.'

'Oh, thanks, Cass.'

'I mean it, The Bath House wouldn't have got up and running so swiftly without you. You've been a huge help. Thanks.'

That lump was almost choking Adira, she was speechless. A tear spilled down her cheek. What was the matter with her? She'd never been so emotional ever in her life.

'Oh, come here!' Cassie rushed from behind the bar to give her a big hug. 'You will be coming back though, won't you?' she looked warily at Adira. Even though the inn had hired another massage therapist, always knowing Adira wasn't a permanent fixture, Cassie had dearly hoped she'd change her mind and stay.

'I… I think so.' She gave a wobbly smile.

'You definitely must, Adira,' Cassie replied in a no-nonsense tone.

Next stop was Fletcher and Lilly. Adira took a deep breath and braced herself. They were still in the drawing room when she approached them.

'Right, I'll be going shortly, so it's time to say goodbye.'

'For now, only for now,' Fletcher told her.

'Yes, for now,' conceded Adira. 'So give me a hug.' She held out her arms.

Lilly was first in, her tiny, fragile frame clinging to her. 'Take care, my dear,' she sniffed.

Then came Fletcher, and she felt safe in his firm embrace.

'Safe trip, lass,' he said with a gruff voice.

'Thanks,' she replied on the verge of tears again. 'And, Fletcher,' she pointed playfully at him, 'I'm giving you strict instructions to hire a cleaner to help Lilly. Do you hear?'

'Aye, loud and clear,' he laughed, then he took something from his pocket. 'Here, I want you to take this.' He handed her a small, silver coin. 'It's a Saint Christopher medal. The patron saint of travellers, to keep you safe.'

'Oh… thank you, Fletcher,' her voice cracked and the tears came tumbling down.

Fletcher watched thoughtfully. Something told her he'd got the reaction he wanted.

'So, you'll be back in a month then?' he coaxed gently.

Adira was unable to speak. Fletcher was naturally assuming she'd be returning when Jasper did. But would it be that simple? A whole month stretched out before her; it seemed an age, which instead of filling her with anticipation and excitement as it should, just didn't. The whole point of buying Sheila was to take off and explore, relish every moment of the unknown. But her emotions wouldn't allow this. The crux of it was she had bonded effortlessly with Lilacwell – and those that lived here. More importantly, she had fallen deeply for Jasper. Despite all the rationalising her head had instructed, her heart had won. She felt defenceless, helpless almost, but there it was. And now she had to go, alone, in the desolate hope that it *could* be that simple, that she'd return in a month, along with Jasper, and all would be well.

But would it? Jasper was returning to Dubai, albeit temporarily, where there was a lot to distract him. Dubai was a playground for the rich, with many temptations. Jasper was attractive, he undoubtedly received a lot of attention... and they were miles apart. A heavy, sick sensation lodged in the pit of Adira's stomach. Never had she been in a situation where sentiment wreaked such havoc.

An hour later, the rain had stopped and Adira was sat behind the wheel of the camper van ready to set off. It was unbelievable to think she had only parked here a few weeks ago; it seemed a lifetime since pulling onto the field through the open entrance. How much had happened in such a short space of time. Still, onwards and upwards, she told herself as she turned the ignition and chugged Sheila into life. Time to move on. There was a big, bold world out there, and she needed to explore it. She was determined to make the most of the time she had sacrificed her career for.

Chapter 29

Fletcher sat comfortably in his armchair staring out of the open patio doors. The showers had cleared and a soft, mellow glow filled the lawns outside. It was early evening and the dew from the rain and now the warm rays of sunshine brought the garden to fresh life. Fletcher breathed in the sweet fragrance of honeysuckle and instantly a memory was triggered. A treasured, precious memory from years back, when he was at his happiest...

It was the summer of 1988 and the midsummer ball at The Laurels. Fletcher had taken extra care in arranging the party – for him, it was to be a game changer. All their lives could change irrevocably: his, Rufus's and Alice's. Subconsciously, way deep down, both him and Alice knew the score. For years, ever since first clapping eyes on each other, the attraction had been immediate, undeniable. For them, the pull was such a magnetic force, it was incredulous Rufus had never picked up on it. But then, Rufus was always so wrapped up in himself, Fletcher had thought, he never paid Alice the attention she so deserved.

Fletcher certainly did. He'd been at pains to seek her company out at every opportunity, that first weekend she had stayed at The Laurels. He remembered how Rufus had assuredly introduced his new girlfriend to the family, gloating at his parents' response. They had been delighted by the dainty beauty on his arm. Alice was charm person-ified, totally enrapturing all of the Hendricks, and most of all the older brother, Fletcher. He simply couldn't take his eyes off her. The way her brunette hair curled smoothly, how her green eyes shone like emeralds and the elegant way in which she held herself, with such poise, a real lady.

She was ten years younger than Rufus, making her much younger than Fletcher, yet he admired the way she handled his family, confidently in her own skin, refusing to be intimidated by the grandeur of The Laurels. She was fun. She was witty and had the most amazing sense of humour. For the life of him, Fletcher was utterly baffled as to how Rufus had managed to capture such a creature. What on God's earth did someone so special as Alice see in his little brother? Rufus was the steady, reliable, boring one. *He* was the gregarious, fun-loving one. Rufus was rather plain to look at and a touch chubby, whereas *he* was good-looking and athletically built. As cruel as it really was, Fletcher had often been referred to as 'the handsome brother'. And yet it seemed Rufus was Alice's choice.

At first, Fletcher thought, quite arrogantly, that nature would take its course, that Alice would be so drawn to him, she would have to come clean with Rufus and declare her true feelings.

Not so.

No matter how much Fletcher encouraged this, Alice would not give up Rufus. But, oh, how he had tried. He lavished her with compliments, gifts, promises of his undying love and finally his hand in marriage. But still Alice wouldn't budge. Whilst she was flattered and enjoyed the attention, it appeared Rufus, for all his dowdi-ness, was what Alice wanted.

Truth be told, Rufus was what Alice *needed*. Because the key attraction for her was stability. Alice had grown up in a family similar to the Hendricks, which was why she'd felt so at home at The Laurels. She had had a father who was the life and soul of the party, who cut quite a dashing figure, with his dark, good looks and roving eye. True, Alice had been attracted to Fletcher, but alarm bells had also rung – knowing full well how someone so handsome and confident couldn't be trusted. Men like her father and Fletcher were attractive to all women and this left them with carte blanche. She'd seen first-hand how her mother had paid the price. So, Alice, rightly or wrongly, stuck with Rufus. He was a decent man, he was honourable, but most of all he was trustworthy. This couldn't, however, stop her strong pull towards Fletcher.

Of course, he never made it easy for her; his gut intuition told him she wanted him as badly as he wanted her, even when stood in the church next to Rufus as best man, watching the love of his life marry his own brother.

As the years tumbled on, Fletcher still waited patiently for Alice to come to her senses. Once or twice, he'd thought he'd come close; he was sure she wasn't happy with Rufus. The light had gone out of her eyes, replaced with a sad, empty reflection. Instincts led him to believe that the time was right to make a final move at the midsummer ball. He sensed this was the ideal opportunity to finally win her over. He'd seen how despondent she'd become, almost like life had been sucked out from her, hardly surprising living with boring Rufus. It killed Fletcher to see how Alice had gradually withered over time. Well, now he was going to change the tide, he was going to do what he should have done years ago and take matters into his own hands.

He'd carefully chosen the music, all Alice's favourites. She had a fondness for swing and nostalgic tunes, so Glenn Miller's 'In the Mood' would get the party started, followed by various other big band and ragtime melodies. It was when the partying slowed down that he intended to strike, then he'd take her in his arms and dance on the lawn, under a starlit sky.

The weather had obliged, giving a still, peaceful evening with a warm, comforting breeze. His house-keeper, Lilly, and her sister, Ruby, had helped decorate the gardens with bright coloured bunting and candles. They'd set up a drinks area in the orangery, along with a trestle table covered in a pink gingham tablecloth for the buffet, while Fletcher's record player would blast music across the lawns.

All was set as Fletcher waited to greet his guests. He stood by the patio doors in the drawing room, breathing in the honeysuckle. Alice and Rufus arrived late, much to his agitation. It was evident by the look on Alice's face and Rufus's tight, thin lips that they'd argued. Fletcher welcomed them with glasses of champagne and waited for Rufus to circulate with the other guests. As soon as they were alone, he looked into Alice's eyes. She avoided his gaze and turned her head. He gently took her chin and moved her to face him.

'He doesn't make you happy, Alice,' he stated flatly.

She didn't answer, but he noticed the first sign of tears. This spurred him on.

'Leave him. Come and live here with me,' he urged. 'I… I love you.' He stared at her intently, waiting for her to melt.

Slowly the tears came – she couldn't pretend anymore.

'This way, follow me,' he whispered.

To his elation, Alice did just that. She followed him from a respectable distance so as not to attract attention, right up the stairs, along the landing, into his bedroom. He locked the door behind them – not a soul on earth was going to ruin this moment he had waited so, so long for. He stared in wonder, completely mesmerised as she slowly undressed, watching how the lemon silk fell gracefully to the floor. Her body was amazing, fragile and petite. He urgently tore off his clothes, desperate to touch her white porcelain skin. She felt soft and smooth as she lay under his body on the bed.

Alice too was revelling in Fletcher's toned, muscular body. She couldn't help but compare it to Rufus's flabby frame, even though he was much younger.

Fletcher wanted to relish the moment, savour every inch of her as he kissed and caressed, but it was impossible, he had to have her.

Alice was ready for him, longing to finally be taken by Fletcher.

Afterwards, Fletcher thought the earth had literally moved.

'Alice,' he croaked, hardly able to speak.

'I know...' she whispered and kissed his lips. Then, they heard voices, totally breaking the spell. They quickly dressed and went downstairs separately. The party was in full swing so they hadn't been missed. Fletcher felt like he was floating on cloud nine. *Finally* Alice had come to her senses.

As the night's sky darkened and the stars came out, Fletcher struck up the last record, 'Moonlight Serenade'. He took Alice's hand and led her onto the lawn, where they danced in each other's arms. Fletcher was past caring who saw; tonight Alice was his.

Chapter 30

Adira had studied the map and decided to head further up to the north-west, edging into Scotland to Dumfries. Research told her it was a lively market town with lots of beautiful coastal villages. She liked the idea of being by the sea and lazing on the sandy beaches it promised. There were also camping sites, which made it easier for her – as opposed to parking on private land, she smiled wryly to herself.

After a few hours' travelling, Adira was well ready to see the 'Welcome to Dumfries' sign and followed directions to Dalbeattie, which is where she planned to stay. There was a small campsite right next to the Sandyhills Beach which would be ideal for her.

Pulling onto the site, she was greeted by an old man in a kiosk waving her towards him. She wound down her window.

'Hello, would it be possible to stay three nights please?'

'No problem, lassie, just a wee moment.' He handed her a form. 'You'll need to fill this in and I'll take payment up front.'

Adira quickly completed her details and took out her credit card. Within a few minutes, he gave her directions as to where to park the camper van.

She was pleased to be high on the west side of the field, overlooking the beach. Looking at the turquoise, glimmering water, she couldn't wait to dive into its coolness. The drive had left her hot and sticky and she longed to feel refreshed.

After a quick bite to eat and a drink of tea, she changed into her swimming costume and headed for the beach. It was filled with young families playing in the sunshine. The beach sloped gently, making the water shallow, ideal for paddling and bathing. A low tide would reveal miles of sand and other secluded bays. Adira breathed in the warm, salty air and her spirits lifted slightly. It was hard not to appreciate such stunning scenery.

She walked straight towards the sea, enjoying the cold, wet sludge beneath her feet. It had been years since she had visited the seaside and once again she realised how dull her life had become, stuck in a mundane existence. Her mind cast back to the office in Goldgate Chambers, imagining it all ticking over like clockwork, everything going on as normal without her. That epitomised it, Adira suddenly thought, the likes of Goldgate Chambers didn't need her; it was merely a machine that would function quite easily with another cog to replace her. Whereas in Lilacwell, she wasn't just another cog. There, she was valued, people genuinely did care. That summed it all up.

As she reached the water's edge, Adira tentatively stepped into its cold ripples, gradually easing the whole of her body against the chilly flaps of sea until she was able to swim. She could taste salt on her lips as she swam facing the sun, letting her face soak in the heat. It was invigorating. Adira stretched her arms and legs in the sea, loving the sense of freedom it gave her. She swam towards the rocks and pulled herself onto a flat slope. Taking great gulps of fresh air, her chest heaved with exhaustion even as she felt more alive than ever. A humid sea breeze drifted through her as she watched the sunlight glisten amongst the blue-green waves. Seagulls echoed in the distance, their silhouettes hovering on the horizon.

Adira turned towards the campsite. Squinting with her hand on her forehead, she could just make out her camper van. Thank God for Edie. If it hadn't been for her, Sheila could well be rusting away in some garage and Adira would be rusting away in London. As it was, here she was on a beach in Dumfries. Yet, even as her happiness soared she couldn't help feeling a pang for Lilacwell.

Later in the evening, Adira ventured into Kippford, a lovely seaside village on Solway Firth, often referred to as Scotland's Riviera Coast. The waterfront was lined with pretty, whitewashed cottages and from there Adira walked along the shore road. Feeling famished, she made her way to a local cafe and ordered fish and chips to take back with her. She wanted to relax in a deckchair on the campsite rather than go out for a meal.

As she ate, a family camping in a nearby tent were setting up a barbeque. She watched, smiling at the excited children running back and forth as their mother ushered them away, while the father stood territorially over the heated charcoal. Adira remembered similar happy days when she'd holidayed as a child. Even then, her gran knew how to make them fun for her, always being the one to buy ice creams, fizzy pop and tacky souvenirs, under the disapproving glare of her mother. She recalled paddling in the rock pools with Edie and filling a bucket with her finds. When Adira had proudly showed it her mother, she had scrunched her face in revolt, not caring for the crabs, periwinkles and seaweed she'd collected. Edie had been the one who'd take her on the funfair rides, while her mother stood by with folded arms, waiting patiently, forever on the periphery, never joining in. Only once could Adira recall making her mother openly smile with pride – her graduation day. The day she stepped up to the platform and accepted her degree certificate in Law. How symbolic, when it was the very thing which had incarcerated her.

'Would you like to join us?' the mother of the family interrupted her thoughts. She'd seen Adira sitting alone and wanted to include her.

'Oh thanks, but I've just eaten,' Adira smiled.

'Well, feel free to have a drink with us later, if you want.'

'Thank you.' She didn't want to commit to joining them. Adira was tired from a long day's driving, swimming and exploring.

Later, whilst getting ready for an early night, Adira contemplated contacting Jasper. Should she? Just a quick message, telling him where she was. She looked at the clock, it was almost nine p.m., making it midnight in Dubai. Even if he was asleep, it'd be there in the morning waiting for him. Why not? After giving it some thought, she typed in the message.

> Hi, made it to Scotland, in a beautiful coastal village in Dumfries. Enjoying the sun, sea, sand and Shella.

There, that was enough, just to let Jasper know her whereabouts and that she was thinking of him. She pressed send.

Within a minute, her phone bleeped with a message. Adira quickly picked it up, her heart thumping. *Undelivered*, it read.

Chapter 31

It had been a very long day for Jasper. Inevitably, leaving his position next month meant a great deal to sort out. The first job had been to inform all his colleagues and clients of his imminent departure. He'd dictated his farewell message, thanking all those he'd worked with, to a very subdued Zara. As he had rattled off the words, rather speedily and without any emotion, she had sat in silence, straight-backed and stony-faced. When Jasper had finished reciting his goodbyes and thanks, he rubbed his hands together and poured himself a coffee. Job done.

Meanwhile, Zara was motionless, in shock. Jasper was leaving her. She couldn't bear it. Why? Why was he going? Panic began to set in. Then those photographs of him with that woman sat on the massage bed flew into focus, making her blood boil.

After numerous meetings and conference calls, Jasper jadedly made his way back to his apartment. His appetite had left him since his return to Dubai, but tonight he intended to make himself a decent meal.

He slammed the door shut behind him and threw his briefcase on the sofa, then headed straight to the kitchen to pour himself a cool drink. One thing for sure he wouldn't miss about Dubai was the lack of alcohol in his fridge. At times like this, he could murder a cool beer.

Instead he made do with icy cold water and a dash of lime.

He went out onto his balcony and took in the splendid beach view. He'd miss this though, sitting in the warmth and looking out at the golden, flat sand and pink skies strewn with lilac. Still, The Laurels offered good views too, and he always welcomed the change of seasons in the UK, as opposed to permanent searing heat.

After a few minutes sat unwinding, Jasper returned to the kitchen and looked to see what he could whip up for dinner. Nesima had dutifully filled the cupboards and fridge with his shopping order, so he had a wide choice. He opted for salad with a cheese omelette, something nice and light, with a ready-made dessert of tiramisu. He thought back to the last time he'd eaten that, in the Italian restaurant with Adira.

Adira. The thought of her filled his senses. Although he couldn't help but feel disappointed she hadn't contacted him. She was obviously busy travelling, he consoled himself.

Having eaten, he turned on the TV and relaxed for a couple of hours. Eventually his eyes grew heavy and he decided to shower and go to bed.

He stared at his reflection in the mirrored bath-room cabinet. He looked knackered; dark smudges under bloodshot eyes, skin pale and drained. He opened the cabinet to get some fresh shower gel when something struck him. The packet of condoms normally discreetly hidden at the back behind other toiletries was lying flat down at the front of the shelf. He frowned. He definitely hadn't left them there. Who had been in here? His mind turned to his cleaner, but again, knowing how careful and respectful she was, he couldn't envisage it being her.

Who, beside Nesima, had access to his apartment?

Then another dark thought crept into his mind like a thief in the night. With a slow, rising inkling, all the pieces were falling into place; the open bedside cabinet drawer, the long dark hair on his bed sheets and now this, evidence of someone rooting in his bathroom. He remembered telling Zara where to find his car keys, little did he know she'd also make use of his apartment key, which was attached on the same key ring. It must have been Zara who had been in his apartment. He also recalled her knowing his favourite coffee, not remembering ever ordering it in front of her. She'd seen for herself on his kitchen shelf what coffee he bought.

How dare she? Fury emblazed him. His initial instinct was to confront her, but that could prove tricky, as her father had a prominent position in the company. Still, she had abused his trust and her position, invading his privacy like this. One way or another, she would face the consequences of her actions, of that he was determined.

Jasper strolled through the enormous shopping mall at the heart of Dubai. His very first visit there had initially left him awestruck. Such was its vastness, with eight floors and hundreds of designer shops. More impressively to him, though, was the gigantic aquarium and underwater zoo, where divers could explore the water and its inhabitants – including sharks – from the safety of diving cages. It had a huge waterfall feature with life-size silver figures diving into it and, most extraordinarily, on one of the floors was an actual dinosaur skeleton from one hundred and fifty-five million years back, perfectly preserved. Jasper had found it mind-boggling, to walk round the colossal bone structure, knowing when it had last roamed the earth.

Yet today Jasper failed to be amazed by any of it. He walked rather subdued from shop to shop, not taking any pleasure in it. He longed to know what Adira was doing, but if she cared about him, she'd have made contact, wouldn't she? He was still seething with anger at Zara and the way she had taken liberties by entering his apartment and having a good look round. It beggared belief.

His eyes were drawn to one of the stalls he'd never noticed before. It contained exquisite jewellery, not the usual bright gold bling, but beautiful glass stones in aquamarines, sea greens and hazy blues. He looked at the necklaces, bracelets and rings and decided to buy something for Adira. Though when he'd see her, he was unsure.

After inspecting the colourful gems, he plumped for a necklace, thinking how it would accentuate the colour of her eyes. God, he wanted her. His desire was growing by the day and not hearing from her only made it stronger.

'Could you gift-wrap it please?' he asked the man behind the stall. He would send it to The Laurels in the hope she would be returning there before he did.

'Certainly.' The man gave a big beam. It always struck Jasper how everyone was happy to please in Dubai; the service was excellent.

Immediately, his mind turned to Colin, The Laurel's estate manager, and how lax he had been. Not any more though, Jasper thought, judging by his latest emails keeping him updated.

He was eager to get back to Lilacwell and really make an impact, not that he hadn't already, but Jasper wanted to be there first-hand to oversee the glamping business he envisaged. He pictured Adira's camper van parked up in the field, then he flashed back to her bathing in the river. That urge came back with a vengeance.

The next day, his bad mood still hadn't lifted as he walked into the office. In fact, seeing Zara sat behind her desk made it plummet even further. He placed the small wrapped parcel in front of her.

Zara's face lit up, thinking Jasper was giving her a present, then it fell like lead on seeing the address label, and more infuriatingly who it was addressed to: *Miss Adira Summers, The Laurels, Lilacwell, Nr Clitheroe, Lancashire, England*. Her mouth pursed, then she looked accusingly at him with blazing eyes.

'Send that special delivery would you, Zara?'

'Yes, Jasper.' She almost choked on the words.

Jasper was still stood looking down at her. 'Zara, I'd like to take you out to dinner, as a thank you for all you've done for me,' he suddenly stated.

Zara's eyes flew to his face, not quite believing her ears.

'Yes... thank you,' she replied breathlessly.

'I'll leave you to make the arrangements. Tomorrow evening suit you?'

'Yes,' she responded immediately, her heart thumping in her chest. This was it. This was the moment she had been waiting for.

'Good.' He gave her a tight smile and walked to his desk, gritting his teeth.

Just looking at Zara got his shackles up.

Zara was in seventh heaven, debating which restaurant to go to. She was thinking high class, of course, and preferably somewhere near to his apartment, because if all went to plan, she'd definitely be invited back for coffee. She imagined them sat in an intimate corner, staring into each other's eyes as he finally let his guard down. Yes, that was it, because he was leaving his position, he could now show his true feelings for her. At last he had realised just what was under his very nose – a beautiful, classy, intelligent lady. She came from good stock, not like the other administrative staff here. *Her* father was regarded very highly indeed within the company, Jasper appreciated that.

Her eyes then focused on the parcel placed on the edge of her desk. Jasper had gone to a meeting, so wouldn't be back for a while. Enough time for her to open it up and see just what Adira Summers was supposed to be getting in the post.

Zara surreptitiously peered over her shoulder to check nobody was passing in the corridor and could see her through the open door. The coast was clear.

Without any delay and with great speed, she ripped open the package. Inside was a black, oblong box. She clicked it open and looked inside. A necklace made of, she examined it closely – glass? Zara pulled a face. How cheap. Not like the expensive gold or diamonds she wore. Then she unfolded the small white piece of paper and read the message, '*Thinking of you, Jasper.*' The fact Jasper was sending this woman jewellery was far too much a personal gesture for Zara's liking. Not to mention 'thinking' of her; which is why she threw the necklace in her bag, along with the crumpled wrapping paper. There was no way Adira Summers was getting *anything* from Jasper.

Chapter 32

Fletcher was in the garden making the most of the bright morning. He had inspected his vegetable patches, which were growing nicely due to the showers and sunshine, and now he was resting on the terrace with a pot of tea and the newspaper. How he missed the hustle and bustle of Jasper and Adira being about the place. Knowing this quiet spell wasn't going to last forever gave him comfort though. But even the warmest of thoughts couldn't take away the steady aching in his body. His whole frame throbbed in pain. Although he hated to admit it, his arthritis was definitely getting much worse. At one time, he'd brush it off, dismissing it with a couple of large whiskies that dulled the soreness, but nowadays a few stiff drinks didn't quite do the trick. He'd tried the same turmeric capsules as Adira had suggested Lilly take, but his arthritis was far more advanced.

Fletcher had to face it, he needed medication. It was debilitating and frustrating in equal amounts. His brain was telling him one thing, whilst his body refused to cooperate. Instead of nipping up the stairs like he used to, now it took him forever to plod his way up, leaving him breathless. Every move seemed so much of a strain, a real effort. Fletcher struggled to get comfortable most of the time.

With a heavy heart, he'd been forced to accept defeat and had rung the doctor's surgery. To his astonishment, he'd been greeted by a young, chirpy receptionist who couldn't do enough for him. Within minutes, he had an appointment booked for the end of the week. Not bad at all, he'd thought with pleasant surprise, fully expecting to have to jump through hoops to get anywhere near the surgery.

He'd found that, in the evening when he allowed himself to drink, his body eased slightly. But lately he'd been drinking more heavily, such were his attempts to block out the discomfort. The hazy, contented state that came with being a little tipsy also brought back those memories from yesteryear. After the other night's farewell dinner, his thoughts had turned more and more to the past.

Fletcher was sat right next to the honeysuckle growing along the stone wall. He'd once heard that the sense of smell was the most receptive trigger point to the memory, and as if on cue, its heady fragrance once more took him back to that glorious night of the midsummer ball…

As Fletcher and Alice had danced closely, he'd made her promise to leave Rufus.

'You belong to me now, Alice,' he'd whispered, kissing her ear.

'But what will I tell Rufus?' she'd hissed urgently, finally accepting where her true feelings lay.

'Tell him the truth,' Fletcher had replied firmly. The music had now stopped and the pair were the only ones left on the lawn.

Alice, suddenly conscious of their whereabouts, had moved from his embrace. 'I'll have to face him,' she'd said, crestfallen. Her guilt weighed heavily, but so did her unhappiness. Alice had married the wrong brother. She knew it. Fletcher knew it. But did Rufus? It was doubtful, due to his apparent lack of intuition. And it was never more apparent as he chatted and laughed with a group of guests, oblivious to his wife and brother, who were walking up the sloped lawn having just shared a romantic, intimate dance. Indeed, nobody seemed remotely interested in them, too busy knocking back the cocktails and champagne which flowed freely.

A little later, the gathering had slowly dispersed, Fletcher bid farewell to his last guests. Alice and Rufus were due to stay the night, however Rufus had suddenly announced he was going to drive home.

'You'll be over the limit, Rufus.' Alice had looked alarmed.

'I'm fine, don't fuss,' he'd dismissed.

'Don't be a fool, man, you're not safe to drive,' Fletcher had harshly interrupted.

Rufus had turned to his brother and looked at him coolly. 'I'll thank you not to interfere.'

Fletcher's eyes had swept to Alice. No way was he letting Rufus get behind a wheel with her in the car. She shook her head slightly, urging him not to create an argument. The last thing she wanted was a scene.

'I'm stone-cold sober, Fletcher.' Rufus was glaring at him, bright sparks of anger prickled his cheeks. He'd taken Alice's hand and pulled her towards the door. Fletcher had fought hard not to punch him. He'd followed them to the hall, where Alice had turned and gave him another pleading look. Rufus had opened the front door with one hand and practically pushed Alice out with the other. Then he'd promptly turned on his heel to face Fletcher.

'This is the last time Alice and I will set foot in this place.' He spoke in a controlled, even voice.

'Is that so?' Fletcher had replied icily.

Rufus had given him one last look of contempt and slammed the door shut.

He'd meant every word. Hell would freeze over before Rufus came anywhere near The Laurels. For all his nonchalance and cheery behaviour in front of everyone, inside he was seething. He'd seen how his wife and brother had humiliated him by dancing so provocatively. Mostly, he was hurt by the look in Alice's face as she'd rested blissfully in Fletcher's arms. The betrayal cut deep. Rufus had always known Fletcher had secretly lusted after his wife. Hadn't it been that way for eternity with his big brother? Forever wanting what he had? As children, Fletcher was the one perpetually in the limelight, constantly seeking attention wherever, whenever he could. *Everybody* loved Fletcher, he went to great lengths to ensure it, with his extroverted, overbearing personality, forcing his bonhomie on all and sundry. Nobody had been more surprised than Rufus when Alice had accepted his proposal, but accept it she did. Alice was *his* wife and he intended to keep it that way, despite his brother's meddling. This was the one time in his life he was prepared to stand up to Fletcher, and it would take more than a quick grope on the grass to end his marriage.

True to his word, Rufus never had returned to The Laurels. Alice had, but not in the way Fletcher had wished. He had longed to speak with her, but feared it may make things harder for Alice. Instead, he sat it out with an agonising hope she'd come to him.

A month after the midsummer ball, she had called unexpectedly one Sunday afternoon. Her face was pale and she looked exhausted.

'Alice!' Fletcher had cried when the housekeeper had shown her into the drawing room. He'd run towards her, then stopped short at seeing her hesitation.

She'd looked at him, then declared in a flat tone, 'I'm pregnant.'

Fletcher had frozen.

'Is it mine?' he'd asked, hoping and praying for her to confirm it was.

'I don't know,' she'd replied.

'But… the timing…'

Her eyes had filled. 'It could be yours, but it could easily be Rufus's too. That night he… he forced himself on me—' She'd broken off in tears.

Fletcher's hands had clenched to fists. He could willingly throttle that brother of his.

'But… a paternity test, that will—'

'Show that the baby's a Hendricks,' Alice had sobbed. 'You're brothers, Fletcher, the result mightn't be cast iron, and how do you think Rufus would react?' Her body had sunk in despair onto the chair.

At that moment, Fletcher knew. A stark realisation had punched him in the gut. She wasn't leaving Rufus. All Alice could offer him was a close relationship with the child that was born eight months later.

It was never discussed again. A silent understanding had been reached; he'd never breathe a word on the matter, and in turn, Alice would make sure her son would know his 'uncle' as closely as a father.

Whose son Jasper actually was remained unknown.

Chapter 33

'Welcome to Drumlanrig Castle, one of the finest examples of late seventeenth-century Renaissance architecture in Scotland,' boasted the tour guide with a wide smile.

Adira stood towards the back of the small group in the marbled hall. Her eyes followed the sweeping curved staircase. A huge chandelier shimmered elegantly, sending spotlights across the pale walls, where family portraits hung, glaring down at the intrusive visitors. The tour guide had every right to be smug. Drumlanrig Castle was indeed a splendid place, with its pinkish sandstone, beautiful architecture, furniture and paintings. As the small party wandered from room to room, the guide kept them interested with stories of the family and their ancestors.

Adira enjoyed the tour. She loved historic houses and listening to their past. Afterwards, she strolled round the country park and Victorian gardens, before deciding to have a coffee in the tearoom. Settling down at a table, she checked her phone for any messages. There was one. With excited anticipation, she quickly opened it.

Oh, it was Rory from the chambers. Adira attempted to shrug off her disappointment as she read his short message.

> Well, Reggie boy's got his comeuppance!

Adira grinned, remembering it was Rory who had taken over the Sir Reginald Demsy case. It looked like things hadn't quite gone to Sir Reginald's plan. Good, she thought. Serves him right. Curiosity got the better of her and she texted back.

> Oh dear, what did he end up with?

A moment later, her phone bleeped.

> Wife got straight 50% cut of everything and remains on the company board of directors.

> Good for his wife, he won't like that.

Adira responded, laughing inside.

> Neither did his bit of skirt!

Adira chuckled. She missed Rory. For a fleeting moment, she questioned her actions. Had she done the right thing, packing in her job? Then shook herself. Of course she had. Not once had she regretted leaving London and her career when in Lilacwell.

But that's because Jasper was there, a sneaky voice taunted her.

Although Adira had been pleased to hear from Rory, she'd rather it be Jasper who had sent her a text. Why had her message come back undelivered? Maybe it was the signal? She got the text back up on her phone and tried to send it again. Within a few moments, the same word appeared, 'undelivered.' She frowned, not knowing why the message wouldn't go through, when he had managed to send her one. An unnerving thought began to simmer, making her feel a little queasy. Was he deliberately avoiding her? Had he changed his mind about keeping in touch? Her eyes prickled with tears.

Trying to stay focused, Adira finished her coffee and thought about where to stay next. Tomorrow she would be leaving Dalbeattie. Having enjoyed Drumlanrig Castle so much, she thought of Edinburgh and the impressive castle there. She tried to whip up eagerness for her trip, but a sadness hovered over her. Wanting to hear a friendly voice, she rang her gran.

'Hello, you,' Edie answered. 'How's it going?'

'Fine. I've left Lancashire and now I'm in Dumfries.'

'Oh, left Lilacwell then?' she laughed. It had tickled Edie that her wanderlust granddaughter had stayed so long in the same place.

'Thinking of going to Edinburgh next.'

'Lovely, Edinburgh's a wonderful city,' enthused Edie wistfully, reminiscing on a visit there from long ago. 'Your handsome laird might be there, waiting for you,' she teased.

'Hmm, maybe,' Adira replied flatly.

'Unless he's in Lilacwell,' Edie added softly.

Adira stalled. Typical of Gran to be so perceptive. She always was one move ahead.

'Anyway, I'll be in touch,' Adira tried to sound casual. Then asked, 'Have you looked for those certificates, Gran?'

'I've asked your dad to get the box of papers from the loft. I'll start searching as soon as he's done that. Safe trip, Adira.'

'Bye.' Adira hung up and stared out of the window, still feeling a bit flat. She decided to ring Cassie and see how she was doing.

'Hi!' Cassie sounded pleased to hear from her.

'Hi, Cass, how's it going?'

'Everything ticking along as normal, besides missing you, obvs.'

Adira was touched. 'The Bath House doing OK?'

'Yeah, great, getting lots of bookings.'

'That's good to hear, your hard work is paying off.'

'And yours! Where are you at the moment?'

'Dumfries, heading to Edinburgh tomorrow.'

'Ah right, I'll let Fletcher know. I'm sure he'll be interested.'

Adira's chin wobbled a little. Then she couldn't help but ask, 'How is he?'

'Oh, he's fine, missing Jasper though.' *Aren't we all?* she thought dully. 'But apparently he's handed in his notice and his company were fine about it, so Fletcher was telling me.'

'Oh, right.' So Jasper had made contact with Fletcher, but not her. That queasy sensation flared up inside Adira. Suddenly wanting to end the call, she tried to sound as cheery as possible, 'I'll let you get back to the madhouse then, speak soon.'

'Yeah, thanks for ringing, bye.'

Adira took a deep breath. Her mind was spinning with all kinds of scenarios as to why she had only received one short text from Jasper. He'd filled Fletcher in on his resignation, didn't she deserve to be kept in the loop? Clearly not.

Chapter 34

Fletcher waited patiently in the doctor's surgery. So far, so good. He'd been given a warm welcome and directed to the comfy chairs in the waiting room, which wasn't too busy. There would be nothing worse than sitting next to somebody coughing or spluttering all over him, spreading all kinds of unknown germs. So, he opted for the single seat directly under the open window, where no one could get near him. He had a quick look round at the new mum with her baby, the teenage boy and a middle-aged woman. He was definitely the oldest here, which depressed him slightly.

He didn't have to wait long before he was called to go through to the doctor. To his utter surprise, a young woman was sat behind the desk smiling up at him.

'Hello, Mr Hendricks, take a seat.'

Fletcher plonked himself down heavily and looked straight at her.

'It's like this, lass, me whole body bloody aches,' he told her somewhat submissively.

'Any particular area?' she asked.

'Mainly me back, but me arms and legs aren't that great either.'

'I see, let's take a look.' She got up from her chair and knelt in front of him. 'Can you extend your legs?'

Fletcher tried as best he could to pull them out and straighten, but with great difficulty and pain.

'And the same for your arms please.' She watched carefully, noting how stiff his joints were. 'Are you on any kind of medication?'

'Nah, never needed 'owt,' he dismissed.

'Hmm, I can see you're in a lot of discomfort, Mr Hendricks,' her forehead furrowed with concern.

'You can say that again, lass.'

'Then why haven't you come to the surgery before?'

Fletcher stalled. 'I… I thought I'd cope.' He swallowed and looked away.

The doctor's tone turned softer. 'But you've suffered, unnecessarily. Your arthritis looks quite bad, and judging by your posture, your back *will* give you a great deal of pain.'

'You could say that,' snorted Fletcher.

'I could have eased this months ago,' she gently chided.

'I know,' he weakly agreed, refusing to give her eye contact.

'Right, well, we'll start with painkillers, that'll ease the discomfort straight away.'

'Good.'

'Then, let's get you a physiotherapist. They can create a structured exercise plan.'

'Eh?' Fletcher looked blankly at her.

'Gentle exercise, Mr Hendricks, it's the way forward,' she replied with a half-laugh.

'Oh, I see.' Clearly, he didn't.

'And a good diet. Let's lose some weight, shall we?' She smiled encouragingly.

'Really?'

'Yes, a healthy weight will improve your carriage.'

'My what?'

'The way you move. If you're lighter on your feet, it'll ease all your joints, which will relieve any stress and therefore ease symptoms.'

'Right,' he replied faintly. He pictured his full cooked breakfasts being replaced with a bowl of muesli and his heart sank. Then a full tumbler of whisky made its way into his mind. 'What about drink?' he asked hopefully.

'The odd tipple won't do any harm.'

Thank God for that, he thought with relief.

'How much do you drink?' she asked.

'Err… well…'

'Every day?'

'You could say that.'

'Try having a few days off, give your liver chance to recuperate.' She smiled again, trying not to sound too authoritarian.

'Oh, me liver and I divorced years ago!' he laughed, trying to make light of the situation.

The doctor didn't react.

Fletcher coughed and shut up. He watched her tap into a keyboard, then tear paper off a printer and hand it to him.

'Here's your prescription for the painkillers and the surgery will be in contact regarding your physiotherapist.'

'Right. Thank you.'

'Goodbye, Mr Hendricks. If there's anything else, don't hesitate to contact me.'

'I won't,' he nodded, then made his way out, feeling somewhat foolish.

Lilly was in the kitchen when Fletcher returned home.

'How did you get on?' she asked, putting the kettle on.

'I've painkillers to take and I'm getting a physiotherapist.'

'Oh?' replied Lilly in surprise.

'Apparently it's the way forward,' he said, making Lilly laugh. 'And I've to lose some weight,' he added drily.

'Oh dear.' Lilly couldn't stop laughing at Fletcher's deadpan expression.

'It's not funny, woman,' he scolded gruffly.

'You're right, it's not.' Lilly strained to keep a straight face. 'Healthy eating from now on. I'll make a nice salad for lunch.'

Fletcher groaned. He'd rather set his sights on a bacon butty. Then, another thought occurred to him. 'Not a word of this to Jasper, do you hear?' The last thing he needed was his nephew laying down the law.

–

Adira had parked at a campsite four miles from the heart of Edinburgh, located in acres of country estate. It combined leafy green parkland with good amenities and had excellent transport links to explore Scotland's capital city.

The following morning, she'd taken the bus route into Edinburgh and was loving the buzz of the culture and vibe it oozed. Resisting the shops and coffee bars, Adira made the steep trek to Edinburgh Castle. She walked through the portcullis gate to the audio booth. She wanted to take her time and discover the magnificent building without being ushered along by a tour guide.

Putting on the headphones, she started her journey with the audio guide, which told her about the history of the castle and the people and events that stood out most in its fascinating past. Adira climbed the Lang Stairs, all seventy of them, which was once the original entrance to the castle. Walking along the Argyle Battery gave sweeping views over the city and towards Fife. The huge six-guns lining up against its walls provided an ideal vantage point for defending the castle.

She went to the prisons of war exhibition, where she learnt that, '*Pirates and prisoners were held in the vaults below the great hall, among them was a five-year-old French drummer boy, captured at the Battle of Trafalgar.*' Poor little thing, Adira thought, hardly believing the cruelty of the past. '*One successful escape attempt saw forty-eight inmates flee,*' continued the audio guide. *Well, I hope that boy was one of them.*

After a solid two hours of exploring, Adira went to the souvenir shops. The exclusive Edinburgh Castle ten-year-old single malt was the perfect present for her dad, while her mum got the traditional shortbread. She bought a soft, wool tartan scarf for Edie, before going into the cafe for a coffee. It was when she was sat still, sipping her cappuccino, that her phone suddenly burst into life. Adira's chest started to thump – was this Jasper? With haste, she grabbed the phone from her bag. It was Cassie.

'Hi, Cass.'

'Adira, so sorry to ring,' she sounded out of breath and frantic.

'What's the matter?' Adira asked sharply.

'We're up shit's creek. The massage therapist's broken her arm!' wailed Cassie.

'Oh.'

'Yeah, fell off her bike cycling to work this morning,' she exclaimed, still irate. 'The thing is, we're fully booked this week. I've managed to postpone all of today's appointments, but—'

'You want me to take over,' Adira finished for her.

'Well… yeah, if that's not too much trouble…' Cassie trailed off desperately. 'I'll pay you double,' she added hopefully.

'I've only just got here.' There was a distinct whine in Adira's voice, but deep down she knew that Cassie wouldn't be calling her unless it was an emergency, which this definitely counted as.

'I know. I'm sorry, but we're desperate.' Adira could hear the anxiety in Cassie's voice and couldn't help but feel sorry for her. The thought of returning to Lilacwell so early didn't faze her, though. If she was completely honest, it almost came as a relief.

'I'll pay you treble,' Cassie begged.

'Stop,' laughed Adira. 'You don't have to pay me double either, I'll come back.'

'Thank you, thank you, thank you!' she gushed.

'But cancel tomorrow morning's appointments. I'll want a lie-in from driving. I'll be there in the afternoon.'

'I will, and thank you so much! You're an angel.'

'I am,' smiled Adira.

'Bye!' Cassie made kissing noises down the phone.

'Bye,' said Adira, shaking her head in amusement.

So, back to Lilacwell. Was she destined to be there?

–

Jasper was on his balcony watching the evening sky turn a dark violet. He was contemplating his dinner with Zara, though how he would manage to eat sat opposite her he didn't know. He was still seething with rage at her audacity. He felt his inside jacket pocket; yes, it was safely there. After checking his watch, he collected his car keys – it was time.

As Jasper pulled up outside her home, he admired the massive, white, flat-roofed villa. It was surrounded by palm trees and greenery, which was unusual for Dubai. Many of the houses just had sun-burned lawns, or decking with pools. Various windows were lit up dimly, but when his gaze turned upwards, towards what were clearly bedroom balcony doors on the top floor, he could make out a silhouette. It was Zara, preening herself in front of a full-length mirror. His eyes narrowed. Would she be taking so much trouble over her appearance if she knew what was in store? He inhaled. He had to remain composed.

Walking up the path, he was again taken by the burst of colourful plants. Sprinklers were installed, which evidently kept all the flowers and shrubbery fresh. Most of the gardens he'd seen were usually sparse and dry from the searing heat.

The door opened before he had chance to knock. Zara's father stood at the entrance looking directly at him.

'Evening, Arun,' greeted Jasper, looking him in the eye. He got the distinct impression that the man was almost warning him.

'Hello, Jasper. I expect Zara to return by midnight,' Arun stated matter of fact, still staring unflinchingly at him.

'Of course,' nodded Jasper. Earlier, he thought, if all went to plan.

Zara appeared behind her father looking rather self-satisfied. Arun stepped aside and after a quick warning glance at the pair of them closed the door.

'Don't mind him,' giggled Zara, 'he's always been very protective of me.' She gave a sweet smile. Jasper resisted the urge to roll his eyes.

After telling him the restaurant where she had reserved a table, Jasper realised it was in fact very near to his apartment.

'Apparently their seafood comes highly recommended,' Zara said, flicking her freshly washed hair over a shoulder. She was wearing a long, burgundy dress with diamanté beads sewn into it. It had a sweetheart neckline and soft folds which tapered in at the waist. Gold, strapped sandals and a gold clutch bag completed the outfit, and as always she was decked in heavy, gold jewellery. Jasper thought she looked gaudy, way too overdone for a simple evening meal. She also had that bloody awful potent perfume on, which made his eyes water. He resented the fact his car would reek of it for days.

They were soon parked up and entering the restaurant. To her credit, Zara had chosen well – its mellow lighting and private booths lit with candles created an intimate atmosphere. Good, thought Jasper, glad of the privacy. The last thing he wanted was an audience.

They were shown to a small table situated in a secluded alcove and Zara looked like the cat who got the cream, such was her smugness as she smoothly sat down opposite Jasper and rearranged her hair – again. Already she was grating on his nerves.

The waiter handed them each a menu. Jasper swiftly scoured it.

'Shall we order starters?' asked Zara.

'No,' he replied flatly, 'or at least I'm not.' He was only going to order a main course. The less time this took, the better.

'Oh,' she sounded somewhat deflated. She'd envisaged them having a long, leisurely meal, basking in each other's company.

'I'll have the grilled salmon with clams and spiced butter,' Jasper told the waiter and snapped his menu shut. 'And a bottle of the house white wine,' he added, not bothering to consult Zara. She chose the same.

'It's my favourite.' She gave another smile and once more flicked her hair back. Jasper gritted his teeth.

A little later, as they sipped their wine, Zara attempted conversation which might encourage him to relax and open up. She noticed he looked tense and arrogantly thought it could be nerves. 'So, Jasper, what are your plans for the future, once you've left the company?' She looked playfully at him, rubbing her finger round the rim of her wine glass.

'I thought it was obvious. I'm going home,' he replied dully.

'Yes… I mean, what will you do?'

He looked at her with a frown. 'I'll manage my family's estate, why?'

Zara was taken aback by his briskness. 'I just… wondered. Won't you miss Dubai?' she asked optimist-ically.

'No.'

The food came after a short while, which filled the silence that had once again started to grow. Jasper checked his inside jacket pocket again. Once they were almost finished eating, he decided to make his move.

'Zara, why did you break into my apartment?' he asked directly.

Her eyes widened and she spluttered on her food.

'I didn't break into your apartment,' she managed to squeak.

'No, you took my key and helped yourself in, didn't you?' He reached into his pocket and threw down a disc. 'CCTV footage,' he explained, 'of you entering my apartment.' He stared at her with a raised eyebrow. 'You then went into each room, including my bedroom and bathroom, and took a good look round, didn't you?' His eyes bored into her.

Zara sat frozen still. She looked at the disc. How could she not have considered the security cameras in the apartment block? She was speechless. Humiliated, she gulped back the tears. 'What are you going to do?' her voice cracked in shame.

'You mean, besides telling your father?'

'No! Please,' she hissed, sharply looking round for eavesdroppers.

Jasper glared coolly at her. 'You should lose your job over this. It was a total breach of confidence.'

'I'm sorry... please don't tell my father,' she pleaded. 'I'll do anything, anything.' Her eyes searched his face.

'Oh please, spare me,' Jasper threw back in disgust.

'All finished here, sir?' the waiter, totally oblivious to the scene, smoothly asked.

'Yes, I'm finished.' Jasper took out his credit card to pay. 'This lady needs a taxi,' he instructed. He then got up, tossed his napkin on the table and stormed out.

Chapter 35

Lilly was stood at the bottom of the stairs.

'Fletcher! Are you up?' He was due his first visit from the physiotherapist. The surgery had contacted him and arranged a morning appointment, much to Fletcher's disgruntlement. A nine a.m. start was hardly his daily routine, usually only rising around ten-ish.

'Yes, I'm up,' he moaned, slamming the bathroom door behind him.

Moments later, he sloped, bleary-eyed, into the kitchen. He looked witheringly at the clock.

'Good God, it's only half eight.'

'Yes, but you want to be ready. They'll be on time. You'll be the first appointment of the day.' Lilly bustled about the kitchen getting breakfast ready.

Fletcher frowned at the two places set. 'You not had your breakfast yet?'

'No I have not. *I* was up at seven o'clock to get here. Somebody had to make sure you were up and raring to go.'

Fletcher rubbed his tired eyes. 'Thanks, Lilly.' He gave a yawn. Then his face dropped as she put two bowls of porridge on the table. He looked at her in despair.

'It's for your own good, Fletcher,' she told him.

'I know,' he replied, staring at it in disgust. How he wished a plate of bacon, eggs, sausage and fried tomatoes was there in front of him.

'Think of your weight.'

'Hmm.' And black pudding. His mouth watered at the thought.

'It's good for your cholesterol too.'

'Hmm.' *And* a side plate of fried bread.

He sighed and picked up his spoon. He didn't regret going to the doctors though. The painkillers she had prescribed had already worked wonders and it was such a relief to sink into bed without creaking in pain. Whereas once he'd dread getting up and having to set his stiff body in motion, now all he had to do was reach for the small bottle of pills by his bedside table and know he'd be helped. However, he did have reservations about the physiotherapy and the 'structured exercise plan'.

'Are you all right?' Lilly looked warily at Fletcher, thinking he was unusually quiet.

'I suppose.'

'You might enjoy it,' she tried to gee him up.

'Well, if the doctor's anything to go by, I'm expecting the physiotherapist will be a young dolly bird,' he laughed, deciding to buck up and make an effort. He remembered Lilly ticking him off last time he got all maudlin.

She smiled in approval. 'That's the spirit.'

They'd just finished their breakfast when the doorbell rang.

Lilly got up. 'You go into the drawing room and I'll see them in.'

Fletcher was sat in his armchair when Lilly entered the room, followed by a young man in a green uniform. 'Tarquin, this is Fletcher.'

The young man beamed. 'Hi, Fletcher,' he called in a sing-song voice and, taking small steps, scurried over to him. Fletcher's jaw dropped.

'I'll leave you gentlemen to it,' Lilly said, the corners of her mouth twitching, and closed the door.

Tarquin knelt down in front of Fletcher and clapped his hands together. 'So, Fletcher, let's take a look, shall we?'

Fletcher blinked and sat still.

Tarquin gave another big smile. 'Let's try to stretch out those legs.'

Fletcher did the best he could, immediately noticing how less painful it was from the last time he'd done this with the doctor.

'Very good!' Tarquin gave another quick clap. 'Now for the arms.'

Again, he managed to lift and extend his arms without the same aching feeling.

'Excellent!' gushed Tarquin. 'Now, I want you to put one leg out,' he glanced around the room and quickly pulled the nearby footstool up to Fletcher, 'and rest it on here,' he tapped the stool. Fletcher noticed his hands were smooth and soft, not hard and callused like his. 'That's it. Now circle your foot.'

It was difficult at first and a crack came from his ankle, making Tarquin's face contort.

'Oh dear, it will get easier, the more you do it. It's all about learning to loosen up those joints.'

'Shame you've no WD40,' Fletcher gave a wry smile.

Tarquin threw his head back in high-pitched laughter. 'Oh Fletcher, you are a card!'

After circling his feet, Fletcher did the same with his hands. After a few clicks from his wrist, eventually the movement eased. Then Tarquin took the footstool away and sat on the chair next to Fletcher.

'I want you to raise each leg and touch your knee-caps with your hands, like this.' Tarquin demonstrated the exercise.

Fletcher tried his best, bringing him out in a slight sweat.

'Now relax,' instructed Tarquin, 'don't want to overdo it on your first day, do we?'

'When I was your age, I'd be up with the lark, making hay until dusk. I had muscles on top of muscles. Now look at me.'

'I'm sure you've still got it in you, Fletch,' Tarquin winked.

Now it was Fletcher's turn to laugh out loud.

And so the session continued, with fun and good humour. Fletcher took a fond liking to the young lad who showed a real sense of care and compassion, and more importantly, laughed at all his jokes. In turn, Tarquin knew that to play along with the old boy meant he was more likely to cooperate. He'd been warned how stubborn Mr Hendricks might be, so had been determined to give a good impression. He'd been trying to come across as a friend, offering a helping hand, rather than a medical figure forcing a strict regime. And it had worked, judging by the light-hearted banter coming from the drawing room. Lilly smiled to herself as she passed through the hall.

–

It was quite late in the evening by the time Adira reached Lilacwell. She had tried to enter Fletcher's field again by the same entrance as last time, but the gate had been repaired and stood solid and bolted, denying access. Colin had sorted it out, she thought with a smile. Then, deciding not to disturb Fletcher so late, she rang Cassie and arranged to park up at the Inn. Cassie had told her to go round the rear of the pub where there was plenty of space. She also promised her a free meal, which Adira was looking forward to, despite being so tired from the drive.

As she entered via the kitchen, the staff looked pleased to see her and Adira couldn't deny the joy she felt at seeing the familiar faces once again.

Cassie was in the reception area when Adira passed through.

'Oh, Adira, come on through. Take a seat and I'll get you a drink. A large white wine?'

'Sounds good.' Adira followed her into the bar and sat down at a small table by the window. The Inn was fairly busy with locals and late diners.

Cassie sat down opposite her. 'There you go.' She placed a cool, refreshing glass of wine in front of her.

'I'm so ready for this.' Adira took a long sip and closed her eyes.

'I'll bet. How was the traffic?'

'Not bad, just glad to unwind though.'

'Well, just tell me what you want to eat and I'll get it.'

'Thanks.'

'And,' continued Cassie with a grin, 'after you've eaten, I've booked a room for you. So you can have a long, relaxing bath and a good night's sleep, on the house.'

'Oh Cassie! That'd be bliss.' Adira closed her eyes again. Oh the luxury!

After a tasty steak and ale pie and another large wine, Adira made her way up to her room. She gasped at its grandeur. The walls were painted a pale duck-egg blue and a large sash window overlooked the river and surrounding hills. Various paintings hung round the room, from local historic houses to rural scenes. There was an antique dressing table at the side of the bed, while a floor-to-ceiling bookcase filled with old, collectable books stood in the corner of the room. The whole space smacked of style and class. It was country living at its finest.

Then Adira opened the en-suite door. It was cream marbled tiled throughout, with a Victorian roll-top bath. Again, the small sash window overlooked the river. She opened it to hear the water flowing and started to run a bath. Even the toiletries whispered elegance, Adira thought, pouring Molton Brown's lime and eucalyptus under the taps.

Adira sank into the deep, scented bubbles and sighed contently. How she'd missed the luxury of a bath. It calmed her whole body, soothing the aching muscles in her neck and shoulders.

After a good soak, she slipped in between the Egyptian cotton sheets of the king-size bed and stretched out, revelling in the sumptuousness. However comfy the camper van was, it was pretty restricting and tonight she was savouring the splendour of the country house, thinking how fortunate the family who once lived here had been. She didn't set her alarm, intending to sleep without any interruptions.

The following afternoon saw Adira working non-stop. Cassie was right, The Bath House had been fully booked.

Adira enjoyed chatting with the clients and also catching up with all the staff. By the end of the day, after she had finished her last massage, she decided to call at The Laurels.

Lilly was delighted when opening the door to her. 'Adira! You're back!'

On hearing Lilly's voice, Fletcher shot out of his chair and shuffled to the hall.

'Hello, stranger!' he exclaimed.

Adira was touched at their response.

'Hello, how are you both?' she smiled as Lilly ushered her in.

'All the better for seeing you, dear.' Lilly gave her a hug.

'Aw, thanks Lilly. It's good to be back.'

'But why so soon?' asked Fletcher. He suddenly frowned. 'There's now't up, is there?'

'No. Well, not for me anyway. Cassie asked me to return to help out at the Inn. The massage therapist's broken her arm.'

'Oh dear. Still, good to see you, lass.' Fletcher thumped her hard on the back.

'Am I OK to park in your field, Fletcher? I notice the gate's now fixed.'

'Of course!' he bellowed. 'I'll have Colin open it for you. Come through, I'll make you a coffee.'

Lilly gave her a surreptitious grin. 'He can actually work the machine now,' she whispered, making Adira giggle.

Chapter 36

The atmosphere in the office hung like a dark, thunderous cloud. To Zara's relief, Jasper was hardly at his desk, he'd been so busy seeing clients and attending meetings. For the first time ever, she was glad of an empty office. After her mortifying dinner, she had returned home, subdued and shaken. Zara had lied to her father, saying Jasper had suddenly been taken ill and so had arranged a taxi to take her back early. Over the next few days, she had kept a low profile by slipping into the office quietly and going straight to her desk. Her head was constantly down, supposedly deep in concentration most of the time. She never went to the water machine in the corridor, or socialised with anyone, or even made coffee for herself or Jasper on the odd occasion he was there. He in turn had avoided any contact with her. He no longer copied her into his emails, and in fact she wasn't included in any of his business now. Zara was well and truly surplus to requirements. It was pointless her being there, as his PA anyway. Part of her contemplated talking to her father to tell him she wanted another position, but she was frightened how that may pan out. Suppose Jasper did as he had threatened and told him everything? She was stuck.

Meanwhile, Jasper was manically trying his best to wrap everything up. Of course, it was even harder not having a reliable PA to call on, but he was damned if he was ever going to rely on Zara again. So far, he had managed, and it was only another two weeks to go before he could wave goodbye to the whole lot – Dubai, the company, the clients and Zara.

It couldn't come quick enough. Not having heard from Adira did nothing for his mood either. Surely, she must have thought about him at some point in the past fortnight? *You contact her*, a niggling voice told him, but his pride was hurt. He *had* texted her, but she hadn't returned a message.

Deciding it was all a bit tedious, he took the bull by the horns one evening and rang The Laurels. Maybe Adira had contacted Fletcher, or even Cassie, and they knew of her whereabouts. It didn't take long for the phone to be answered.

'Hello.' It was Fletcher. Jasper immediately relaxed at hearing his uncle's voice.

'Hi, Fletcher.'

'Jasper! Good to hear you. How's it all going?'

'OK. Just tying up a few loose ends, then I'll be home.' How good it was to say that.

'Excellent. Can't wait to see you.' Jasper felt a lump in his throat. He swallowed it.

'Has… has a parcel arrived in the post, addressed for Adira?'

'A parcel? For Adira? No, why?' asked Fletcher, surprised.

'I sent her something.'

'Oh, well no, nothing's come.' A short silence followed. Fletcher sensed a degree of awkwardness. 'She's back here in Lilacwell you know.'

'Is she?' Jasper didn't know what to think. If she wasn't occupied travelling, why hadn't she contacted him?

'Have you two not spoken?' Fletcher bluntly asked.

'I texted her when I arrived in Dubai, but heard nothing back.'

'So you just left it at that then?' Good God, what was wrong with the man? Fletcher rolled his eyes.

Another short silence followed.

'I'll—'

'Get your affairs in order?' Fletcher's voice was more encouraging than dogmatic.

He was right, of course he was. Uncle Fletcher always knew best.

'I will,' replied Jasper firmly.

Later that evening, his mind kept going over what Fletcher had said. Jasper had every intention of contacting Adira, but it was too late to do it then. It did puzzle him though, why she hadn't returned a message, especially at remembering how upset she was when they'd parted. He stared for a moment at his phone on the glass coffee table. Then he pictured it on his desk a couple of weeks ago, when Zara was hovering over it. That familiar sense of foreboding began to rise up him.

He grabbed the phone off the table and searched his contacts. Adira was the first name to come up. His eyes narrowed, as his thumb pressed away at the touchscreen to reveal that Adira had been blocked. Zara had blocked Adira from his phone. But why? Because she happened to be the first female name she'd come across? This was outrageous!

He unblocked her and searched the text blocked history for any possible messages that he hadn't seen. There was one, sent days ago. He held his thumb down to restore it, then up it came:

> Hi, made it to Scotland, in a beautiful coastal village in Dumfries. Enjoying the sun, sea, sand and Sheila.

He beamed. She *had* contacted him. Then his smile faded at the thought of what Zara had done. Once again, she had acted appallingly by meddling with his phone. The woman knew no boundaries. Well, that was it. Enough was enough.

The next morning, he strode into the office, stopping at Zara's desk.

'Did you send that parcel?' His voice had a steely edge to it.

Zara looked up sharply. 'Yes,' she lied.

'It hasn't arrived.' He stared at her evenly.

'I'll chase it up,' she replied in a small voice.

'You'd better.' He then turned on his heel and went to Abbas's office. He tapped on his door and was called in.

'Good morning, Jasper.'

'Abbas,' he nodded back. 'Can I speak to you, in confidence?'

'Of course.' Abbas cleared the papers he'd been reading to the side of his desk. 'Is there a problem?'

'Yes,' Jasper answered directly, making Abbas sit up, 'but it's more of a personal nature, than business.' Jasper then outlined Zara's unprofessional behaviour. Abbas's eyes widened in shock as he listened. This was grave indeed. Zara was the daughter of a very prominent member of the board. The situation had to be handled with care and extreme discretion. 'I have a copy of the CCTV footage, if needed,' Jasper told Abbas.

'Yes, I think you'd better leave that with me.' He was absolutely staggered by what he'd heard. 'In the meantime, I'm removing her from your office.'

'Yes. I think that's for the best,' agreed Jasper.

—

Adira was sat at the bar with Cassie. They were enjoying a break from a hectic morning.

'The Bath House is the best thing that's happened to this place,' Cassie told her. 'I can't believe how well it's taken off.'

'It certainly has.' Adira sipped her fresh orange juice. She loved being back at the Inn. At one time, she'd have needed a glass of wine in her lunch break to see her through a working afternoon. How things had changed.

There was just one nagging doubt that troubled her. Jasper.

'Penny for them?' Cassie eyed her thoughtfully.

Adira looked at her. Why not confide in Cassie? It may make her feel better and Cassie was fast becoming one of Adira's closest friends as they spent more and more time together.

Sighing, she answered. 'It's Jasper. He hasn't been in touch. Only once, to say he'd arrived in Dubai safely.'

'Really?' frowned Cassie. 'Have you not contacted him?'

'Yes, but the message came back undelivered.'

'That's strange. Have you got a landline number for him?'

'He did give me his office number.'

'Well, try it then,' Cassie said, almost in exasperation. She reached over the counter and picked up the phone behind the bar. 'Use this, try it now,' she urged, putting it in Adira's hand. 'Go on!'

'OK.' Adira reluctantly looked up Jasper's office number on her mobile and tapped it into the phone. After a few crackles, it rang. Adira's chest was pounding. She looked at Cassie for moral support, who winked and left her to it.

'Good afternoon. Jasper Hendricks' office,' said an efficient female voice.

'Hello... could I speak to Jasper please?'

'May I ask who's calling please?'

'Adira. Adira Summers.'

'I'm sorry, Mr Hendricks isn't in the office at the moment.'

'Oh... could you tell him I've rung please?'

'Certainly. He's taken his girlfriend out for lunch and won't be returning for the day, but I'll tell him tomorrow when he's next in,' the proficient voice told her. Adira felt like she'd been punched in the stomach.

'Thank you,' she choked and put the phone down. Her head felt dizzy, and she gripped the bar to steady herself.

–

Zara smiled spitefully. One last parting shot before leaving his office. Served him right – and her, the common hussy. After being summonsed into Abbas's office and told of her imminent move, she was past caring. Zara knew she couldn't possibly be dismissed, just moved on, which is what she wanted in any event. If Jasper couldn't see what a fantastic catch she was, more fool him.

Then another malicious thought crept into her mind, one which made her smirk with glee. Little did Jasper know, but she still had access to his apartment. She'd had another key cut to his front door, and she knew when the cleaners came. As before, she'd pretend to live there and simply wait to follow another resident through the corridor. As long as she acted confident and self-assured, they wouldn't question her. She had managed it last time without a problem, so why not again? Jasper was in a meeting and would be for some time. If she was going to do it, she had to do it now. Well, what had she to lose?

Chapter 37

Fletcher was restless. It bothered him to hear Jasper down-hearted. Reading between the lines, he knew all wasn't well with the lad, despite trying to sound upbeat about his job. Whilst he was glad to hear all was on track professionally and he'd be back in a fortnight, Fletcher knew that Jasper's personal life wasn't quite so rosy. Once again, he felt the compulsion to intervene. What was it with these youngsters? He shook his head in despair. Just then, he heard the door slam, and Lilly called out.

'Fletcher, are you ready?'

'Yes!' he called back. He was due another physiotherapy session.

Lilly came into the drawing room.

'What time is Tin-Tin coming?' Fletcher asked.

'You know perfectly well his name is Tarquin,' chided Lilly, 'and he'll be here any minute.'

Fletcher smiled to himself. He rather enjoyed his time with Tarquin. The banter between the two had grown and often Lilly could hear either Tarquin's high-pitched shrieks, or Fletcher's low, rumbling laughter coming from the room. She was pleased he'd taken to the treatment so well and had noticed a change in his mood. No longer was he moping about the place, pining for Jasper, but he seemed more upbeat. He obviously wasn't in as much pain now either, which could only help. Plus, having Adira back had also brightened him up.

Lilly was also pleased Adira had returned; she was glad of the female company. She was expecting to see her at some point that day, after she'd asked to use the washing machine.

The front doorbell rang.

'That'll be Tin-Tin,' Fletcher grinned, rubbing his hands together. 'I wonder what he'll have in store for me today.'

'Stop calling him that,' Lilly scolded lightly and went to answer the door.

As predicted, the rest of the morning was filled with good humour as Fletcher, who was making steady progress, managed to complete all the exercises Tarquin set him.

—

Adira's morning had been busy too. She was tired and the last thing she had wanted to hear was her alarm. Sighing, she'd pulled back the bedcovers to turn it off when she saw it.

One missed call.

From Jasper.

She must have been asleep when he'd rung, late in the evening for him. But then, he'd spent all day with his girlfriend, hadn't he? she thought bitterly. Deciding to ignore the call, she washed and dressed, then made her way to The Bath House.

It was now approaching noon and to her relief there were no more appointments booked that day. But now she had time to think about Jasper. Why was he ringing?

For a friendly chat? His secretary must have passed on the message of her ringing him, he was probably just returning the call.

When Adira told Cassie about her conversation with Jasper's PA, she pulled her face in disbelief.

'A girlfriend? Since when?'

'That's what she said.' Adira shrugged.

'Well, he's never mentioned a girlfriend before and he's leaving Dubai for good, so—'

'Maybe she's coming back with him?' Adira interrupted. The thought filled her with dread.

'No. There's been some misunderstanding. It doesn't make sense.'

It did puzzle Adira why Jasper had acted the way he had with her, especially if he had somebody waiting for him in Dubai. Cassie was right. It didn't make sense.

Cassie was looking at her with an expectant expression.

'I'm not ringing him,' Adira stated flatly.

'Sure?'

'Yes,' she replied firmly.

How glad she was with her decision not to ring two hours later. Especially when she received the picture on her phone.

Adira's eyes widened in horror at what she had just opened. There, lying completely naked with a knowing smirk on her face, was a woman on a bed. Jasper's bed. She knew that because a picture of Fletcher was clearly visible on the bedside cabinet. Whoever this was, she definitely wanted her to know she'd been with Jasper. His girlfriend. It was Jasper's girlfriend warning her off. Adira wretched and only just made it to the toilet before throwing up.

Later that afternoon, Adira had called at The Laurels with all her laundry, feeling sick to the stomach and dazed. She was bending down, piling it into the washing machine, when Fletcher came into the kitchen.

'Ah, just the lady.'

'Hi, Fletcher,' she mumbled over her shoulder.

'Jasper rang.' Adira froze. 'He wanted to know if a parcel's arrived for you.'

'For me?' She stood up straight to face him.

'Yes,' nodded Fletcher, seeing how guarded she was looking. 'He sent you something.'

'Oh right,' she frowned.

'But it's not arrived yet.' Fletcher eyed her and folded his arms.

'Did he say what it was?' asked Adira.

Fletcher let out an infuriated sigh. 'Don't you two talk?' Then he marched into the hall. 'Follow me!' he called over his shoulder as he picked up the phone. Squinting, he read Jasper's number which was written out in large numbers on the pad next to it. Adira panicked as she realised what he was doing. 'You, here,' he ordered, pointing his finger at her.

Adira tentatively walked towards him.

–

Jasper was in a board meeting when his phone vibrated in his pocket. He discreetly took it out to see The Laurels flash before him. Instantly he stopped. What was wrong? Had Fletcher had an accident? He rose and quietly made his apologies for leaving.

Outside, in the corridor, he answered.

'Hello?'

'Jasper, it's me, Fletcher,' boomed his uncle's voice. He sounded fine, thank God.

'What's the matter?' he asked urgently.

'I've somebody here to talk to you.' Fletcher handed the phone to a hesitant Adira. She swallowed, then spoke in a quiet voice.

'Hi, Jasper.'

At hearing her, Jasper's shoulders relaxed and a warm feeling whooshed through him. 'Hey you, I called last night.'

His voice sounded warm and friendly, genuinely pleased to hear her. She wanted to cry, the deceit! And how naturally it came to him. Had she ever really known the true Jasper? The liar. Bastard.

'I rang you yesterday, but your PA said you were out.' Then she added with force, 'With your girlfriend.' It was out in the open now.

She heard an impatient snort come from Fletcher.

'My girlfriend?' Jasper frowned. Then it dawned on him. Zara, again. He could cheerfully strangle that bloody woman. He closed his eyes for a moment before speaking. 'Adira, there is no girlfriend. Believe me.'

'Really? Well, she's just sent me a rather intimate picture which tells me otherwise,' she replied, her voice rising, causing Fletcher to look alarmed.

'Listen, I'm in the middle of a meeting, but I'll ring later. OK?' Jasper pleaded, whilst trying to work out what the hell the deranged woman had done.

'Not OK,' Adira said with force.

'Please, I can explain, honestly,' Jasper assured her.

She looked at Fletcher, who was still standing over her with his arms folded. She wanted to run out of here as far away as possible. Angry, hot tears stung her face.

'Adira? Adira, are you there?' The concern in Jasper's voice just made it worse and she couldn't speak, a huge lump forming in her throat. She just stood, frozen, looking at a confused Fletcher and listening to Jasper's pleas. 'Adira, don't go! Please…'

But it was no use, Adira slammed down the phone and bolted, practically running down the hall.

Fletcher stared blankly with his jaw dropped as she bolted out of The Laurels. *What the hell has gone on?*

His first thought was to ring Jasper back, but then a more worrying one followed. Adira could be leaving this place right now and they may never see her again. The very notion made him cold. Without hesitation, he went after her, as fast as his poor old, arthritic legs would let him. Fletcher panted and heaved his weary body with might and determination to the field where Adira had parked her camper van. Thank God it was still there. He made his way over, his chest wheezing heavily. The door was open. He pushed it further, expecting to see Adira frantically packing, but to his utter dismay, he saw her flopped on the seating, in floods of tears.

'Oh lass! Whatever's happened?' He came to sit next to her.

'This is what's happened, Fletcher.' Adira passed him her phone, with the photo of the woman, lying naked in Jasper's bed.

Fletcher squinted to examine the picture.

'How do you know this was taken in Jasper's apartment?' He refused to believe the worst of his nephew. He just knew there must be a reasonable explanation.

'Look at the framed picture on the bedside table,' she replied flatly.

Fletcher's eyes glanced sideways. Sure enough, a picture of himself was there. It must be Jasper's bedroom. His heart sank.

'I can't believe this of Jasper.' Fletcher was almost talking to himself in disbelief. 'Wait till I get hold of him.' He put his arm round her shoulders. 'Promise me you won't set off driving in this condition?'

'No, but I will be going,' Adira replied resolutely.

Fletcher nodded his head sadly. He felt like crying himself.

–

Jasper could have cried, with rage, as he began to comprehend what had gone on. He *had* to speak to Adira. But what if she'd already left? The vision of her setting off into the sunset, leaving Lilacwell behind, never to return, made his blood pump.

Taking a deep breath, he tried to think logically. If he rang her, she most probably wouldn't pick up.

Somebody had to tell her the truth. Fletcher? No, it was too uncomfortable trying to justify how some woman was in his bed.

Cassie! He'd get hold of her. She'd be the most likely person who would know where Adira had gone, if she had left.

With a shaking hand, he rang the inn and prayed Cassie was there to take his call.

–

Dusk was edging in on the quiet, calm evening as Cassie walked through the field. Still in shock by Jasper's call, she tapped on the camper van's door. Adira answered, with red, swollen eyes.

'You look like death warmed up,' Cassie said, half smiling.

'Thanks, I've had better greetings.' She stood aside to let her in.

Cassie entered then turned, suddenly looking serious.

'Sit down, Adira, I've something to tell you.' She then outlined everything that Jasper had told her about how his warped, unhinged PA had behaved.

Afterwards, they both sat still, muted, taking in just what had gone on. Adira's mind was on overdrive. Instantly, her barrister's intellect was assessing the facts, cross-examining what she had learnt. Could Jasper be lying? *But why would he?* her astute brain reasoned. Why would he choose to return to Lilacwell if he was in a relationship in Dubai? Could he have slept with this lunatic, simply because he could? *Again, why?* Her rationale kicked in. If Jasper used people for sex, he would have tried harder with her. Of course Jasper was telling the truth. It was the most plausible, reasonable conclusion which reflected his character.

True to his word, Jasper did ring later in the evening. He outlined what Zara had done to his phone and how she had lied to her about him being out with a girlfriend, not to mention entering his apartment. Adira was naturally still shocked, but Jasper pointed out that Zara was well off the scene now. Not even her father could save her from the disciplinary procedure she was due to face.

'If anything, this has made me more determined than ever to leave Dubai,' he told her. 'And what about you? Are you pleased to be back in Lilacwell so soon?' She could hear the amusement in his voice and it warmed her, now that she knew full-heartedly where she stood in Jasper's eyes, she felt reassured.

'Yes. I got as far as Edinburgh, before being dragged back,' she laughed. There was a slight pause.

'I've missed you.'

'I've missed you too.' Then remembering what Fletcher had told her she asked, 'Jasper, what have you sent me?'

'Ah, it's a surprise.'

'Hmm, am I likely to get it, if psycho Zara's supposed to have sent it?'

'Don't worry, you'll get it.' He smirked to himself. Too right she would. 'Goodnight, Adira, speak soon.'

'Goodnight.'

She drifted off into a blissful, heavenly sleep and dreamt of being held in warm, solid arms, gazing into chocolate brown eyes and being thoroughly kissed.

Chapter 38

Fletcher couldn't sleep. Tossing and turning, he heard the grandfather clock in the hall strike one. His mind was wide awake. Pulling back the duvet, he swung his legs onto the floor and pushed his feet into his slippers. He took his dressing gown from the hook on the door and put it on. He'd make himself a cup of Horlicks, that may put him to sleep. Usually, the whisky he drank after dinner would help him nod off, but as he was cutting back on alcohol, he now remained clear-headed when he went to bed. He wasn't sure if this was a good thing or not, because a clear head meant sharper memories. Sharp, vivid images of scenes from the past which haunted him.

Fletcher slowly made his way down the creaky stairs. The hall was lit with moonshine beaming in through the large window overlooking the front garden, its silvery streaks giving it a magical feel. Fletcher went into the kitchen to put the kettle on. As he waited for it to boil, his eyes gravitated to the key rack, where bunches of keys hung carelessly, mainly house, car and outbuilding keys. All except one, which hung separately on its own, tied up with red ribbon. An antique bronze skeleton key with a long, elegant neck, it had a fancy loop at the head where the ribbon threaded through.

Fletcher clenched his jaw. He promised himself he wouldn't do this anymore, but he couldn't stop moving towards it. His shaky hand lifted up the key, unhooking the ribbon, fingers closing around the cold metal. He shut his eyes tight for a moment. Then, not even bothering to make his drink, he went back up the stairs, along the landing and stopped at the bedroom door opposite his.

The lock was a touch stiff as Fletcher turned the key and edged his way in. The room was in total darkness and a slight smell of dampness hung in the air. He felt for the lamp switch on the table nearby and soon the room was filled with soft light.

Fletcher took a good look round. Everything was the same, just as it had been the last time he had been there. Nothing touched, nothing changed; the cast-iron bed perfectly made, the French-polished dressing table with mottled mirrors, the marble fireplace with silver candlesticks and the wardrobe, where a beautiful lemon silk gown draped elegantly on the door. Alice's dress. He pictured her in it, dancing with him on the lawn to 'Moonlight Serenade'. Then he turned to the bed, where his most revered memory had taken place. Here Alice had become his, the two of them as one. If Jasper was his, this is where he had been conceived.

In his heart, he knew Jasper was his son, always had. He suspected Alice thought so too, but he loved her enough to obey her wishes. Alice had chosen to stay with Rufus. He had to accept it. It seemed a ridiculous request at the time to ask for her dress, but it was important to Fletcher to make that night sacred and retain every detail, every memory.

He walked to the wardrobe and touched the silk, now faded and dusty. Fletcher's eyes filled. How different it could have been.

Chapter 39

The days passed pleasantly for Adira and having finally had contact with Jasper made all the difference. As was usual for her now, working at The Bath House kept her busy and most evenings a message or a phone call was made to and from Dubai. Together they had established a routine and it was only a matter of days before Jasper was due to come home. Fletcher too seemed a lot happier, knowing all was well between them.

It still amazed Adira how seamlessly she had slipped into her new lifestyle at Lilacwell. Life here was almost unbelievable compared to the rat race in London which she'd endured for years until a few short months ago. The relationships she had made also warmed her heart. Adira felt like she had always known Fletcher, Lilly and Cassie, and the staff at the Inn were friendly, accepting her as if she was a local. The affinity she had with Lilacwell was real. She once joked with Cassie that she must have lived there in a former life.

Adira noticed that Ruby had booked another appointment with her. Hopefully that meant the last Indian head massage must have helped with her headaches. She was just preparing the room for her when there was a quick knock at the door before Lisa came into the room.

'Hi, Lisa.'

'Hi.' Lisa scurried over and whispered, 'Thanks.'

Adira looked at her for a moment, then gave a big smile. 'For...' not wanting to presume too much, in case her instincts were wrong.

'I'm pregnant,' she hissed, 'but keep it to yourself.' As if the joy lighting her face wouldn't give her away, but Adira refrained from commenting.

'Oh Lisa, that's brilliant news!' She hugged her.

'I can't tell you how grateful I am.'

'I only told you to be less stressed, and I give that advice to most of my clients no matter what their ailment!' laughed Adira.

'I know!' Lisa laughed too. 'But it did the trick.'

'Well, I'm not so sure, but it was advice I remember my gran giving years ago.'

'Did it work then?'

Adira thought for a moment. 'Yes, actually it did. It was a neighbour.' She remembered Mrs Gardner giving birth to twins, but she didn't tell Lisa that. 'I'm so pleased for you.'

'We're over the moon. But remember, keep it quiet for the moment. Early days and all that.' She raised crossed fingers.

'Mum's the word,' winked Adira.

Lisa left the room with a spring in her step as Ruby stood at the doorway.

'Ah, Ruby, come in.'

'Hello, dear. How are you? Glad to see you're back.'

'I'm fine thanks and it's good to be back. How are your headaches, Ruby?'

'Much better, thank you. Although my neck and shoulders still feel a little stiff.'

'Right, let's give them a good massage.'

A few minutes later and Adira's hands were digging and probing into Ruby's muscles, easing the tension from her tight muscles. She could feel the old lady relax under the gentle pressure.

After half an hour, Adira gently stopped. 'All done, Ruby,' she told her softly.

'Ah, that's much better, thank you,' Ruby said, her eyes fluttering open. Then she sat up and circled her head. 'I've thought about having physiotherapy. Lilly says it's working wonders for Fletcher.'

'Yes, he does seem a lot better,' agreed Adira. 'I believe Lilly's encouraged him to embrace it,' she laughed.

Ruby gave her a pensive look. Adira paused for a moment, suddenly recalling the last conversation they had had about Fletcher. Ruby had mentioned how he had forever held a torch for someone, never realising how Lilly was his perfect match.

'Lilly has always had Fletcher's interests at heart,' Ruby told her.

'Yes, I believe so.' Then curiosity got the better of her. 'Ruby, do you know who Fletcher had a soft spot for?'

'Yes, I do. We all do, it was plainly obvious,' Ruby replied with a sad sigh.

'Who?' Adira couldn't resist asking.

'Alice.'

'Alice?' Adira frowned, wondering why the name seemed familiar to her. Then it clicked. 'You mean—'

'Jasper's mother,' Ruby replied, looking straight at her.

'Oh.' Adira was stunned.

'Yes,' sighed Ruby, 'the silly man hankered after his brother's wife when he could have had Lilly.'

Not knowing what to say, Adira stared at her in shock.

Walking home later that afternoon, Adira was still pondering over Ruby's words. Did Jasper know that his uncle had always loved Alice? If love was the right word, which she supposed it must be. Why else had Fletcher not settled with anyone? She debated whether or not to say anything to Jasper, it was a sensitive issue after all. Maybe it was common knowledge amongst the family but something that was never discussed. The proverbial elephant in the room? She couldn't help but feel such sadness for Fletcher, and Lilly too. It was all such a tragic shame. Adira agreed with Ruby, her sister would have been ideal for Fletcher.

Chapter 40

Jasper had started his packing. It hadn't taken him long to fold his clothes into cases. His books, CDs and set of golf clubs he'd bought in Dubai were boxed up and ready to be shipped back to England. The apartment had come fully furnished and he was going to leave the water cooler he had installed.

He was on the balcony, his favourite spot, overlooking the beach. It was strange to think this time next week his views would be very different. He'd miss watching the sea glint with bright sunlight and the flat, golden sand stretching out for miles. He'd miss the constant cloudless blue sky and the warm, balmy nights; the sweet smell of perfumes in the souks and the hustle and bustle of the markets; yoga on the beach, horse riding, golfing on the lush courses and dining out in the stillness of the night under pink skies. But it wasn't home. He didn't belong. Dubai had served its purpose and he would always think fondly of it. But now, he thought of Lilacwell and The Laurels and all those loved ones waiting for him. It touched the soul – something Dubai could never do.

Tomorrow would be his last working day. He hoped there wasn't going to be too much of a fuss made, preferring to simply slip away quietly. Jasper had already received lots of emails from clients and colleagues giving thanks and sending their best wishes. It was reassuring to know he'd made such a good impression. Abbas had spoken to him that morning and praised him for all his hard work. He had also given him a glowing reference and apologised for Zara's behaviour.

'It's not your fault,' Jasper had responded.

'Zara is a member of this company and, as such, I feel responsible for her actions,' Abbas had solemnly replied. Jasper had nodded. The least said about Zara, the better. He was just looking forward to getting on that plane and never looking back. He'd booked his own flight, no longer having a PA to do it for him. He was due to land in Manchester early evening in two days. Jasper didn't want to spend any more time than necessary in Dubai, he was just eager to get back home and see Fletcher and, of course, Adira.

Once again, he reflected on how strong his feelings were for her. It truly was a first. Never before had a woman got under his skin the way Adira had. Jasper, being the pragmatic, logical type, tried to analyse why she had had such a profound effect on him. Looks-wise, it was clear why the attraction had sparked, but he'd encountered several beauties in the past, who had blatantly showed interest in him. There was far more to it. Adira was intelligent, having gained a law degree at Oxford, but again, he had come across many an intellectual woman in the workplace. Adira had compassion too. She had shown a real kindness to Fletcher and Lilly. He recalled how she had helped other villagers as well with her herbal knowledge and had travelled all the way back from Edinburgh to help Cassie out at The Bath House. He smiled ironically at how he had originally been suspicious of her and questioned her motives for befriending Fletcher. She had practically turned The Laurels around, without taking a penny from his uncle. But the one underlying factor for his affinity towards Adira stood out for Jasper; Fletcher had given her his stamp of approval.

As if on cue, his phone rang. It was his uncle.

'All set?'

'Yep. Ready to go.' A surge of excitement shot through Jasper at hearing his own words.

'You definitely think you're doing the right thing?' asked Fletcher a little warily. He hated to think he'd pushed Jasper into anything.

'Absolutely,' replied Jasper resolutely, 'it's time to come home.'

A lump rose in Fletcher's throat. For a moment, he couldn't speak. He coughed.

'I'll… I'll be here waiting. Safe trip, Jasper.'

'Thanks. See you soon, Fletcher.'

Jasper collected all the framed photographs dotted about his apartment (including the one of Fletcher which Zara had moved) ready to pack up. He examined the picture of his parents. Only once had they come out to visit him. His mother had embraced Dubai and all its attractions, whilst his father had taken a more reserved attitude, refusing to be impressed by any of it. Jasper had half wished he hadn't bothered to come, noticing how he had dampened the whole holiday.

As expected, his mother had been delighted to hear of him coming home. She'd been surprised, knowing he had signed another two-year contract. When he had explained why, because of Fletcher's health, a short silence had followed. 'I see,' had been the delayed reply, causing Jasper to frown. What did she expect? His mother, more than anyone, ought to understand his predicament. From the moment he'd been born, it was understood he was the sole heir of The Laurels and its estate, so why should she sound so stilted? Did she resent him coming back for Fletcher and not her or his father? This had prompted his next question.

'How's Dad?'

'Oh, you know, same old,' she'd batted back neutrally. There'd been no suggestion to talk to him from either of them.

He could just imagine how his father would smother her joy once learning of his return. He doubted he'd be there welcoming him home with open arms – the absolute antithesis to Fletcher. No wonder they had little contact with each other; they were miles apart, in every sense.

'I'll let you go, darling. Take care,' she'd said, interrupting his thoughts.

'You too, Mum, bye.'

Jasper looked at the photograph of Fletcher, his face creased with laughter, smiling widely into the camera. How buoyant he looked, so full of love and life. Was he doing the right thing? his uncle had asked. Too damn right he was.

Chapter 41

'Oh, it's beautiful!' gasped Adira, holding up the necklace. The parcel Jasper sent had arrived that morning and Fletcher had taken it to the Inn for her to open. She'd been having a coffee at the bar with Cassie when in he'd walked with a grin on his face. He, more than anyone, wanted to know what was inside.

'It certainly is,' agreed Cassie, admiring the deep blue and aquamarine glass gems. 'Put it on. Here, let me fasten it for you.'

Fletcher sized her up with a smile. 'It makes your eyes sparkle,' he remarked. It did indeed highlight the colour of her eyes. 'That's why he bought it no doubt,' he chuckled.

Adira blushed at the scrutiny, making Cassie suppress a smile.

'What time will he get back?' she asked.

'This evening about nineish,' cut in Adira before Fletcher had chance to reply. She was so excited to see Jasper and had arranged to be at The Laurels to welcome him home.

'I bet you can't wait,' Cassie looked at Fletcher, who was beaming like a Cheshire cat.

He nodded. 'I'll be glad to see him.'

'You should have a welcome home party, Fletcher,' she teased. 'Your summer balls were legendary, I believe.'

Adira sighed and looked wistfully into the distance, 'How lovely it would be to see The Laurels in its former glory.'

Fletcher's eyes narrowed in contemplation. Maybe they had a point. It certainly gave him food for thought. Adira was right. It would be splendid to see The Laurels bursting with vitality and life, like the old days. He could picture it now: the gardens sparkling with fairy lights, the sound of music, chat and laughter, as people sipped cocktails and danced on the freshly cut grass. His imagination ran wild, then inevitably his mind wondered back to the past.

'You OK, Fletcher?' asked Adira. 'You look like you're in another world.'

'For a moment I was,' he said quietly, making her frown. 'Well, I'd better get going,' he smiled and took himself off.

Adira looked thoughtfully on.

'I bet we've got him thinking,' Cassie said with a grin. 'Lilly and Ruby used to rave about the summer balls at The Laurels.'

'Did he have them every year?'

'Apparently yes, up until about thirty-odd years ago.'

'Hmm,' replied Adira. *So why did they stop?*

–

Fletcher's mind span into overdrive. The more he thought about it, the more appealing it became. Of course, why didn't he think of it before? A good, old-fashioned knees-up, that's what the place lacked. It would be good to see everyone enjoying themselves – Jasper, Adira, Lilly, Ruby, Cassie and all the rest of the staff at The Inn. Hell, he'd even invite Tarquin and the doctor too! Fletcher rubbed his hands in glee, he was on a mission.

As he entered the back door, Lilly was in the kitchen, she'd just been washing up.

'Lilly, I've had the most amazing idea,' he told her with gusto.

'Oh really?' She looked up, surprised.

'The Laurels is about to host another summer ball!' he exclaimed in delight.

Lilly blinked. Another summer ball? After the last one? Her mind took her straight back to that night many years ago…

She and Ruby had taken great care over their appearance. For weeks, they had been deciding upon outfits. Finally, Lilly had chosen a powder-blue tea dress with an elegant rouleau button-through front and full sleeves, a flattering waist tie and a swishy skirt. It was cool, ladylike vintage and suited the mood of the party perfectly. Her hair was done up quite elaborately with ringlets gently spilling down the sides. She'd sat still as a statue while Ruby did her make-up, paying particular attention to her pale, grey eyes. The mascara and liner made them stand out strikingly. Lilly had hardly recognised herself when Ruby proudly stood her in front of the full-length mirror.

Her sister had known a lot was hinging on the night. To her, it was plainly obvious how Lilly worshipped Fletcher. It had perpetually been the case. Lilly and Ruby had grown up with Fletcher. He, being a few years older, had always kept a watchful eye on them, like an older brother. They enjoyed his company, the way he had them in hysterics and made them welcome at The Laurels, while his younger brother Rufus used to look at them disapprovingly, as though he resented them being there. Fletcher had been the ultimate gentleman, forever seeing they were safely escorted home after a night out and warning off any unwanted advances.

But it was so much more than neighbourly friendship for Lilly. She had made her mind up to marry him from the wise, old age of four – her first day at school, when Fletcher had taken them each by the hand and led them confidently into school. He was her hero. Her knight in shining armour.

When Lilly had first passed her driving test, she had driven her battered, second-hand Mini through the winding country lanes to a standstill. She'd run out of petrol. Fletcher had flown past in his open-top Triumph, halted, then reversed back to check on her. He'd burst into laughter at seeing the fuel gauge at zero.

'Hop in, lass, we'll get you some juice!' he'd called, opening the passenger door.

It had always been like that, Fletcher never too far away, on hand and ready to assist. Lilly felt sure he knew of her crush on him. That's what Ruby called it, a mere crush. To Lilly it wasn't, though – it was love.

So, she was determined to look her absolute best that night. Time was pressing on and still Fletcher hadn't married. Neither had she, so tonight she was determined to make it count. Enough was enough, no more shilly-shallying, she was going to make her feelings clear and tell Fletcher exactly how she felt about him. With a bit of luck, he would wake up and smell the roses, and see what was in front of him.

'You look beautiful, Lilly.' Ruby had held her shoulders, smiling into the mirror at her. 'He better appreciate you,' she'd warned playfully.

Lilly had had a few glasses of champagne for Dutch courage, leaving her rather light-headed and cheerful. She'd looked through the crowded orangery to catch a glimpse of Fletcher, but there was no sign of him. Lilly went onto the lawn and weaved through the dancing couples, but still there was no Fletcher. She'd decided to head back indoors and ventured into the drawing room where he often sat, but he wasn't there either. Out in the hall, one or two people chatted by the staircase; then she did see him, looking faintly dishevelled and rosy-cheeked, coming down the stairs. He was straightening his tie and smoothing back his hair. She was just about to call him when she then saw Alice follow him at a distance. The guilt oozing from her face and the uncomfortable demeanour had left Lilly in no doubt as to what had been going on.

Fletcher and Alice?

A whoosh of shock had jolted through her. Lilly was transfixed, monitoring their every move. She'd watched in despair and anguish as they'd danced on the lawn to 'Moonlight Serenade', gazing into each other's eyes. At that moment, she knew Fletcher would never be hers and slowly the tears had started to fall.

A warm pair of arms had embraced her.

'He doesn't deserve you,' Ruby had hushed as she'd hugged her sister protectively.

Lilly was still gazing into space, contemplating Fletcher's announcement.

'Well, what do you say?' he asked, face full of excitement.

'I... I... Sorry, what?' she asked faintly.

'A summer ball! Here at The Laurels, what do you think?'

'Oh! Yes... but, why?'

'Because it's what this place is short of, Lilly!' he exclaimed. 'It'll give us all a lift.' Then, pointing his finger at her, he added, 'It'll give you a boost and I think you deserve it.' He looked into her eyes with such sincerity it melted her.

Could this be the summer ball she had wanted all those years ago?

Chapter 42

Jasper sat back in his seat as the plane thundered down the runway and gradually lifted into the sky. He took a deep breath – at last, he was on his way home. His final journey back. He'd spoken to Adira last night and her excited tone had lifted his spirits. Evidently, she was as eager to see him as he was her. After the debacle with Zara, Jasper was determined to have honest communication with Adira. He cursed himself for not being as open as he should have been before he'd left for Dubai. If it hadn't been for his uncle's counsel, encouraging him to contact Adira, things could have ended so differently. The idea of her travelling in that camper van meeting new people in different places, never giving him a second thought, churned his stomach. But that wasn't the case, he reminded himself. Adira was safe in Lilacwell with Fletcher, waiting for him.

A warm glow flowed through him. It also made him realise the changes he would have to make at The Laurels. For a start, he'd need a decent bedroom. Whilst he loved his room in the eaves, it desperately needed a revamp. It was small. It most definitely required a king-size bed and an en-suite bathroom, plus double glazing in the windows. He'd thought of knocking through to the empty room next door to give him the space. He also fully intended to rip out the kitchen, which must be at least fifty years old, and replace it with more stylish units, whilst still retaining the country-house look. He'd seek Adira's advice, she'd know exactly what to choose.

Then there was the estate to think about. Colin, the manager, had certainly stepped up to the plate, constantly keeping him up to date. Jasper wanted to get as much of the land back in working order as possible. The orchards needed looking at, clearing any dead trees and repairing the barns where the picked fruit was stored. He had plans to grow fresh crops and plant more vegetables. The fields by the river were where he would set up the glamping site. He thought shepherds' huts would be compact and easy to maintain and he'd partition off an area for campers to bring their own tents, caravans or camper vans. Already, he had earmarked the nearest outbuildings for utility blocks.

Jasper aimed to capitalise on the area of outstanding natural beauty they lived in and saw it as an ideal holiday location. He envisaged the prospective holiday brochure, showcasing the stunning scenery, photographs of the twee shepherds' huts, local attractions, pictures of the village and the Inn. He wanted to utilise The Laurels, really turn it into a brand. It was a magnificent country house and whilst he didn't want public intrusion, certain areas could accommodate events. Jasper visualised the orangery decked with bunting and farmhouse tables laden with home-made cakes. Visitors could sit on the lawns and enjoy afternoon teas. In winter, he'd considered opening the library and drawing room for sherry and mince pies and have the local choir sing Christmas carols, or hosting murder mystery nights and involving the local amateur dramatic society, maybe arranging painting weekends for artists? He'd need to get Colin to start advertising for staff, because they were certainly going to need them. But first things first – he wanted his home in shipshape condition for his family.

–

Adira had just finished her afternoon appointments at The Bath House and was making her way back to the camper van. All day, she'd been looking at her watch and thinking of Jasper travelling back. A nervous, excited tingling fizzled inside her. She was heading for The Laurels later, to be there when he arrived home. She smiled imagining how Fletcher must be at fever pitch.

By eight thirty that evening, Fletcher was pacing up and down the hall like a caged tiger. He was on high alert, listening for any sound of Jasper's taxi pulling up to the house. The back door slammed shut, making his head turn sharply. Adira came through to join him.

'Hi, not long now,' she smiled up at him.

'Aye.' He looked at the grandfather clock in the hall.

'Fancy a drink?' she asked, thinking it might calm him down a little.

'Good idea!' He strode into the drawing room. 'What will you have, lass?' he called over his shoulder.

'A stiff gin and tonic please,' she laughed, also feeling the need to steady her nerves.

They'd soon sunk their first drink when the sound of a car made them stop and stare at each other.

'He's back.' Fletcher put down his glass and paced back into the hall. Adira quickly followed him. Fletcher had already opened the front door. 'Jasper!' he bellowed, his arms outstretched.

There he was, wheeling a case, with a rucksack on his back, wearing a huge grin. He embraced his uncle, then looked directly at her. Their eyes locked.

Fletcher moved to go back up the front steps, clearing Adira's way as she stepped into Jasper's arms. She buried her face into his chest, breathing in that reassuring, familiar scent of him.

'Welcome home,' she whispered huskily.

'Come here,' he said, tipping her chin up to kiss her. His lips were soft and inviting.

After several blissful seconds, Fletcher coughed. 'I'll put the kettle on, should I?' he called, before making himself scarce.

Jasper and Adira faced each other and laughed.

'I hope you're not thinking of returning to Sheila tonight,' he said with a glint in his eye and a raised eyebrow.

Chapter 43

Fletcher, Jasper and Adira had enjoyed a lovely evening, catching up and exchanging stories, whilst the drinks were merrily slung back. Fletcher had been on top form, fully basking in the company, but by midnight he'd burnt himself out. His eyelids were practically closing as he bid them goodnight and made his way to bed.

Jasper turned to Adira. 'Alone at last,' he smiled and reached out to run his hand through her hair. Adira melted under his touch and her heart started to beat wildly. He pulled her closer to him on the settee and she lifted her mouth to meet his in a gentle kiss. His tongue glided over her lips and he cupped her face as the kiss became more urgent. Their hands stroked and explored each other's bodies, until they were frantically undressing.

Afterwards, Adira hugged him tightly, sinking her face into his shoulders.

'Jasper,' she croaked, hardly believing what had just happened.

'I know,' he breathed heavily, gently rolling to her side. Propping up his head, he looked down at her. 'That was amazing.' He bent to kiss her. Then, a playful grin hovered over his mouth.

'What is it?' Adira asked.

'Your body is as heavenly as I remember.'

Adira frowned, then the penny dropped, making him openly laugh. 'You mean... you *did* see me bathing in the river then?' she asked, trying to sound outraged, but spluttering with laughter too.

'Yep. And what a memory that's been. It's kept me going for weeks,' he teased, before kissing her protests away.

She pushed him light-heartedly, then ran her finger over the scar on his shoulder. 'How did you get this?' she asked. It had piqued her interest since massaging him.

'Ah, now there lies a tale,' he winked.

'What?' She sat up eager to hear, wrapping her arms round her legs.

'A gang fight. I was nearly butchered.'

Her jaw dropped in shock, then seeing him burst into laughter, realised he was joking. 'Very funny. Go on, how did you get it?'

'I did it here, as a kid chopping wood. Fletcher nearly had a heart attack.'

'I bet he did.'

He moved to sit next to her and put his arm across her shoulders. 'Come on, let's go to bed.'

'Could be a tight squeeze,' she smiled.

'Good.' He ran kisses across her collarbone.

'Jasper?'

'Hmm,' he carried on, moving his lips up her neck.

'What do you think Fletcher will think, you know, about me staying the night?'

A low snigger escaped him. 'What took you so long, probably.'

Adira was right. It had been a tight squeeze in Jasper's bed, but still one of the best nights she'd ever spent. Together they had whispered and giggled, hugged and made love until the early hours. In the morning, despite having had so little sleep, they both awoke with the joys of life.

Fletcher, too, it seemed was still very much on good form. As predicted, he hadn't blinked an eye when seeing Adira at the breakfast table, almost as if he'd been expecting to see her. It was a comfortable, pleasant atmosphere as he made them all cereal and toast. Jasper was surprised not to see a full cooked English breakfast greeting them. When querying it with him, Fletcher gave a rueful look.

'Aye, well, I've decided to watch me diet a bit.'

'I see,' replied Jasper, looking at him thoughtfully.

'Hmm. I... I also see a physiotherapist now,' added Fletcher a little cautiously.

Jasper frowned. 'For how long? You never said.'

Adira gave Fletcher a knowing look and raised her eyebrow.

Oh damn it, he thought, *I might as well tell him*.

'I went to see the quack,' he confessed.

Jasper immediately stopped eating, giving his full attention. 'When?' he retorted.

'A couple of weeks ago. It's nothing to worry about, just went for something to ease the old aching bones.'

'What did the doctor say?'

'Well, she gave me painkillers, which have helped a lot, and told me to watch my weight and exercise a little to loosen my joints.' He stared almost defiantly at Jasper, as if challenging him not to make a fuss.

Adira intervened. 'It's worked wonders for you, hasn't it, Fletcher?' She placed a hand discreetly on Jasper's lap, willing him to be tactful.

'Good. I'm glad to hear it, but I wish you'd told me, Fletcher,' Jasper said with concern.

'Bah, I'm fine. Fighting fit.' Then he frowned and looked at the kitchen clock. 'I thought Lilly might be here by now, she was so looking forward to seeing you.'

Adira was surprised not to see her as well, especially given the late hour. All three of them had had a good lie-in, recovering from the late night. Usually Lilly would have been at The Laurels pottering about by now.

Just then, the phone rang.

'I'll get it.' Jasper stood up and went into the hall. Fletcher and Adira remained silent, straining to hear who had rung. 'Oh no. How is she, Ruby?'

Fletcher and Adira looked sharply at each other. Fletcher's face suddenly drained colour as they stilled to hear the conversation.

'I see. Yes, yes of course, I'll tell him. If there's anything I can do, Ruby, please just ask.'

Fletcher shut his eyes and put his head in his hands.

Moments later, Jasper sat back down with a grave expression. 'Lilly's had a fall. She's been taken to the hospital,' he told them.

'Oh poor Lilly,' cried Adira.

'Will she be all right?' asked Fletcher grimly.

'She's badly bruised, in shock, but stable,' Jasper said quietly.

Fletcher's chin started to wobble, Adira covered his hand with hers.

'Don't worry, Fletcher, I'm sure she'll be fine,' she tried to console him.

'How can you be sure?' he snapped back, making her flinch.

Now Jasper put his hand on her back, in support. 'Let's all stay calm,' he spoke gently.

But Fletcher started to cry, making Adira's eyes fill too. 'Lilly… my Lilly all bruised…' he sobbed, his shoulders shaking uncontrollably.

'Oh Fletcher,' Adira rushed to his side and put her arm round him. Then she turned to Jasper. 'Can we see her in hospital?'

'Yes. Ruby asked if I'd take her this afternoon—'

'I'm coming,' interrupted Fletcher.

'Of course, we'll all go,' Jasper reassured him.

Later that afternoon, the four of them drove to the hospital. Ruby explained what had happened on the way there.

'She was just walking down the stairs when she tumbled on the last few steps. I saw her…' Ruby's face crumpled in anguish. 'She was flat out for a minute or two before I rang for an ambulance…' She started to sniffle.

Adira grabbed her hand, they were both sitting on the back seat of the Range Rover, as Jasper drove solemn-faced. Fletcher stared out of the windscreen, still looking dreadfully pale.

'It's all right, Ruby, we'll soon see her,' comforted Adira, praying that Lilly would be OK.

When they entered the hospital, Jasper considerately held back with Adira.

'We'll let you two go first,' he told them. 'We won't all be allowed to go in together.'

Fletcher nodded and ushered Ruby into the ward where Lilly had been admitted. Jasper and Adira took seats out in the waiting area.

Fletcher's eyes swept round the room. He saw her by the window at the end of the row.

'This way, Ruby.' He took hold of her arm and strode up the ward. Lilly was asleep, laying small and vulnerable like a child. Fletcher's chin started to wobble again, before he fought for composure. He had to be strong for Ruby. He pointed to the chair beside the bed. 'You sit down,' he motioned to her.

'No.' Ruby turned to look him in the eye. 'If she wakes up, your face will be the first thing she'll want to see.'

Fletcher stared, open-mouthed.

'You do realise,' she continued in an icy cold voice, 'she asked for you when regaining consciousness. *Fletcher*, she said, *where's Fletcher?*'

'Oh Lilly...' he whimpered, looking at the frail, old lady lying in bed before him. Tears stung his eyes again, threatening to fall any second. He gulped back the emotion.

Still, Ruby just stared aloofly at him. 'You were all she ever wanted, Fletcher,' she stated flatly.

Chapter 44

The next few days went by in a bit of a blur at Lilacwell. All the villagers were shocked and saddened to hear the terrible news of Lilly's fall. Whilst making steady progress, she still remained in hospital to fully recuperate and allow the swelling to go down. Lilly had been delighted by the army of visitors who had continually come to sit with her, showering her with presents, concern and promises of assistance once she was discharged. Fletcher had been at the hospital every day on vigil. It killed him having to leave her there at night, wishing he could safely see her home. The Laurels was empty without her. Even having Jasper and Adira there didn't fill the gap of not having Lilly wandering about in the background, forever chatting to him. He'd been staggered at Ruby's words in the hospital. Did he really mean *that* much to Lilly? It was times like this that made him realise just how precious Lilly was to him. Something Ruby would be quick to point out, he thought.

Never having missed a visit since her fall, the nurses had all grown fond of him, as he joked along with them and the rest of the patients, trying to inject a little humour into the place. Lilly's face lit up every time she clapped eyes on him, which warmed his heart.

'Once you're well enough, let's have that summer ball, shall we?' he half-teased, loving the look of enthusiasm she gave.

'Oh yes!' she squealed, taking him utterly seriously. 'We could all do with a boost.'

How right she was, reflected Fletcher, anything to make her happy.

That evening, he voiced his thoughts to Jasper.

'I think it's a great idea,' he said. 'But let's hire help, instead of trying to do it all ourselves.' He'd seen it as an opportunity to set the ball rolling with his business ventures. They would need to employ a small team of staff to assist with future events.

'We've always managed before,' replied Fletcher.

'Yes, when you were all thirty-odd years younger, not riddled with arthritis or recovering from a fall.' Jasper looked at his uncle sternly.

'Yes… you're right.' Fletcher cursed himself – of course Lilly couldn't help, she was far too fragile. And could he really see himself lugging chairs and tables round? He laughed to himself. What had he been thinking? A classic case of the mind willing, but the body unable.

Adira was thrilled to hear of the summer ball when Jasper told her of his conversation with Fletcher the next day.

'It'd be lovely to see The Laurels host a party again.' She stared dreamily into the distance, 'I can just imagine how it used to look in the old days.'

Jasper smiled, loving her passion. 'Well, it's a good opportunity to see how future events will pan out. I intend to start hiring staff. We'll need assistance setting up a marquee, plus catering and waiting on.'

Adira's eyes sparkled with anticipation. Then as quickly as it flared up, it faded. She was suddenly very aware of her position at The Laurels. In fact, in Lilacwell full stop. What was she now? A local, or still a traveller waiting to move on? Jasper and Fletcher had been at pains to make her welcome at The Laurels, almost one of the family, but she wasn't family, was she? Whilst Jasper insisted she stay with him, something inside Adira prohibited her from doing so; and it wasn't just the small bed they'd been snuggled into. *I don't want to outstay my welcome*, she thought, or even worse, have people think she was taking advantage.

Jasper saw the expression on her face and paused. What was going through her mind? Alarmed, he thought she might be having second thoughts about staying in Lilacwell. Had she changed her mind about travelling? Then he reminded himself of his vow on the plane home – *open communication*.

'What is it, Adira?' His eyes searched her face.

She gulped at the sincerity in his voice and the way he was looking at her. 'It's just that… I'm not sure where I fit in… I mean, all this talk about the future for the estate, your ideas…' Her voice cracked.

'Hey.' He reached out and held her face in his hands. 'You belong here, with me. That's if you want to.' He stared into her eyes, searching for a hint of what she might be thinking.

'Yes, of course I do,' she replied in a small voice.

'Then why do you insist on returning to Sheila most evenings?' he asked, a smile hovering round his lips. He suspected she still felt a touch embarrassed in front of Fletcher.

Taking the initiative, she held his gaze. 'Because it's your childhood bedroom we're sleeping in. I don't feel I belong.'

Right, that's it, thought Jasper.

'OK. It's time it was renovated into an adult space,' he stated firmly. 'And with a bloody king-size bed,' he added, making Adira laugh. Then he took hold of her. 'Listen, we'll do it together, make it our room.' He was looking earnestly at her. 'I want you to feel at home in The Laurels, do you understand?'

'Yes.' She gave a shaky smile, emotion suddenly filling her.

Deciding to seize the moment, Jasper told Fletcher of his plans later that day when Adira had gone to work.

'The thing is, it's too small. I want space, enough room to share it with Adira.'

'I bet you do,' chuckled Fletcher. Then he eyed him. 'I take it Adira is going to be a permanent fixture at The Laurels?'

'I dearly hope so… That's providing she wants to be.' He was ever mindful that Adira hadn't actually completed her year of freedom that she had so yearned for original-ly. After all, that's what had put them together in the first place, wasn't it? If it hadn't been for her wander-lust, they would never have met. This whole sequence of events wouldn't have happened. The very thought gave him goosebumps. It would have been a travesty. Now he wondered, did she want to follow through with her plan and continue travelling? He didn't want to hold her back or get in her way, but he longed to have Adira by his side. For him, she was his future – his home, as much as The Laurels was.

There was a moment's silence before Fletcher quietly replied.

'Perhaps you'd better ask her then.' He looked directly at him.

Jasper's mouth twitched, his uncle just couldn't help himself.

'I'm on the case,' he returned, looking straight back at him.

'Good. Good,' nodded Fletcher.

—

Fletcher swilled his whisky round the tumbler, then knocked it back. Tonight he needed the courage and, more importantly, the reassurance of alcohol. All this talk of changes at The Laurels had quite resonated with him. It brought into sharper focus how significant the future was, not the past. He'd come to realise just how much his memories had played a part in his life, and not always in a positive way. He now understood how he had let history control him and how he had sacrificed too much, for the sake of one revered night. Yes, it had been the most cherished, sacred memory, but he had allowed it to determine his very being. He could have made himself a life, carved out a more promising, brighter future when Alice had refused to join him.

He now knew, with extreme bitterness, he had played it wrong. Fletcher strongly suspected his brother was infertile – why else had Rufus and Alice not had any other children? He was bloody certain he'd sired her only child, and as Jasper's potential father, he should have laid down the law, demanded she tell Rufus. At least that way Jasper would have known the truth. And now what of his future grandchildren? Would he be denied them too?

No way. Enough was enough, it was time to take matters into his own hands.

He poured himself another drink, slung it back and went into the kitchen to fetch the key. Jasper was just making a coffee.

'Hi, do you want—'

'Follow me please,' he cut in, sounding the most serious Jasper had ever heard him and instinctively he made his way up the stairs behind Fletcher. He watched his uncle open the bedroom door – the one he had snapped at Adira to leave alone – and flick the light on before calling him in. Jasper had never been in this room, just assuming it was used for storage. His eyes adjusted to the dim light, taking in the picture of his mother on the bedside table. Frowning, he turned to see a silk dress hanging from the wardrobe door. He recognised it as his mother's, from seeing photographs of the last summer ball The Laurels had had. Then he looked at Fletcher, knowing something monumental was going to happen.

Fletcher was shaking slightly, but he was steadfast. Swallowing, he cleared his throat. 'Jasper, I believe you were conceived in this room...' He paused. 'By me.'

Time stood still as the revelation of his words hit Jasper.

'You mean... you and Mum...'

Fletcher slowly nodded his head.

'Why wasn't I told?' Jasper asked incredulously.

'I wanted to. Alice forbade me, she always maintained we couldn't be sure I was the father. It's remained a secret... until now.'

Jasper stilled, his eyes widened in shock. Images of his childhood rapidly flashed before him: being packed into the car with a suitcase every summer to stop at The Laurels with Uncle Fletcher; learning to ride a bike with Uncle

Fletcher; fishing, swimming, horse riding – with Uncle Fletcher; being taught to drive and getting his first car, all with Uncle Fletcher. Never with his father. He recalled his father's impatience with him as a small boy, the lack of interest in him as he grew up, how dismissive he was of his achievements and suddenly it all fell into place. Jasper's gut feeling told him Fletcher *was* his dad.

They stood motionless, staring at each other.

'In my heart, you've always been my son, Jasper.' Fletcher ceased shaking. A huge wave of relief engulfed him.

Jasper nodded. 'I've felt it too,' he replied huskily. Then, with tears running down his face, he strode over and held tightly onto Fletcher.

'It's all right, son,' Fletcher soothed, cradling him, 'it's all right.' He closed his eyes, finally the truth was out.

Chapter 45

It had been a long time since The Laurels had seen such activity. As instructed, Colin had advertised for staff and put together a small team of estate workers to assist with the summer ball and forthcoming events. The fields next to the river had been cut and new boundary ropes sectioned off the glamping site. Jasper and Adira had looked at shepherds' huts made by a local craftsman and ordered five, which were being delivered imminently. The utility blocks were almost complete and the dilapidated outhouses half crumbling on the estate had been demolished. The marquee for next week's summer ball was being erected and the orangery was in the process of having a good clean. The terracotta tiled floor had been power washed, as had the windows, which now sparkled. All the lawns had been tended to and were looking splendid.

Fletcher couldn't take it all in – things were moving at such a pace.

'I hardly recognise the place!' he exclaimed, whilst gazing at the manicured gardens, blooming with colour from the French doors.

'It all looks beautiful. Jasper has done an amazing job,' Lilly replied, sitting comfortably in Fletcher's chair. He'd done nothing but fuss and tend to her since her discharge from hospital. He had contemplated asking her to come back to The Laurels, where he could keep an eye on her, but realised this may offend Ruby, so had just visited their cottage every day, thoroughly getting on Ruby's nerves.

'He certainly has,' said Fletcher, his head moving from side to side, watching all the activity outside.

'Sit down, Fletcher,' chuckled Lilly. 'I'm sure they all know what they're doing.' How he did kerfuffle, not just over all the arrangements, but also her. She'd been touched at how attentive he had been, with his daily visits, constantly asking how she was feeling and bombarding her with gifts, not to mention the huge bouquet of flowers which took up most of the bay window in the cottage (completely blocking the light, Ruby had complained). The slippers, dressing gown, books and toiletries she supposed Adira had chosen. Still, it made a very pleasant change to be waited on, instead of her tending to Fletcher. Her sister would argue it was too little, too late, she had no doubt, but Lilly didn't care. She was happy to wallow in the attention, whilst it lasted.

Adira and Jasper were in the library, leaning over the desk, covered in stationery samples for the glamping site. It was to be called 'The Laurels Hideaway' and they were discussing which style of font and logo to choose.

'What about this one?' Adira pointed to a plain cream sign with a simple picture of laurel leaves entwined with black calligraphy writing.

'Yes, I like it. Minimal, but effective,' agreed Jasper.

Luckily, they had very similar tastes, which had proved convenient whilst redecorating 'their' bedroom. In the end, they had decided not to renovate Jasper's eaves room – he hadn't the heart to change his childhood bedroom, full of happy memories. Secretly, he planned to make it a nursery but hadn't voiced this with Adira, yet. Instead, they had refurbished the 'locked' room opposite Fletcher's bedroom. The time had come to give it a new lease of life.

Jasper had quietly taken Adira into the bedroom and outlined the whole revelation to her. She had listened in silence, not disclosing what she had already been told by Ruby.

Jasper had been pragmatic about it. Once the dust had settled and he'd taken stock, he had come to appreciate that, actually, nothing had changed. In fact, it had answered more questions. He saw little to be gained in telling his mother that he'd learnt the truth. What would be the point? It seemed futile, and would only lead to upset within his family. So, on the surface, it was business as usual.

Adira thought his approach was absolutely the right one. Her eyes had darted round the room, resting on the elegant lemon, silk dress. Although covered in dust, there was no denying how striking Alice must have looked that night at the ball.

'It's exquisite,' she'd said, running her hands over the soft folds.

'Take it,' Jasper had replied, 'I'm sure once it's cleaned, Fletcher wouldn't mind you wearing it for our summer ball.'

'Oh, I couldn't.'

'Of course you could. What's the point of it hanging there?'

Adira looked at the dress again. It was a touch too long for her, with a deep frill around the edge. Perhaps if she had it shortened and took out those puff sleeves it would be more her style? And in a sense more *her* dress than Alice's?

Indeed, Fletcher had seen little point in the dress, or the whole room, acting as some kind of talisman to the past. Onwards and upwards was his new mantra, determined to make up for lost time. He categorically refused to stay locked in the years gone by and was throwing himself into the future and all that encompassed. He didn't think it would be too long before grandchildren were on the way, although he discreetly kept that to himself, for once.

—

The summer ball was the talk of the village. Invites had been sent and accepted. Most of Lilacwell was about to descend upon The Laurels and witness it in all its glory.

Adira had invited Edie, her parents and then, as an afterthought, Rory. As he was from the north, she thought he'd appreciate the gesture. He'd been thrilled and had booked one of the shepherds' huts to stay overnight. If anyone could give them honest feedback, it was Rory, she'd laughingly told Jasper.

'Good, because we'll need it,' he'd said, then turned to face her. 'No regrets?' He couldn't help thinking he'd dropped her in at the deep end with all the commotion of running the estate and starting up the new business ventures. He was accustomed to working at full pelt, but was he expecting too much from Adira?

'Absolutely not.' She'd put her arms round his neck and kissed him. 'I wouldn't want to be anywhere else.'

Chapter 46

The sun had decided to put in a guest appearance for the summer ball, as The Laurels team of staff had worked tirelessly throughout the day. The marquee was looking magnificent, draped with ivy. Inside were trestle tables covered with cream linen cloths and vases of bright flowers from the gardens. The orangery dazzled in the sunshine with its sparkling windows and fresh painted white frame. A bar area had been assembled at the back and new comfortable seating had been installed. Bunting swooped across tree branches covering the immaculate cut grassed lawns.

It was now early evening and the guests would start appearing any minute. All the residents of Lilacwell had been invited, but never being one to miss a business opportunity, Jasper had also sold tickets to people outside Lilacwell. His aim was to have the place full and showcase The Laurels off to as many as possible. He'd had flyers printed to hand out with the new logo on, advertising The Laurels as an ideal venue for all occasions, even business conferences. He'd also created Instagram and Facebook accounts to bring in guests from further afield who might be tempted by photos capturing the natural beauty of the place.

The Laurels Hideaway was completely finished now and was looking very professional with all the signposts leading its campers to the glamping site. Sheila was still parked proudly by the river.

A small jazz band gathered together under a gazebo in the far corner of the lawn and began to strike up the music. Jasper stood by the French doors in the drawing room looking devilishly handsome in his black dinner suit. He sipped a whisky whilst assessing the scene outside. Everything ought to go as planned. He'd meticulously gone over the arrangements with the staff that afternoon. They'd all been schooled, given exact instructions with attention to detail. He expected the best from them. A lot was hinging on the summer ball. It was The Laurels first event and it had to be a roaring success.

He turned at hearing Adira enter the room. His gaze took in her slim figure, beautifully complemented by the silk, lemon dress. It fitted her perfectly and the re-style suited her down to the ground. Instead of putting her hair up in a fancy, elaborate style, she had opted to have it free to cascade past her shoulders and it looked stunning.

'All set?' she grinned. Looping her arm through his and kissing his cheek.

'As much as we'll ever be,' he replied with a smile. 'You look amazing, by the way.'

'Hmm, you don't look so bad either,' she teased, admiring his broad shoulders in the black dinner jacket. His pristine white shirt contrasted well with his tanned skin. Adira caught the faint aroma of his bergamot after-shave as he lowered his mouth on hers, quickening her pulse. Their kiss was interrupted by a loud cough.

'Don't mind me,' said Fletcher as he entered the room. He too was looking very suave in his dinner suit. His hair was neatly combed in a side parting.

'Fletcher, you look wonderful.' Adira was truly impressed. It wasn't hard to imagine what a heart-throb he would have made in his younger days. He was looking more energised than she had ever seen him.

Just then, in came Lilly.

'Ah, here she is!' announced Fletcher, his face beaming. 'And how lovely she looks.'

Lilly did indeed look lovely in her silver-grey, velvet gown. It had a sweetheart neckline and three-quarter-length sleeves. Her hair was done up into a pleat and diamond drop earrings delicately glinted.

'Lilly!' exclaimed Adira, rushing over to hug her.

'Will I do?' Her eyes twinkled mischievously – she was certainly back to her old self again.

'I'll say. You look fantastic,' she gushed.

'The best The Laurels has ever seen,' Fletcher proclaimed, then pointed to his chair. 'Sit down, Lilly, don't overdo it, lass.'

'Oh for goodness sake, Fletcher. I've only just got here,' Lilly laughed, totally loving the attention he gave her. There was still no sign of Fletcher easing up on his attentiveness.

Jasper smiled. It was good to see the old boy enjoying himself. Then he discreetly checked his inside jacket pocket for the small box which he'd placed in there.

The music was in full force now and it was time to greet the visitors. Jasper opened the French doors and led them all outside. The staff were doing a sterling job circulating with the cocktails.

Adira saw Cassie looking very elegant in a bronze off-the-shoulder gown and waved. She looked towards the front gates, eagerly awaiting her family's arrival. Edie and her parents had been introduced to Jasper and Fletcher that afternoon and had been totally impressed with the place, not to mention Fletcher, who had had them all entertained with his bonhomie. They were staying at the Inn, which had met Cleo's high standards, much to the relief of her husband. Edie had also been blown away with the country charm it oozed.

Cleo had been astonished. Whilst she'd had grave reservations about Adira quitting her career to go off travelling, she had, under her husband's strict instructions, tried to remain neutral. Say nothing. But upon entering Lilacwell, Cleo had been charmed by this quaint, little village tucked away in the Forest of Bowland. She had been even more impressed by The Laurels and its surrounding estate. Her estimations had grown further when meeting Jasper, a fine young man with prospects and impeccable manners, and as for his uncle, well, he couldn't be more welcoming. Cleo could now see first-hand how well her daughter was thought of and how well she fitted in. It was all so promising, but, most important, Adira was *happy*.

Tonight, as Cleo approached her daughter, she saw that she radiated utter joy, which Cleo had never seen before. Her girl had found herself; without any help or interference.

A smile hovered over Cleo's lips. *Good for Adira*, she thought. That tiny baby which they had very nearly lost, had well and truly made it. Tears stung her eyes.

'You OK, Mum?' Adira asked with concern.

'Yes of course.' Cleo quickly wiped her eyes and coughed. Then she turned to face her. 'Well done, love, I'm so pleased for you,' her voice cracked.

Adira blinked, not accustomed to seeing such emotion from her. 'Thanks, Mum,' she smiled, then kissed her cheek.

Pat looked on with a great sense of relief. At last, the women in his life were united, in every way. He too was touched at how well things had turned out for his daughter.

Later, Edie had taken Adira to one side and squeezed her hard.

'I've never seen you so happy,' she smiled. Adira was bursting with glee and vitality.

'I am happy, Gran,' she replied.

Edie slightly hesitated, then reached for Adira's hand. 'Darling, I've delved into the paperwork my father left me.'

Adira's head turned sharply. She'd been keen to ask her gran about it but was reluctant to mention it in front of everyone. Now that Edie had broached the subject, she was all ears.

'His marriage certificate was there.'

'And?'

'My parents were married in Clitheroe.'

'Clitheroe! That's the nearest town, Gran,' she replied with excitement. 'It's got to be our Grace Conway, surely. I'm going to dig deeper, get the full picture.'

Edie smiled. 'I think you were meant to find Lilacwell, don't you?'

Adira gave her a quick hug. Out of the corner of her eye, Adira saw Rory, nonchalantly walking up the side entrance from the glamping site. She couldn't help grinning to herself. Although dressed smartly, he never quite managed to pull it off, with his tie lopsided and his shirt slightly untucked. Still, he was here and she was so glad he'd made it.

Adira went to welcome him. 'Hello, you.'

'Hi!' He gave her a hug.

'Come and meet Jasper.' She glanced round and called him over. The two men shook hands.

'It's good to be back up north.' Rory breathed in the country air.

'Ever tempted to move back?' asked Adira.

'Very, but not sure I've the backbone to pack my career in, unlike some.'

'We do have barristers up north, you know,' replied Jasper, grinning.

'Yeah, think big, Rory,' chipped in Adira. 'You could set up your own chambers.'

Rory's head titled to one side in thought, then he suddenly became side-tracked. 'Tell me, who is that adorable creature?'

Adira and Jasper followed his stare.

'That's Cassie. I'll introduce you,' laughed Adira.

The drinks flowed, the music played and a dark, peaceful night sky appeared, dotted with stars. Candles gently flickered on the tables and lanterns glowed from the trees. A warm breeze filled the air. The band struck up a lazy, lingering tune.

'May I have this dance, Lilly?' Fletcher held out his hand.

'You may,' she promptly replied.

'Just the one. We don't want you getting tired.'

'Oh stop,' she smiled.

Together they made their way onto the lawn and joined the other couples slowly moving together.

Jasper held Adira close, then whispered in her ear. 'Follow me.'

Adira looked up surprised. 'Where are we going?' she asked, as he took her hand and guided her towards the side pathway.

'You'll see,' he smiled over his shoulder.

He led them to the field by the river where Sheila stood. He walked them towards the campervan and opened the door. As they stepped inside, Adira gasped. It was decorated with balloons and fairy lights. On the table was an ice bucket filled with champagne.

Jasper reached inside his pocket and pulled out the box. Adira stared, wide-eyed. He opened it to reveal the most exquisite diamond solitaire ring. 'Marry me?' He looked deeply into her eyes. 'I know it's soon, and if you still want to spread your wings and travel, I'll wait. But I know without a shadow of a doubt that you were meant for me, and we are meant to be together. You've changed me, Adira, for the better. You've changed us all, you're part of the family and belong at The Laurels with the rest of us. I never want you to leave. I love you.'

Adira's hands flew to her face, overcome with emotion. A million thoughts raced through her mind – yes, it was early, they'd only just officially become a couple! But, like Jasper, her heart had never felt so sure.

'Yes…' she choked, before flinging her arms round him. 'Destination reached,' she whispered in his ear, 'I've found what I've been searching for.'

An owl smoothly glided down and rested on top of the camper van roof. Not wanting to disturb its occupants this time, it calmly sat and took in the evening's surroundings. It seemed Sheila, the camper van, had truly proved to be a safe haven.

Author's Note

Ever wanted to just get away from it all? I certainly have. I watch with both admiration and envy at those appearing on various TV shows, who have literally sold up and escaped to follow their dreams. Whether it be a chateau in France, a cottage in the country, or a bolthole by the sea; if only I had a miniscule of their courage and adventure!

Occasionally I kid myself that I'll do it. I *will* sell my house, my chattels, pack in the day job and *just go*. Then, reality kicks in. As do my husband's wise words, because it's all well and good having dreams and aspirations, but do they match your partner's? I think it's extremely fortunate when both parties have real conviction in their actions, without any hesitation. That together, they can absolutely fulfil their life-time ambitions. Whereas I love the idea of packing in the rat-race and living a simpler, more fulfilling existence, could I really do it?

Adira, the main character in this novel, could. As a young, free and single woman, having had enough of working all hours in a stressful job, decided to take the plunge. She made the monumental choice to radically change her life. Adira does all the things I wistfully wish I had. She buys a Volkswagen campervan and takes off exploring. Off she goes, leaving the city and all its trappings – the high-flying career, prospects, money and a chambers full of perplexed barristers who simply do not understand.

It's not long before Adira reaches Lancashire, the glorious county where I live. This is what makes *Escape to Lilacwell* a personal favourite of all my books to date. It's set on home turf. The village I've based Lilacwell on, is in fact Whitewell, in the beautiful Forest of Bowland AONB. There is an Inn at Whitewell, which is also based on the Inn in my novel. Allow a little poetic licence for all the quaint street names and the high street with artisan shops, but Puddleduck Cafe really does exist…and has been visited by the Queen herself!

It's not all local countryside, Dubai also gets a mention. This brightly lit city, full of luxury and glamour couldn't be more different to Lancashire's rolling hills and valleys. But again, as my son now lives in the UAE, it has personal connections.

I often get asked as a writer, if any of my characters relate to people I know. I can honestly say 'no' to this question. All my characters genuinely are complete imaginary figures. However, Fletcher Hendricks, the kind, old man in this story does resonate with my late father-in-law, Geoff, whose voice I can hear in Fletcher. Like Fletcher, Geoff was a wise sage, who spoke his mind and gave good advice in that strong Lancashire accent, peppered with 'Aye' and 'Lass'. So, for all these reasons, I'll always have a soft spot for *Escape to Lilacwell*.

Did Adira find what she was looking for? Absolutely she did, after meeting a few quirky locals along the way. She fell under Lilacwell's spell and I hope you, the readers, did too. I hope this charming, little Lancashire village enchanted you as much as it does me.

As for my escape, well I'm part way there. We have moved to a coastal village in Lancashire, which does have equally quirky characters like Lilacwell. It has a rural community, with flat open landscape looking toward the Bowland Fells, the Lake District mountains and Morecambe Bay. My village has age-old traditions which I find endearing, coming from the suburbs, such as the 'Coffee Feast'. This dates back to days of yore when coffee was part of the contraband smuggled in off the coast and all the villagers enjoyed such luxury. A parade, led by Morris Dancers and the Village Jubilee Silver Band, proceed through the village and return to the church for the crowning of the Coffee Feast Queen. How quaint is that?

Whilst I haven't quite given up the day job, I have reduced my hours and spend half the week writing, my passion. My husband has at last relented and made us a garden room, where we can relax and enjoy the nature on our doorstep. Also, we're in the process of planting vegetable plots, so hopefully should be harvesting our very own fresh produce soon. So, I suppose I've semi-escaped.

Acknowledgements

I'd like to give a big shout out to Canelo, my fabulous publishers, particularly my editor, the wonderful Emily Bedford. It's thanks to Emily that Lilacwell has come to life and made it into print. Her meticulous editing has made it a novel to be proud of, which I am. I'd also like to thank Jade Craddock, copy editor; proof reader, Rachel Sargeant; Diane Meacham, the book cover designer (love that cover!); and all the fantastic team.

Most of all I'd like to thank you, the readers. It's lovely hearing from you and your kind words mean the world.

Bye for now. I'm busy writing the sequels, but do keep in touch.

Love Sasha x